Best of British Science Fiction 2020

Best of British Science Fiction 2020

Edited by Donna Scott

NewCon Press
England

First edition, published in the UK July 2021 by NewCon Press

NCP 261 (hardback)
NCP 262 (softback)

10 9 8 7 6 5 4 3 2 1

Cover art by Alex Storer
Cover design by Ian Whates
Text layout by Ian Whates and Donna Scott

Contents

Introduction

Donna Scott

Welcome, dear reader, to my selection of stories the *Best of British Science Fiction 2020*. Before you plunge into these pages, please do take a moment to think about that strange year that we all just went through, and all that we are *still* going through, and let's take a collective scratch of our heads.

As I write, the leaders of seven of the most powerful nations in the world are gathered in Cornwall, and the Red Arrows just flew past my window in Northampton on their way to London to celebrate the Queen's birthday. I mean, just reading that sentence back again seems weird, but that really is what's going on, and where the news is concerned today, that's just the mild stuff. It's one of the hottest days of 2021 so far, and just to re-cap, we're in the second year of a global pandemic. Not only are a good proportion of the public eager and determined to get out in the sunshine and return to 'normality', they also seem to be quite satisfied to pretend that the absurd hyperreality of our times is also... quite as things should be. Right now though, we are about to pause on the rollercoaster of data that will determine whether the government says we can safely remove all legal limits to social contact, and rush down the track screaming joyously into 'freedom', or – like some friends of mine were when the Oblivion ride opened at Alton Towers, and they were first on it – stay horribly and uncomfortably stuck up on the top for quite some time.

Somewhat paradoxically, though we are frequently reminded by the press all the time just how abnormal things are, and how our lives are 'on hold', there are robots waiting at the crossings every day to take people their shopping, and I seem to have spent many of the clear nights in the past year watching Starlink rockets shoot overhead, and watching SpaceX on YouTube as they have tested their reusable technology prototypes at Boca Chica, and sent astronauts on the Crew Dragon to the International Space Station.

There is as much of a sense of the future rushing forward whether we want it to or not, as there is of our personal progress being impeded… though perhaps it really isn't.

I'm also looking forward to the time when Covid-19 no longer has a hold on our day-to-day goings on, but the virus continues to impact every country in the world, and has even affected the putting together of this anthology, as I myself fell ill with the virus a few months ago, and I also lost my dad to the disease. So, I hope you forgive me even mentioning the pandemic in this introduction, as I know we are all heartily sick of it, but it is the elephant in the room, coughing away, and wearing its mask incorrectly (under its trunk).

I'm afraid to say that the pandemic has also affected my taste in science fiction. At the start of Lockdown last year, I had to stop watching the TV series *War of the Worlds* with its empty streets and deathly encounters with aliens in supermarkets. Plus, after the grimness of seeing anti-vax protests in London, I found I was quite done with zombie apocalypses. Watching *Contagion* though, was quite useful in a way, as Kate Winslet gave some excellent advice in it about handwashing and not touching your face. Not that it did any of the characters much good until they were all vaccinated…but anyway, once you've seen *Contagion*, you really don't need to see *Pandemic*. Or *Flu*. Or anything else along those lines, really.

Whilst I did not want to watch any programmes that cut too close to the bone, the same could not be said for everyone, and some people also had a taste for literary reflections on the virus that I did not share. I don't know if it was due to some rashly announced calls for submission early into Lockdown, but from my reading pile it seemed an awful lot of writers were inspired to take the real spread of infection and simply extrapolate with horrific negativity, and to echo what a disgruntled sacked special adviser claimed someone said last year, "let the bodies pile up".

So, you will notice I have not put many overtly virus-inspired stories in this collection. There are notable exceptions: "The World is on Fire and You're Out of Milk" by Rhiannon Grist is here because it is superbly witty and very funny; also "Infection" by Liz Williams, which takes an askew glance at proposals for infection control from the point of view of a young would-be superspreader, and gives us a story that is deliciously tongue in cheek and far from derivative. Lavie Tidhar's "Blue and Blue and Blue and Pink" is slightly reminiscent of *Catch-22,* with pilots taking on dangerous missions to zones of infection, but believe me, it's brilliantly nuts, and one of my absolute favourites, probably of all time.

Thankfully, many writers have been inspired by our times to reflect on much more diverse topics, such as humanity's place in the world – and its intrusion into nature; the progress of AI consciousness; considerations in health and social care, and the meaning of those things that are unique in their significance to mankind: the true meaning of love, and the linearity, or not, of time. And it's a breadth and wealth of such ideas that you will find here. From M.R. Carey's disturbing tale of a soldier dealing with the victims of a time-bomb in London, to Val Nolan's drowned and radioactive Aberystwyth, with signs evoking the Cofiwch Dryweryn (Remember Tryweryn) graffiti wall, painted in the 1960s to protest the flooding of the Tryweryn Valley by Liverpool Council. From AI tanks disappearing to live wild in the jungle after the madness and confusion of war in Fiona Moore's "The Lori" to robot companions sharing a meet-cute by a green grocer's stall in "Pineapples are Not the Only Bromeliad" by RB Kelly. Here, too, is the adorable and thoroughly deserving winner of the BSFA Best Short Fiction Award for 2020: "Infinite Tea in the Demara Café" by Ida Keogh, a multiverse romance that also celebrates café culture and food in its scrumptious prose.

There is plenty to celebrate in short fiction from this most peculiar and *science-fictional* of years. I hope you enjoy these stories. May they be a cautious hug for your soul, or an elbow bump if you're especially cautious.

Donna Scott,
Northampton,
June 2021.

War Crimes

M.R. Carey

Someone had moved in London. So of course the site manager voked the emergency line, and Emergencies routed it to my unit without a second thought. The orders were the same as always. Do what has to be done, then forget that you did it and how you did it until the next time.

The movement was an infinitesimal thing, much too small to register on the unaided human eye, but there were sensors in place for just this purpose. The sensors had 300% overlap and they were so sensitive they could track dust motes drifting through. That wasn't what they were there for, though, and that wasn't what made the alarm bells jangle on this bright May morning, just before the park opened.

Somewhere in the stretch of London between Oxford Street and the Thames, one of the former inhabitants – or exhibits, or whatever you want to call them – had shifted position by a thousandth of a thousandth of an inch. I know that sounds trivial, but when pressure builds up behind a dam the first cracks are going to be on that same microscopic scale. Something had to be done before the whole situation went from micro to macro. And when I say something had to be done, I mean I had to get out there and do it. Temporal weapons and their toxic legacy are my specific area of expertise, so this crisis landed in my lap with the same inevitability that once attended death and taxes.

It landed hard, too. I woke with a sense of urgency (that was not my own) jangling inside my head.

"Ow!" I muttered. "Off!"

The desperate need to be up and doing faded slightly, but it didn't go away.

"I said off, Tally. Not mute."

"Sorry, Lieutenant. You didn't voke, and I had my mike off."

I didn't voke because I'm in the habit of dropping out when I go to bed. Some people can't sleep without the murmur of distant conversations, like waves on a shore a mile from your bedroom window, but I can't sleep with it. Drift is fine. Drift is just emotional substrate, connecting you to the world like an umbilical. It's something else again to have people talking in my ear when I'm dozing off. Or maybe having secrets you can't ever share makes you come at your voke from a different angle; inclines you to put up your guard before it's needed.

(I know. It shouldn't ever be needed. But still.)

I didn't bother to explain any of this to Tally. He's twenty-three and he's got so much idealism washing off him that I have to wear sunglasses every time we work in the same physical space. I voked on and asked him what the trouble was. I was already bracing myself, because his drift had urgency, scale and immediacy threaded all the way through it, right underneath the purely personal anxiety. You didn't need words to gauge the likely volume of shit that was involved.

It's London, Tally voked. *I mean, London 21.*

The memorial. Not the actual, living city but the chunk of amber at its heart.

Sensor went off?

Just before start of day. Nobody on the ground but the cleaning crews, fortunately, and we got them out fast. We told the management to lock down for the foreseeable, but to wait for us to take a look-see before they made any announcements. Obviously we didn't want anyone to be upset or afraid if it turned out to be nothing.

Which was a good instinct, but also a typical example of Tally's idealism hitting the real world at a slightly skewed angle. He really thought the staff at the memorial park would turn off their drift as well as their vokes, putting a perfect seal on the information as he had politely requested.

You there right now, Tal?

Yeah.

Of course he was. *What are you seeing?*

Umm... I'm at the front gate. By the orientation desk.

And?

There's a crowd here that stretches back as far as Regent Park.

I let out a breath I hadn't known I was holding. It emerged as a sigh.

Sorry, Cap. I could ask them to move back a way...

Which would be nice, to be sure. But I didn't have it in me to treat these people as if they were just an impediment to my working day. Some of them were only there out of curiosity, but others almost certainly had personal or humanitarian agendas that were almost bound to come to nothing. They deserved courtesy and kindness at the very least. Outside of that... well, there was a limit to what I could offer.

And there was Tally himself to consider. He'd been assigned to Temporal for almost a year now. It was past time I put him through the next stage of his training – the one that hurts, and leaves a scar. Perhaps I should take the opportunity this situation offered, but that would bring its own stresses and complications.

One way or another, it was going to be a long day.

No need to move them, I voked. *Not yet, anyway. I'm coming over.*

Which meant getting dressed. My husband Martin was sprawled half-in and half-out of the covers, on his stomach as always and with one arm thrown up over his head as if he was hedging his bets on a surrender. I kissed him on his cheek, and got a fuzzy burst of loving, confused drift, but he didn't wake. I left him an engram to say I'd gone to work and might need to isolate when I got home. Then I grabbed some clothes out of the closet – and the black plasteel carrier that looked like a camera case and was coded to my DNA – and got dressed in the kitchen. No time for make-up or other niceties, with London on the move. I gulped down some coffee, forced a brush through my hair and got on the road.

The road was busy, but running smoothly anyway. I ambled my way over to the fast lane and found a clear spot between a group of children on their way to school and a carrier leading a group of six enormous freight-mechs. The schoolkids were sitting cross-legged on the moving roadway, wide eyes taking in the landscape as it passed. Their vokes were on a closed group-loop, but they emitted a constant drift of excitement and curiosity that was very pleasant.

When I got to my exit I felt quite sorry to leave them – especially in light of what was coming.

Then I realised they were stepping off the road along with me, and all that updrift went out of the window as the realisation hit. The man and woman walking alongside the kids were their teachers. They weren't going to school, they were on a day trip. And given our shared direction of travel, there was really only one place they could be headed.

I voke-flagged the woman, and after a glance in my direction she opened a channel.

Hi. Can I help you?

Hello there. Are these your kids?

She smiled. *Only from nine to three-thirty.*

And you're going to London 21?

We are indeed. Down from Leeds. Primley Park Communal. We've been studying the ante-com era for half a term, and this is the big finale. The woman frowned. My drift was locked so she wasn't getting any emotional commentary from me, but she must have read something in my face. *Is there a problem?*

Potentially, yes. The memorial park is closed at the moment, pending my inspection. Lieutenant Husnara Begum. Huss to my friends. I voked an ID-flash, so she would understand what "Lieutenant" meant, but it didn't help as much as I'd hoped. Some people don't realise we still exist, and they don't like it when they find out they were wrong. The woman tilted her head, squinting as if the ID-flash was standing in the air in front of her and she could bring it into better focus.

Is that a joke?

I hope not. If it is, it's on me.

But... we don't have an army. We haven't had an army for decades.

True. For the most part. It's just us, now. REME. The Royal Electrical and Mechanical Engineers. "Royal" is an obsolete word denoting approval and status. They keep us around for emergencies involving old ordnance. Sometimes things crop up that require a very specialised skill set.

Such as...?

I switched to spoken word. That question went a long way into dangerous territory. It was best if the answer took us straight back out again. "Bombs. Grenades. Things of that nature. Look, why

14

don't you stay close to me? I'll make sure the staff at the park find a space for your class that will be comfortable and safe. At least until we know whether they'll be able to reopen today."

I walked on ahead while the teacher voked with her colleague. A few moments later the local drift filled up with the kids' very strongly felt disappointment and dismay. They had come a long way to be turned around at the gates. I hoped it wouldn't come to that. I hoped this would turn out to be a machine fault, and I could go home without ever taking that skill set I'd mentioned out of its black plasteel box.

We were pushing our way through quite a big crowd now, but because I'd turned my voke off it was weirdly silent. All I was getting was the emotional backwash, and I muted that too as it became too strong and strident to think through.

The gates of the park loomed ahead of us. I voked Tally and had him tell the duty manager to prep that room. By the time we got there, a nervous assistant – I mean he looked nervous, he wasn't broadcasting in front of the public – was waiting to take the children and their teachers off to somewhere comfortable and private.

"If we do have to go back…" the male teacher ventured.

"If it comes to that, I'll commandeer an army transport for you. You can go back on old road. Static road. I imagine the kids have never done that before?"

"No," his colleague said. "Neither have we, for that matter. I didn't know the old roads were still there."

I smiled. "It's a day for surprises, isn't it? The government maintains a separate transport network for infrastructure repair. Most of the time the roads are empty."

"Thank you," the male teacher said. "Can I ask…?"

"Yes?"

"Why is the park not open?"

"There's a potential safety issue. We have to check it."

"I heard someone moved," a young woman near us called out. Presumably the same thing was being voked by hundreds of other people all around us, but with my own voke turned off I didn't need to acknowledge or respond.

"A safety issue," I repeated.

"Whose safety?" a teenaged boy demanded. He was wearing a t-shirt that read TIME STOPS, LIFE DOESN'T — the slogan of a protest movement dedicated to an impossible cause. Not that they're wrong, exactly. It's just that what they're asking for can't ever be granted.

"The general public's," I said.

"Would you care to voke that?"

This was not a conversation I wanted to have. I'd chosen to let the teacher know who I was, but I wasn't keen on revealing or justifying the military's involvement in the situation to the crowd at large. Not until I had at least got a chance to see what was what. So I turned that invitation right back on the boy, shutting him down with what you might call a show of force.

"Are you attempting to initiate voke contact with me when I've chosen to withdraw?" I asked him mildly.

He was outfaced at once. He was blond and pale-skinned, so his blushing showed to quite impressive effect. "No!" he blurted.

"Because my right to privacy is absolute."

"Of course it is! I didn't mean…" He faltered into silence.

"Then let's unask the question," I said. "No hurt or blame to either. I'll tell you this. I'm an expert in these matters, and I head a well-trained team. If we do our job competently — which we will — there is absolutely no danger to anyone here. And no disrespect or injury will be done to any of the time-stopped unless it's absolutely necessary in order to prevent a catastrophe."

I moved on quickly, leaving the boy to come down from that painful public embarrassment and the teacher and his class in the care of the park officials. If all went well, they'd still get their day trip. If not, I would do my best to see them safely home.

I met up with Tally a little way inside the gates. He was doing his best to look inconspicuous, which of course meant that he stood out like a hippopotamus in a henhouse. Seeing me coming, he let his shoulders slump. I opened my drift just in time to catch the tidal wave of his relief.

"Lieutenant! It's just been getting crazier!"

"I saw. Have we got a pinpoint on the source, Tally?"

He nodded. "Quite a long way in. Near the centre."

That was bad news. It raised the possibility of a fail cascade – and made it that much more likely that we would have to intervene.

"Show me."

Tally led the way and I followed. We passed through the gate, with its exhortation to REMEMBER THOSE WHO FELL, AND THOSE WHO STAND FOREVER.

I'd been to London 21 as a child, and what I mostly remembered was being bored. I'd been too young. The ineffable strangeness and sadness of the place hadn't registered with me, only the silence. The weight of it, like time made solid and pressing down on me. Actually that wasn't too far from the truth.

As an adult, I was more profoundly affected. The piece of old London that was frozen stretches from the middle of what used to be Tottenham Court Road in the north to the Strand in the south, and it extends about a mile to the east and west. The entry gate feeds you past an imposing ancient structure called Centrepoint into an avenue of buildings that are mostly rendered in stone, baked brick or poured concrete. No perma-weave extrusions at all, and very few hydrogel ceramics.

The roads are all static, of course, so you walk on your own two feet – which gives you plenty of time to look in the windows. Quaint and curious emporiums offer goods whose use it's almost impossible to imagine, even with the aid of the download foci that are scattered around. What was the fastest ever 5G network, and why was it considered a good thing? Who went into the Scientology Life Improvement Centre, and what did they find there? So much of our past is opaque to us.

I have to admit, though, that looking at the shop windows was mostly a way of not looking at the people. It might surprise you to learn that a temporal engineer is capable of that kind of squeamishness, but there it is. I've seen literally thousands of time-stopped in the course of my work. I know exactly what they are, and what they're not; what was done to them, and how. I've been briefed extensively on their ontological state by people who've gone down to the sub-atomic level to verify their hypotheses. I know where I stand.

None of which makes it easier for me to look at them, or walk among them.

There's just something intrinsically wrong in the spectacle of people – children, men, women – caught in such a hideous snare. Trapped and held in a mood of joy or misery or boredom that should have been transitory, murdered without ever knowing it, and made to recapitulate forever the last moment of their lives.

Most cities where time weapons were deployed have gone the same way we did and turned the detonation sites into public monuments and memorials. There are those who argue that they should be closed off to the public and treated as actual burial grounds, but that has always been a minority view. Most people feel that we own this tragedy and should acknowledge it rather than hiding from it, however painful that may be.

Tally was walking briskly ahead, but now he turned to look at me and pointed. "It's this way," he said. "Bayley Street." The look of surprise on his face told me he'd voked the words first. He must have thought my reticence was just for the crowds outside, when actually it was for him too. I still hadn't decided whether or not I was going to induct him, today, here, into our profession's last and ugliest mystery.

We turned a corner and crossed another street into a small square. There was a fenced-off garden space in the middle, trees and benches, an archaic lamp post, a statue of a Victorian gentleman now surrounded by living statues from two hundred years later.

On the day the time-bomb fell, the square had been full of people. Most of them were alone, or else walking in twos. The exception was a single large group on the far side of the garden, heading for its open gate. A young woman led them, carrying a long slender pole with a square of bright yellow card or plastic mounted on it. A tour group, I assumed, following their guide. If my voke was on, I could have accessed the contextual notes from any of several nearby download foci, but this really wasn't the time.

Tally pointed. Fifty yards ahead of us was a man wearing a formal suit of eye-catching drabness, grey with a pattern of narrow blue lines almost too faint to see. His head was bald, his lean face austere and calm. He was clean-shaven but he had missed a spot on the right side of his jaw, leaving a blue shadow. There had been no way for him to know, when he went through his ablutions on that long-gone morning in the mid twenty-first century, that this was the face he would be presenting to the world for centuries to come.

Most of the people here had been taken while they were walking. This man had stopped where the square met the street from which we had entered. He was staring off down the street as though he had come there to wait for somebody and was impatient for them to arrive. Whoever it was, perhaps they were among the frozen figures we had already passed. Or perhaps some other business kept them away that day and they were spared.

We came up on either side of the time-stopped man and I made a more careful appraisal. Sitting next to him on the ground was the squat silver bulk of a baffle rig in its shock-proof box, presumably lowered from an aerial carrier. Public roads didn't extend into the time-stopped areas.

"Is he moving now?" I asked Tally.

"I didn't check. I waited for you."

"You took a baseline, though?"

"Oh. Yes. Of course. Can I…?"

"Send your stats to my Offhand."

The Offhand is a dead storage. It doesn't connect to your sensorium unless you tell it to, and you can pick and choose. It's a way of receiving voked messages without voking back. Again, I was insulating myself from Tally while I decided how to handle this and how much to tell him.

I found his send in the Offhand and brought it up. It was a map of the square with every physical distance flagged to an accuracy of 0.3 Angstroms.

Using that as a reference point, I took my own measurements on a Chiang-Voss gauge, which I check and recalibrate every two or three days. I read the distances and ran the check again. Then I ran it a third time.

"Is everything okay?" Tally asked. His anxiety and confusion were painful to see. Like many people – the majority, even – he's a bit clueless at reading faces with no drift to go on.

"No," I said shortly. Everything was far from okay. There had been a seven-picometer slippage in the space of less than an hour. The situation was fluid, as they say, and we had even less leeway than I'd been assuming.

There was one final test I needed to carry out. The odds were in my favour, but I'm fatalistic at times like this. I always assume the worst. I reached into my pocket and took out a tiny metal disc like an antique battery. A touch was enough to unfold it, turning the disc into a lattice of slender metal rods shaped like the skeleton of a glove. It slid across my right hand and affixed itself there, each filament in its proper place. The rods were only a sixteenth of an inch thick, but they were marked along their length by thousands of puckered indentations. Psionic amplifiers.

I touched my hand to the forehead of the time-stopped man. I closed my eyes and sub-voked the command. *Open.*

What I was hoping for was nothing. Nothing at all.

Which was just too bad for me.

"Lieutenant Begum!" Tally yelled. "Huss!" Again, he must have voked first and went for speech as a last resort, but I'd switched off everything as a precaution before I made contact with the time-stopped man.

Some time had passed, but probably only a couple of seconds. I'd bitten through my lower lip, and there were lacerations in my left palm where my nails had punctured the skin as I clenched my fist. I had slumped against the time-stopped man, and he was the only thing holding me up, but I hadn't dropped to my knees or lost control of my bodily functions. It could have been worse.

"Are you all right?" Tally blurted. "It looked as though you were going to faint!" He reached out a hand and I grabbed hold of it, switching my weight from the frozen man to him. For the time being I was going to have to let his question hang in the air. It's hard even to think after the kind of battering my mind had just taken, let alone speak.

I made my decision there and then, as I slowly got my balance back and stood upright again. I would have to truncate immediately, and if I was going to do that then I was going to tell Tally the truth. All of it.

I hated to do it. I might have sounded flippant when I talked about his dazzling idealism, but let's be clear: that's just one more defence mechanism on my part. What I was about to take away from him was a thing that was precious, and that ought to be inalienable. But because he'd chosen a military career, it wasn't.

"Tally," I said, "Voke the crowd outside. Tell them to disperse to a half-mile distance. Then alert local police to maintain that perimeter."

He frowned, and hesitated for a moment. Uncertainty made him blink rapidly, four or five times in succession. "Will you ride the call, Huss? I mean… in case I miss anything out, or…"

"Absolutely." *I'm here. Go ahead.*

Tally concentrated hard. *Attention,* he voked. *If you're in the vicinity of London 21, you need to draw back until you're at least half a mile from the gates. One of the time-stopped in the park area is breaking out of stasis. If the field fails, and the energistic recoil isn't contained, there will be an uncontrolled emission of localised temporal distortion. People caught in the recoil could age years or decades in the space of a second. Medical complications include cardiac events, aneurisms and renal failure. There's a substantial risk of immediate death. We're going to erect a baffle rig now, but in case the stasis field fails before we can contain it you all need to be well out of range.*

Tally looked to me, anxious, wanting approval.

I nodded. *That was great. Now the police, and the park management.*

While he was busy with that I set down the plasteel carrier I'd had with me all this time, opened it up and performed a quick inventory of its contents. The brace and brackets, the drill, the bolt and the detonator. My instruments of murder, all in place.

Shall I set up the baffle rig? Tally asked me. He was a lot happier now that we'd made the announcement. There was still nervousness in his drift, but much less than before and outweighed by a sense of calm; of events unfolding in a clear, predictable way. I was about to upset that apple cart. I was about to smash that apple cart into smithereens.

Never mind the rig, I said. *Come over here.*

I deactivated the connector. It shrank back down to a disc.

Hold out your hand.

Tally obeyed without question. Military discipline doesn't change, even now the army is pretty much a vestigial institution. I dropped the tiny device into his palm. It unfolded again, and he drew in an audible breath as it fitted itself to his sensorium.

What is this thing? he demanded. He wasn't afraid, only curious. With a hundred training simulations and seven actual mission outings under his belt, he thought he knew our field kit inside out.

The first little apple, falling off the cart.

It's a drift connector, I said. *And an amplifier.*

A connector? But… everyone is already connected to…

Stay with me, Tally. The time-stopped lived in an era before drift was a thing, right?

Tally was still staring at the angular, spider-legged thing that had spread across his palm and up his fingers. *Right?* I voked again.

Right. Of course. But…

The only emotions they felt were their own. The only thoughts they could access — their own. We see them as being locked away from us in a bubble of frozen time, but when you think about it, their everyday experience was already one of isolation. Exile. Solitude.

Tally was looking at the rest of the equipment in the carrier now, and his calm mood was considerably ruffled. *That looks like a gun,* he said, pointing at the bolt.

It is a gun. Tally, listen. I'm explaining something to you, and it's important. I took his hand between both of mine. *What do you feel?*

He stared at me, puzzled and unhappy. *Nothing.*

Nothing at all?

He shook his head.

Why do you think that is? If it's designed to force a connection, and to amplify the emotional signal, why are you feeling nothing from me?

The corners of his mouth tugged down as he thought. Seeing this as a test, he wanted very much to pass. *The setting?*

Good. Yes. The amplifier is incredibly sensitive, but it's stopped down to a very particular, very narrow wavelength. I'd be lying if I said I understood the physics, but what matters is the effect. It can penetrate a stasis field. It can pick up the thoughts of the time-stopped. After a moment I amended that last statement. *If they have any.*

Mostly they don't. More than three-quarters of the people caught in a stasis event are hit so hard by the field that all thinking and all affect just stop dead in the same moment that their bodily movement stops. Ego-death occurs instantaneously, and when you touch them with the amplifier you get nothing but silence.

Those are the lucky ones.

The rest...

The rest are still awake. The time-bomb froze their bodies but not their minds. They had a partial immunity that has never been explained or understood. They continued to think and to feel, inside bodies that had been turned into form-fitting coffins.

I imagine for a time what they mainly thought was "when is someone going to come and help me?" But no one did, or could. The time-stop effect renders the affected person or object impervious to any external force. Divorced from the pulse-beat of entropy, they can only endure.

At some point, after weeks or months or years, madness invariably set in. The trapped mind locked itself into a cycle of panic, rage and pain that fed on itself and grew stronger with each iteration. That was what I felt when I touched this man's mind. The voiceless, substanceless shriek entered me, filled me, tore at my skin from the inside out.

I nodded at the time-stopped man. *Touch his forehead*, I said. *Lightly*.

Put your hand in the mincing machine. Turn the handle.

It took Tally a long time to recover. To be fair, not as long as it took me when my captain, Angelo, inducted me for the first time. But as with me, it came in stages. The shock first, then the panic. "He's hurting! He's hurting so much! Lieutenant, you've got to help him!" And finally the stunning grief as the implications slowly sank in. We sat together on the edge of the pavement, his head against my chest, and I held him until he came back from that abyss.

There are thousands of the time-stopped. Thousands on thousands, all across the world. Some are only statues. Funeral architecture. The rest are like this man – bottomless reservoirs of suffering.

"Something's got to be done," Tally said, his voice muffled by tears and fabric. "We can't just leave them."

"We don't have any choice," I said, gently. "Nothing we've got can even touch them until the stasis field starts to break down. Nothing, Tally. They're out of the world. Until one day they're not, and then they're a lobbed grenade in a crowded room. We can do exactly one thing for this man, now. We can put an end to his pain. Come on. I'll show you how."

I took him through the mechanics of it. The harness attaches to the head of the time-stopped child, woman or man by four carefully placed brackets. The bolt attaches to the harness. A sensor measures the integrity of the stasis field continuously, tracking gradients and updating projections faster than any human mind could react. The instant the field falls, the bolt is fired. The time-stopped individual lives again, for the tiniest fraction of a second. Then dies, as the detonator is triggered and the bolt shoots home through the basal ganglia of the brain.

It's all we can do, I told Tally. It's tragic and it's terrible and there is absolutely no alternative, no choice, no other way to play this.

Because the voke and the drift were what dragged us back from extinction, at the ragged edge of the eleventh hour. After thousands of years of killing each other, torturing each other, suddenly there we were all up inside each other's defences, knowing the stranger as well as we knew ourselves. Hate was impossible. Misunderstanding was impossible. Loneliness was impossible.

We surrendered to empathy as a last resort, and we were each other's salvation.

Now every child that's born is born in the drift. Cossetted, embraced, known and protected by the collective mind. We've never known the desolation of being alone in the dark, crying out ceaselessly for help as hope curdles inside us and turns us into monsters.

The time-stopped are our forebears, our family, but if we open our arms to them they will destroy us. Their fears and hatreds and agonies will poison the drift for generations, perhaps forever. We will become what we were before. We will fall into the ancient pit, and perhaps this time we won't be able to climb out again.

So we invented that lie, about the temporal distortion wave. Keep your distance, or be Rip Van Winkled. And we invented a non-existent piece of technology, the baffle rig, to justify engineers like me – and like Tally – stepping into the breach and containing all that dangerous energy. When we're done there's nothing to see. The unfortunate time-stopped has been sublimed away, rendered into dust and loose atoms. Actually they're laid down, in the big steel box that's supposed to contain the baffle rig, and lifted out by a robot transport. They get a hasty burial on Ministry of Defence land, with no funeral rites and no grave marker. And the world goes on.

As for us, the keepers of the secret, I suppose we're doing the same thing soldiers have always done. We kill for the state, and we tell ourselves that somehow, in this one instance, killing isn't a crime or an atrocity but a needful thing. The past lives on, not just in the time-stopped but in us.

Trust me. You don't want any part of it.

Blue and Blue and Blue and Pink

Lavie Tidhar

Purple clouds roiled on the horizon and the old Cessna Centurion came in low and fast, riding the tailwind. Giorgio, on the ground and looking up, took shelter behind a crude half-shed of corrugated iron and lit a cigarette with a Zippo he'd once bought in the Talat Sao back in Vientiane. It was supposedly owned by a downed Air America pilot during the Secret War.

He stared at the plane coming in from the border. Smoke was coming out of the engine and half a wing looked like it'd been strafed, and Giorgio wondered who it was flying it. One of the Israelis, maybe.

The plane, trailing smoke, dove down low as it lined up to the landing strip. All the pilots came out to watch. The Cessna struggled in the air, then righted, the engine whine louder now. The Cessna hit the strip with a bump and Giorgio coughed smoke, but then it came down safely and coasted the rest of the way and came to a halt.

Everyone cheered.

The pilot – Avi, or Eli, or one of those – took off his belt and fell out of the open door. He looked dazed.

"Pink!" he said. "Blue and blue and blue and pink!"

The ground crew opened the hoses then. Avi – that was his name, Giorgio was almost sure it was that – rolled on the ground as the laced water hit him. Giorgio took a drag on his cigarette. Avi screamed. The other pilots, having been through this exact routine too many times before, lost interest and drifted off. Avi's two buddies waited anxiously until the jets of water stopped and the pilot stopped screaming. They ran over to him and helped him up.

"Decontaminated," the guy who passed for ground crew foreman said. He stowed away the hose and he and his team went to the cargo hold and began off-loading the contraband. Giorgio put out his cigarette and went to join the other pilots in the sole shack that served as bar and tuck shop.

"Did you hear about Johnny Luck?" Sam Cheng said, passing him a bottle. Giorgio twisted off the cap and took a swig. The beer was cold, at least.

"No," he said. "What about him?"

"Came in three, four days ago from a run, got deloused and everything, but he must have been careless on the other side. Started showing yesterday morning. He's in the isolation tent."

"Shit," Giorgio said.

"Yeah. Me and some of the boys are going over there later, sing him out. You should come."

"I... all right."

Giorgio downed the rest of his beer and tossed the bottle onto the heap with the others. He didn't want to go see Johnny Luck.

"How many does that make now?" he said.

Sam Cheng shrugged. "Five the past month."

"Shit."

"It's the job. It's why we get the danger pay. And who else is going to hire us? American Airlines? This is the only job that's going. You know this, Giorgio."

"It's a shit job."

"But it's flying."

He handed him another beer. Giorgio nodded.

"It's still flying," he said.

There were twelve of them outside the isolation tent that evening.

"Enough for a minyan," one of the Israelis said. Giorgio looked at him blankly.

Johnny Luck was inside the tent. Giorgio tried to remember what he knew about him. Not much. Recent arrival, one of the oldest at twenty-seven. No one on the squad expected to make it to thirty. Not if they stayed. He thought Johnny was South African. There were a lot of South Africans running missions over the line.

"Ready, boys?" Chaplain Buzz said. He wasn't really a chaplain, but before he became a pilot, he went to seminary school.

They started singing "Danny Boy." The pipes were calling across the night and inside the isolation tent Johnny Luck was slowly, well – whatever it was that happened after you were exposed, it was happening to Johnny Luck.

After the song they all raised a drink for Johnny, and then they poured some on the ground outside the tent. Then they drifted off. Someone started a campfire and someone else strummed a guitar. Giorgio lay under the mosquito net in his tent and tried to sleep. He'd run, what, nineteen, twenty missions over the line, easy? Never had a problem. Always observed the protocols. Never been exposed.

But everyone's luck runs out sooner or later.

Giorgio fell asleep. In his dream he was back home in his parents' farmhouse. Vines grew over the pergola columns and roof and bunches of grapes hung down, purple and green. He reached up and plucked a grape and put it in his mouth and it tasted blue and blue and blue and pink. His mother came out of the kitchen where she had been cooking and saw him.

"Giorgio!" she said. She wiped her hands on her apron. This was very strange to Giorgio, since he grew up in a small flat, not on a farm, and his mother never cooked.

His mother looked at him curiously.

"How much you've grown!" she said.

"Mama," he said. He went to her. She looked good. But hadn't she died in the last major outbreak, five years ago? And she was never this large or this homey. His mother was thin as a rake and smoked long menthol cigarettes and worked in accounts. "You look good," he said.

"Come give Mama a hug," she said. She put her arms around him. It felt good to be held by his mother.

"Snuggly-wuggly," she said, nuzzling him close. "Snuggly-wuggly-woozy-woo."

"No, no," Giorgio said. "No, mother."

Mother was turning blue.

"Snuggle!" she cried. Her arms lengthened, wrapped around him. Blue and blue and blue and pink.

*

Giorgio woke into early dawn. He was drenched in sweat and his teeth were clenched tight, and there was a bad taste in his mouth. Mosquitoes buzzed outside the net, and in the distance someone was still playing the damn guitar.

Giorgio took a sip of warm water and gurgled and spat it out on the ground. He stole out of the tent into the rising sun. The sun rose over the line, on the other side. Some of the other pilots were already awake and about. Nothing came from the isolation tent. Over at the tuck shop, Sam Cheng was frying eggs.

Giorgio ambled over and got a burrito. Sam poured him a coffee, which he brewed in a giant can that once housed pickles. He said it gave the coffee a kick. The coffee was vile, but it was the only coffee around, so Giorgio drank it.

He grimaced.

"Bad dream?" Sam said sympathetically.

"Bad coffee," Giorgio said.

"Sure, boss. Whatever you say."

A plume of dust rose in the distance. Giorgio watched it come closer and soon heard the sound of the engine. The jeep came into the pilots' encampment and stopped, and the woman from the company stepped out. She wore field boots that were more expensive than Giorgio's plane. She had goggles on and a face and nose mask, and she wore gloves. The ground crew foreman came over and they spoke briefly, then the foreman nodded. Another plume of dust came across the horizon and soon one of the company's big unmarked trucks arrived and the ground crew started off-loading contraband and loading the stuff the pilots brought back on their runs in its place.

The woman walked over to the tuck shop. She looked at the hand-chalked menu, at Sam Cheng, and at the coffee. If she made a face it was behind her mask. She nodded to Giorgio.

"Pilot?"

"Aha."

"Got a job for you."

"Why me?"

"You're present."

Giorgio nodded. "What's the run," he said.

She motioned for him to come. The ground crew had unloaded all the contraband off the big truck. Giorgio saw that the isolation tent was down. A sealed plastic box the size and length of a coffin sat by the waiting truck. He felt a little queasy at the sight.

"Knew him?" the woman from the company said.

"A little."

"All right." She handed him a chart in her gloved hand. Giorgio took it. He frowned. The flight path was longer than he'd expected.

"A deep dive?" he said.

The woman from the company shrugged.

"I'll have to take on extra fuel," Giorgio said.

The woman from the company shrugged.

"What am I taking?" he asked her.

"The usual."

"All right."

"It's a bonus flight," she said, apparently taking pity on him. "Double the usual pay. When you get back."

Implied in her tone was that failure to return would just save the company costs.

"All right."

She nodded. "Get to it, then," she said.

The ground crew loaded Johnny Luck's coffin onto the truck with the rest of the contraband the pilots brought in from beyond the line. Giorgio didn't know who the company really was, or why it was still trading over the line, when no one should have been crossing the line for any reason. The whole place was under quarantine.

Giorgio went to his plane. The ground crew had already loaded the cargo. Giorgio said, "I need extra fuel."

The foreman said, "Already done."

The foreman never said very much. He was a company man. Like the woman from the company he wore goggles and a face mask, though unlike hers, his boots weren't worth shit.

"All right."

"See you, Giorgio."

Did he know the foreman's name?

"Yeah, see you," he said. He climbed into the cockpit. Did the check. Started the engine. Taxied to the runway. Saw that one plane had already taken off, ahead of him. Starting early that morning.

He took to the air. This was the best part. The moment the wheels left the ground and the whole improbable thing happened, of leaving the earth and rising into the skies. The airfield grew small below, tents and parked airplanes and the company truck. Bad coffee and bad dreams.

He climbed and then eased the stick until he was flying at a fixed altitude. He looked down. Fields and small rivers and clumps of houses here and there. Roads. He checked the compass and the map, but he didn't really need to.

As he approached the line, he dropped down low. He flew over grassy hills and old abandoned roads. Once he thought he saw a patrol convoy and skirted 'round them. Then he was over the line, with no discernible change on the ground below.

He followed a river for a little while until it reached a fording and a small abandoned mill, and then he flew north-easterly for a while. He rose high again. From the skies the world over the line looked the same as on the other side. He saw roads and he saw houses and once he passed a small town, though no one walked in the streets and the playgrounds were abandoned. But he could sense eyes in the windows, and he knew people still lived there.

Carl, he thought. That was the foreman's name.

The sky was very blue and blue and blue, with only a blush of pink on the horizon. Giorgio passed over a small village and turned northeasterly again. He didn't recognize the land below any more; this was outside of the regular route the smugglers took. A crackling of static came on his headphones.

"...Everywhere..." a male voice said in panic.

Giorgio turned the dial, trying to dislodge the moronic voices that kept coming up on the old VHF.

"...Overwhelmed..." A woman's voice this time. Giorgio turned the dial.

"Mama loves you, Giorgio," a woman's voice said very clearly in his ear. He gritted his teeth. In life his mother barely showed her emotions, mostly she was disappointed in him, his hair that had been too long, his choice of girlfriends, his choice of career. "Giorgio, it's me, love, can you hear me, over?"

"Over and out," Giorgio muttered. There was no point trying to turn off the radio. The voices came on regardless, this side of the line.

He dove low, spotting the target in the distance. A white farmhouse just like the one in his dream, and a dirt track running parallel to it, which he'd have to use for landing.

The attack came fast and sudden on his right. He felt the thud of multiple impacts against the belly of the plane. He banked sharply left and then right, trying to dodge them. He looked down, saw muted shadows in the vegetation and arrows flying into the sky. He rose and the arrows reached the upmost point of their trajectory and fell back down to the ground with a strange, forlorn grace.

The farmhouse grew close. Giorgio glided, looking it over, but he could see no movement. An old truck stood next to the farmhouse and crates had been left haphazardly on the ground.

Giorgio wondered if he should just go back. But then he wouldn't be paid, and would have to take on the cost of the extra fuel besides. So, he went down for a landing.

The dirt strip was straight and flat, surprisingly so, and the plane landed smoothly. Giorgio turned the plane around for take-off and taxied near the drop point, then stilled the engine. He sat in the cockpit for a moment, looking, but nothing moved, and everything seemed peaceful. He put on his standard-issue surgical mask and gloves and climbed down from the cockpit.

The sky was very clear, and the sun was warm. Empty snail shells lay on the ground under a clump of gerberas. Giorgio walked slowly to the farmhouse.

The cargo was waiting for him on the tarmac. He noticed some of the lids on the boxes were ajar and the contents caught the sun. They glinted like gold.

"Hello?" Giorgio called. "Hello?"

Nobody answered. Giorgio shrugged.

"All right," he said.

He went back to the plane and began off-loading the shipment of contraband by himself. It wasn't unusual to never see anyone. It was better this way. It was hot, though.

He took down boxes of useless stuff – toilet paper, soap, board games, toys, stuff the company picked up in bulk for pennies on the other side. He stacked the boxes against the white stone of the farmhouse. The walls were crawling with ivy.

Giorgio went back to the cockpit. He picked up his bottle of water and took a long swig. Then he went back to work.

The return contraband was heavy. He figured it was old gold coins, pieces of jewelry, stuff like that, which was of no further use on this side of the line. It didn't matter to Giorgio. It was only when he was lifting the final crate, straining against the weight of it, that he heard the fuzzy.

"Hug?" the fuzzy said hopefully.

Giorgio put down the crate. The fuzzy was blue and blue and blue and pink, with large curious eyes and a round, cuddly shape. It stood in the sunlight less than two meters away, blinking.

"Hug!" the fuzzy said.

Giorgio took a careful step back, and then another. The fuzzy didn't move any closer, but it looked hurt at Giorgio's retreat.

"Snuggle-wuggle?" the fuzzy said. It blinked again.

Giorgio knew he should get away from the fuzzy, but somehow he didn't take another step back. He stared at it. Back when he was four or so his mother bought him one just like this one. He loved it and fell asleep with it every night and took it with him everywhere he went.

"Huggy-bugs," the fuzzy said pleadingly.

"No, no," Giorgio said.

The fuzzy hopped in place. Then, somehow, it was too close to Giorgio, even though Giorgio didn't see it make the leap across the distance. Now it was *too* close. Giorgio felt warm foolish love suffuse him.

"Huggy-wugs," he said.

The fuzzy felt warm and natural in his arms. He held him close, remembering that odd sensation when you loved something so much you wanted to just squeeze it and squeeze it harder. But the fuzzy didn't mind. The fuzzy was soft and pliable and endlessly huggable. Its huge eyes stared lovingly into Giorgio's.

"Snuggle-wuggle," it said. It nuzzled Giorgio's neck and buried its face in the crook of his shoulder.

Giorgio got back into the cockpit, the fuzzy in his arms. It was too late to turn back now. He stared at the fuzzy.

"Take... with?" the fuzzy said. "Help... Fuzzy-wuzz!"

How long did he have? He thought about Johnny Luck in his box. He wasn't going to go that way. He could stay behind the line. Some pilots never came back, and their missions were written off. The company didn't care as long as the deliveries kept running. And there were always new pilots to carry them through.

He put the fuzzy in the jump seat and strapped them both in. The engines came alive, and the propeller spun, and the fuzzy and Giorgio accelerated across the dirt track. The plane jumped into the air, and the fuzzy warbled something Giorgio didn't catch.

The steady drone of the engines was calming on his nerves. He flew back the way he'd come, over a small village with blue and blue and blue and pink flowers growing in a profusion over the roads and in the gardens and in pots on the windowsills. Giorgio smelled menthol cigarette smoke from the back seat of the plane.

"Watch where you're going, Giorgio!" his mother snapped. He turned his head and saw her sitting there, puffing on the long thin cigarette with quick jerks of her hand, the way she had ever since he could remember.

"Mama," he said.

"Watch the road!"

"This isn't a car, Mama," he said. She only ever came flying with him once, reluctantly. He had been so proud, having just got his wings. She had complained the whole way to the airfield and then sat mute in the small plane the whole half hour they were airborne. Giorgio had felt a vague sense of disappointment then that he never quite managed to put into words.

He flew over the small town again and then, just like that, he went over the line. He looked behind, but of course there was nothing there, and the jump seat was empty.

He felt fine. The sky was blue and blue and blue and pink. Soon the airfield came into view, and the tents, and the parked airplanes. The jeep of the woman from the company was still there. Giorgio eased the stick, aligned with the landing strip. The landing was smooth. The ground crew sprayed him with delousing water, but he didn't feel a thing. They off-loaded the cargo and Giorgio went off to change his wet clothes. The fuzzy was in the corner of his tent as Giorgio put on a fresh shirt and trousers.

"Huggy?" it said hopefully.

Giorgio looked into the crooked mirror over his washbasin. There was nothing there, just the back of the tent, and the dim light, and a mosquito. He finished buttoning his shirt and stepped out of the tent. He went over to the tuck shop.

"Could I get a beer?" he said.

The fuzzy pushed the bottle inexpertly across the wooden counter.

Giorgio took a sip, but the beer tasted like bubble gum, and he put it down. A shadow fell on him then, and he looked up and saw the woman from the company.

"Did you get the cargo?" she said.

Giorgio shrugged.

"Sure," he said.

"Sit up straight when I'm talking to you," the woman from the company said. She smelled of menthol cigarettes.

"Yes, Mama," Giorgio said. The fuzzy jumped into his lap. It looked up at Giorgio with big bright eyes.

"Huggy-wuggy," it said.

"Yes," the woman from the company said, quite seriously. She knelt down and put her arms around Giorgio. He felt like he was four years old again, and everything was better.

"Snuggle-wuggle," the woman said.

And everything was blue and blue and blue and pink, forever.

Infinite Tea in the Demara Café

Ida Keogh

Henry first suspected he was in a different universe when his waitress told him coffee didn't exist.

He had found himself at his usual corner table in the Demara Café, affording him a full view of both the establishment and the street outside where the morning traffic was making haphazard progress towards central London. Or rather, at first glance it looked like his usual table. But it didn't feel like it. Without thinking, he straightened the cutlery. It felt too light.

He inspected his surroundings. Over by the counter a couple giggled softly at a shared joke, their heads almost touching. At the next table a woman filled pages with turquoise ink, her eyes not leaving her notebook as she reached for her teacup. As he gazed at the twin reflections of looping lines in her glasses he had a momentary vision: a searing flash, and a wall of heat. For a split second the air smelled acrid.

China clinked. He had knocked over his cup and was gripping the table. A spreading pool of vibrant green liquid advanced towards his blanched fingers. He stared at it, open-mouthed, because he had no idea what it was.

"I'll get that, Henry." His waitress leaned over and mopped up the virescent spillage with brisk efficiency. He was sure she hadn't been standing there a moment before. She had kind, dark eyes, and skin the colour of a salted caramel latte when all the froth has melted into its depths. But she was not the waitress who served him coffee every morning.

"I'm sorry, have we met?" he enquired.

The girl tapped her name badge. "Liara," she said, with a half-amused pout. "I've been working here for nearly a month, remember?"

He did not and could only stare at her blankly.

"Why don't I get you a refill? On the house." She reached over and patted his hand, an alarmingly familiar gesture.

"Thank you," he said. He glanced at the green-soaked cloth. "Coffee, please."

"Coffee?" she said, her tongue playing with the word. "What's that?"

"You don't have coffee?" He could feel his mouth going dry.

"I've never heard of it," she said. "I'm pretty sure it doesn't exist!" Her face rumpled with concern. "Henry, you order the same thing every day – the house blend matcha, milky, two sugars. You ordered one not five minutes ago."

"Matcha? What's that?" he asked. "It sounds Japanese."

"Korean, actually," she replied, pointing at the menu.

Now Henry knew that something was very wrong indeed. The menu was headed 'Demara Tea House'.

It was only then he noticed that the lady with her notebook and the laughing couple had completely vanished.

Now he sat alone in this strangely quiet lull somewhere between breakfast and lunch, wondering how he had got here and contemplating his not-coffee. There was a fuzziness to his thoughts.

Liara was bustling behind the counter, arranging colourful little balls he couldn't identify into perfect trios, plainly unaware people were popping in and out of existence. Perhaps it was not them, but him? Was he somehow being flung between parallel worlds?

He wondered what Liara would make of this grey-haired fool forgetting both her name and how he took his tea. Who was back in his reality, enjoying his morning coffee and his maple pecan Danish? He had a sudden pang for his daily indulgence, with its soft pastry and glazed nuts and the lightest crème pâtissière. He wanted to suck the stickiness from each finger and allow the hot, bitter roast to mingle with the lingering flavours on his tongue.

While he thought of this comforting ritual, Liara looked up from her confections, gave him an encouraging smile, and promptly disappeared.

In an instant the café filled with people and noise and the sharp tang of unfamiliar spices. Chairs scraped and a group burst out laughing and spoons struck porcelain. The matcha was gone from Henry's hand. Instead there was a bowl before him filled with noodles and garish vegetation submerged in a translucent broth. A whiff of vinegar and fish rose to assault him. He scanned the room in a panic.

Finally, he saw Liara, taking an order with quick flicks of shorthand. He had to speak to her. If he could start to pin down differences between one universe and the next he might find a focus to return him to his own world, to his simple, ordered life.

He waited patiently while she distributed plates adorned with delicacies, steaming bowls, and a dozen pots of tea trailing a bouquet of smoke and citrus. He caught her eye as she cleared a table, and tentatively raised his hand to beckon her over.

She strode towards him, frowning. "Something wrong with your Kimchi Nabe, Henry?"

Now she was here, Henry was unsure what to ask her. Even from their brief previous encounter, though, he could tell something was different. Liara's face was drawn, her graceful efficiency worn down to the point of abruptness. He would ask about that, then.

"Is everything all right? You look tired."

Her expression softened, then sagged, then her dark eyes welled.

"Mum's test results are back," she blurted. "Henry, she's fading, and I don't know how to tell her." A teardrop brimmed over and tumbled down her cheek.

"I'm sorry," Henry mumbled, knowing nothing about Liara's mother at all.

"If you're not in a rush I'm on a break soon? I thought maybe, with everything you've been through... with your wife..."

Her words hung burning in the air, stealing all the oxygen in the room. Henry couldn't breathe. His wife, Camille, had passed away twenty years before. He had cherished her, and mourned her, and finally buried his dearest memories of her under years of hard work and then, in his retirement, a carefully constructed routine which left no time to dwell on the past. Now, in this world, some version of him had spoken about her to a complete stranger. Much worse, it hadn't occurred to him to consider whether in these other worlds she would still be gone – or whether there might be a world where she was still alive?

And with that thought, Liara, and his cooling bowl of Kimchi Nabe, and the clamouring crowd surrounding him were gone.

Henry travelled across worlds in a daze. Waiters and waitresses came and went, and with them the scents of jasmine, cabbage, cinnamon, sizzling pork. When he asked them to look up Camille, the very question seemed to force him on to the next world, and the next. Outside, black cabs became mauve, then ochre. In some worlds he asked for coffee. One stranger after another looked at him with bemusement and concern before evaporating out of existence. In one loud world where he couldn't get the waiter's attention at all he took his plate of what looked like jellied tentacles and threw it to the floor in frustration. As the smashed and gelatinous remains unpicked themselves from reality and a fresh plate appeared on the table before him, he wept.

He felt a cool hand on his shoulder and opened his eyes. The table now sported a pristine, blue tablecloth. He had moved on again. A waiter with a pallid complexion and a black apron was standing over him, holding a tall glass of steaming matcha on a saucer painted with koi carp.

"Did you know Ruby, then?" the waiter asked, setting the beverage down.

"I'm sorry, did I know who?"

"Liara's mother, Ruby. It's her funeral today. You looked upset, I assumed… It's Henry, isn't it? Liara told me to look out for you."

"She did?"

"Yes, she said you'd been so kind to her in the past few weeks. You'd given her the strength to say goodbye." He paused, pointing at the glass. "She told me how you take your matcha. I hope I got it right."

"Thank you," Henry replied, wiping his eyes with his shirt cuff, embarrassed. The waiter loitered beside the table. Henry realised he was waiting for him to try the tea.

The bright green concoction swirled gently beneath the glass as Henry lifted it. He turned it this way and that, not knowing what to make of it. He raised it to his lips, and inhaled fragrance like a herb garden after rain. He took a sip. It flowed fresh and clean over his tongue, leaving an unexpected trace of bitterness and a delicate hint of toasted grains.

"It's perfect," he said, and meant it.

The waiter nodded and turned to attend to his other customers.

"Wait," Henry cried out. "Do you know where the funeral is being held? Do you think I should go?"

"I'm sorry," said the lad, "I don't know. Liara did say she thought of asking you but..."

"But what?"

"I think she didn't want to impose. She said you're pretty strict about your morning routine. I'll tell her you asked after her."

Henry glared at his cup. Even though the delicious brew wasn't his and he had never met this Liara, he couldn't help feeling a sense of guilt that he wasn't there for her. At least in these worlds his doppelgängers had tried to reach out, to open up to a young woman needing guidance. But in every universe, he realised, he had come to rely so heavily on an unchanging regime that he couldn't escape when it mattered most. He had become a stubborn old goat. Camille would have been ashamed of him.

There was no more he could do here, he thought, but perhaps there was another world waiting for him where he could do better. He closed his eyes and thought of Liara. The air felt warm, and a tingling sensation spread from his heart out to his fingertips. He knew that this time he would traverse to another reality by choice.

A high falsetto lilted over rapid hand drums. Henry breathed in a heady mix of cumin, ginger and coriander. Opening his eyes, he found that the walls of the café here were painted a deep vermillion and hung with bold canvasses. A stylised elephant in slick lines of silver swept its trunk towards gold dusted chillis and star anise on the adjacent wall. His onward gaze led him to Liara, sitting at a table in front of the crimson petals of an open lotus flower, cradling a large, steaming mug.

He hesitated for a moment, then took a deep breath, stood up from the corner table and walked over to her.

"May I join you?" he asked, his hands becoming clammy.

Liara looked up at him with faint surprise. He noticed her eyes dart across to his familiar seat. "Of course, Henry, please," she said, gesturing at the chair across from her. She gave him a half-smile as he sat. He saw now, with dismay, that her eyes were rimmed with red. They sat for a moment in awkward silence.

"How are you?" he said, finally.

Liara took a gulp of tea, then sighed. "I'll be all right. I just miss her desperately," she muttered. She looked up at him. "I haven't had the chance to thank you for –"

"Wait," Henry interrupted. "I have to tell you something. That wasn't me. That was a different Henry."

"What are you talking about?" She looked astonished, hurt.

"Please, let me explain. I think I only met you, or a version of you, a few hours ago. Or a few days perhaps; it's hard to keep track of time. I've been travelling through worlds. Sometimes you're there and sometimes you're not. The first occasion we met, you seemed happy. You had only ever made me matcha, but I hadn't tasted it before."

"Matcha? What's that, Japanese?"

"Korean, actually." He smiled. "I don't know why, but I think I was meant to meet you. This you."

"Henry, you're not making any sense. We met weeks ago. I moved here to be closer to Mum and we got talking about your wife, Milly... Are you telling me I imagined all that?"

"Camille," he corrected. "I only ever called her Camille. Liara, that was a different version of me. I think I've taken over from the Henry you know, and perhaps he's somewhere else, on a new path."

Still nervous, he began moving cutlery and napkins to align precisely with the checkerboard tabletop. Liara watched him curiously, as if seeing him for the first time. Which, in truth, she was.

"You're really not the Henry I know, are you?" she mused. "You're telling me there are truly parallel universes out there? That somewhere my mother is alive and well?"

"I think so, yes. Though I tried to find a world where Camille was still alive, and I never could."

Liara sat back, thoughtful. She sipped from her mug. "But if you found her, she wouldn't be your Camille, would she? She would be a different person, with twenty years of history you hadn't shared."

Henry frowned. "You're right," he said. "It wouldn't be the same. I loved my Camille, and I lost her. I thought I had moved on, but I'm starting to understand I just hid her memory away. In one universe after another that has only ever led to a dull retirement where the best thing about my day is a good cup of Arabica. Or matcha. Or whatever all the other Henrys have every morning. What do I drink here?"

Liara quirked an eyebrow. "Darjeeling. Every day."

"Liara, don't become like me. Remember your mother with gladness. Celebrate her life, and yours."

She scrutinised him, as if trying to appraise the worth behind his weary eyes. "I will, Henry," she said at last. She drained her mug and smacked her lips. "You know," she continued, "Mum would have liked you. This you. I hope you find a universe where you might meet. You can tell her that in every possible reality her daughter loves her very much."

With unaccustomed boldness, Henry reached across the table and squeezed her hand. "If I ever meet her, I will be sure to do that. Would you tell me about her? How she laughed? What she loved?"

"I'd like that," Liara said. "Can I get you something first?"

"What was that?" he asked, gesturing to her empty mug.

"Masala chai," she said. "I add an extra sprinkle of black pepper. It will set your soul on fire. Have you ever had it?"

"No," Henry smiled, "but I think I'm ready to try."

Many worlds and cups and dishes later, a woman his age with familiar dark eyes popped tiny, sticky balls into her mouth, washing them down with a glass of something vividly pink. When she saw him, she beamed, her face crinkling with happiness, and he knew deep in his bones he would not be moving on again.

"Henry! How lovely to see you."

"You too, Ruby," he replied warmly. "I have a message for you."

"Oh? Well come tell me all about it. But first, let's order a fresh pot of tea."

All I Asked For

Anne Charnock

Alice performs ten movements in twenty-five minutes, including two strong kicks, plus a shoulder roll and what I can only describe as a shiver. I am so proud of her. She flexes the muscles in her arms, more so than yesterday. And with her hands relaxed, her fingers curled inwards, she looks as though she's play-boxing. I make a note – *10 in 25* – in her activity diary, just as the doctor ordered.

Noah turns to me and grins. "I've been looking forward to this all day, watching her movements, and counting," he says. "Let's do it again." We always do.

This has become our routine since Alice turned twenty-eight weeks. Noah and I sit together at home twice a day and check her activity – specifically, how long it takes for her to make ten movements of any kind. We view her, at many times her actual size, on our sitting room screen. Alice in her dream state – a live feed from a camera focussed on our baby in her baby-bag, fifteen miles away in a gestation ward. Alice in a clear plastic womb of sorts, gestating in a fluid close to natural amniotic, her umbilical cord connected to a plastic tube. Her own little heart pumping the flow of blood. And an overhead monitor with flickering green and red against black, revealing her vital signs.

"She's always more lively in the evening, isn't she?" I say. "I reckon they feed extra nutrients to her at this time to simulate a mother's evening meal."

While at work today I tried to check on Alice and her activity because she seemed a little sluggish yesterday. But the office was manic. I slipped out at lunchtime to buy a sandwich and took a quick peek at her on my phone. She seemed fine and, to be honest, I'm glad I didn't make an actual count. It's something Noah and I enjoy doing together.

We sit side by side and watch for any movement. I place one hand on my belly, and when Alice kicks, I imagine her kicking inside me. Or at least I try. I don't tell Noah I'm imagining this because he might feel left out, or he may wonder if I'm regretting our decision.

When I look back it all seemed so rushed, and I wish now I'd insisted on waiting another week or two. I should have stood firm, because it seemed unfair to migrate the baby before I felt her first kick. My pre-emptive caesarean occurred at twenty-two weeks. Alice left me behind. She became free, to reach her ideal birth weight, with perfect nutrition, in the gestation ward.

Just one kick. That's all I asked for.

"It's so much better being able to see her," I tell Noah in a show of solidarity. He leans towards me and kisses my forehead. His gentleness breaks me, and I wipe away tears. We met only three years ago and didn't expect children to come our way. Our Alice. My first pregnancy. When Alice is born, I will be forty-six years old.

My doctor referred me straightaway to the hospital. An automatic referral, she said. Standard practice for a person of advanced maternal age. At the initial appointment, the consultant talked me through the elevated risks of older mothers giving birth prematurely. His tone seemed to say, *Look how much you and your baby could cost us.* At the second appointment, he looked at my scans and repeated his concerns. It's difficult to argue when you are lying on your back on a gurney. He stood over me with a nurse by his side. I asked, "What about the danger in transferring the foetus? You seem to be swapping one risk for another risk." I am sure the nurse tutted. The consultant, his hands spread, seemed too nervous to lower them onto my modest bump, as though the simple act of touching might precipitate disaster. He didn't trust me, he didn't trust my body to hold onto my baby. He kept on about "the appalling chronic conditions" visited upon a child born super-premature. I told the consultant that I felt perfectly healthy and preferred to take the risk, to carry the pregnancy. I remember the way his top lip curled. He said, "Do you really think that's the correct attitude? We must do what's best for the baby."

With his hands flat on my belly, he told me that one day most babies would gestate from conception in an artificial womb. "But for now –" he sighed "– we must do what we can for high-risk cases. Migration to a baby-bag is a huge step forward."

Noah and I go to bed early because tomorrow is visiting day. Noah often likes to be little spoon. But tonight, and most nights since I became pregnant, he's big spoon to my little one. He squeezes me tight, kisses me on my neck. "One more sleep," he says. And we both giggle. Momentarily, I glean a premonition of a house filled with laughter when Alice arrives.

Only two months to wait. Sixty-three days to be precise. We will attend the birth – the opening of the bag. The umbilical will be cut and clamped exactly as happens with a natural delivery.

On my bedside table, I keep a small screen linked to the camera feed from the ward. I kiss my fingertips and touch the screen. "See you soon, Alice. Sleep tight and I'll sing to you tomorrow, something new."

Earlier in the day, I recorded myself singing a song – one I'd considered cheesy until recently. I emailed the recording to Alice's playlist, now full of similarly cheesy songs that now completely melt me. I close my eyes. Together forever.

If I wake in the night, I will gaze at her for a few moments before slipping back to sleep.

We sign in, sanitise, show our parent badges to two security guards and enter the baby ward. We see Alice in the hospital only once a week, and this is our ninth visit. If I had a choice, I would come here every day, but the hospital restricts the number of parents in the baby ward at any one time. So, for six days of the week, my chest aches with the loneliness caused by our separation – a voluntary, if not totally willing, separation. During the six non-visiting days of the week, I distract myself by working extra hours and pounding the treadmill at the gym. Anything to speed from one visit to the next.

As we enter, a nurse approaches us through the semi-darkness of the ward and leads us to Alice. She's in a different bay to her usual one, with five other foetuses rather than the usual four. A familiar anxiety breaks surface. I check the labels attached to her baby-bag.

"It's definitely Alice," says Noah.

"Just checking."

He thinks I worry too much. And I know the hospital has systems and processes that everyone deems fail-safe. But, to me, it's easy to imagine a mix-up. I don't understand how Noah can be so trusting. After all, full-term babies look similar to one another, so these foetuses must be difficult to differentiate for the medical staff.

"We can tell it's Alice now. Look at those ears. Just like mine, poor thing," he says. It's true. There's no mistaking those ears.

I don't tell him, but I suspect my anxiety over a mix-up has a deeper root. The way I see it, if I gave birth the normal way, I'd know for sure that the baby was mine. As soon as the baby was delivered, I'd hold her. There could be no doubt.

The nurse says, "Alice is doing so well. No problems at all. She seems very sensitive to touch this week."

I step forward and place my fingertips against her back. Her legs make a cycling motion. I want the nurse to leave us. I don't want anyone to speak.

"She hasn't much room. What happens if she grows too big for the bag?" asks Noah.

"She'll be fine," says the nurse. "It gets pretty cramped in a real womb."

Noah says, "We posted a new recording this morning."

"Well, I'll leave the three of you to enjoy it. I'm at the other end of the ward with some new arrivals. Just wave if you need me."

I glance across and notice, at the far side of the ward, a row of baby-bags arranged close together without any separation into bays. I wonder if Alice's move is part of some reorganisation.

Noah pulls over two chairs and we sit as close as we can to Alice. We lean forward and take an earpiece each. After a few minutes of older recordings, the new song begins. I laugh, embarrassed, when my voice fails to hit the top note. And at the same moment Alice's limbs seem to quiver as though she's excited.

"Look at her. She loves it," says Noah.

We take it in turns to place a palm on the bag, close to Alice's body. And as Noah removes his palm, Alice appears to swim. I reach out, touch the bag and feel her elbow press against the ball of my thumb. My voice misses the top note again.

Yes, better days lie ahead. This is the sweetest moment, and I bend down so that my face is an inch away from Alice.

"Better say our goodbyes soon," says Noah. "Visiting time is nearly over." On cue, the nurse appears. "Not rushing you, but another parent is due to visit this bay in ten minutes," she says.

We overlapped with another parent last time, and I felt uncomfortable sharing the space. I always feel self-conscious when other parents are around even though we're all in the same boat. It's obvious that I'm an older mother, and so it's clear that I had little choice. But the young mother I met last time seemed eager to tell me she had no choice either – cancer treatment. Questions otherwise hang in the air, and I'm sure we're all aware of them. Is your baby-bag strictly necessary? Did you fake a phobia about childbirth? Did you want a baby-bag to protect your career?

"Are you reorganising the ward?" I ask the nurse. "I'm wondering why Alice has been moved. And I see there's a row of baby-bags, which you haven't grouped into bays."

"Just temporary. A bit of overspill from the ward next door. That's the ward that doesn't receive visitors."

She raises her eyebrows, and I know she's referring to terminations, and foetuses rescued from chaotic homes.

"That's a shame," I say. "Not having visitors. Is their world silent? No voices to listen to."

The nurse leaned into me. "Unofficially, the nursing staff read stories to them and sing songs. We make the recordings on our own time. No one asks us to do it, but it only seems fair, doesn't it?"

I find myself suddenly welling up. "We could share our recordings, couldn't we, Noah?"

He stares at me. Without answering.

"Jeez, that came out of nowhere," says Noah as we leave the hospital. "I didn't know what to say."

"Sorry. It just came out. I felt sorry for them. I mean, why should Alice have songs and stories, while they only hear the sounds of the ward – trolleys clunking, the nurses chatting to one another. Those foetuses don't know they're any different."

We slip into silence for the journey home. We love our visits to see Alice, but it's a deep dread feeling to leave her behind. An abandonment.

My own mum says I don't know how lucky I am. She only had me. A difficult birth. She claims I'd have a dozen brothers and sisters if baby-bags had been invented sooner. Slight exaggeration, I know. But if Mum has told me once, she has told me twenty times that childbirth can't go on. She mentions the Stone Age. She barely listens to me.

Noah places my dinner on the table. He takes care of me even though I'm not pregnant, as though my burden has simply shifted from a physical dimension. I carry brittleness rather than weight.

"I keep thinking about the other foetuses. The other babies," I say.

"I'm sure they'll end up in good homes. Listen, let's do another count before bedtime. I think Alice is really responding to your new song."

I pick at my meal. I'm off my food. No one will ever say to me, *You're eating for two now.*

Ten movements in twenty-three minutes. I make a note. Another record breaker.

Noah says, "When she is here, we'll forget all this. Alice will be born at full term, and she'll look forward to a long, healthy life. We owe her that."

I want this to be true. But I fear I'll never lose that feeling of dread when we leave our baby with the nurses, strangers really. And I still believe we could have waited. I deserved to feel Alice kick. But clearly, it's not about me.

The Savages

David Gullen

Afternoon shaded towards evening, the hour before dusk. Up in their room Jin could not concentrate. Worms coiled inside their soft carapace, a trembling anxiety. The inevitable was coming. Tomorrow or the day after, perhaps by some miracle the day after that. The course of their entire future was about to be set, their own desires counted for nothing.

Yet it was still a normal evening. The sun slid towards the horizon, a cloud of tiny az-men fluttered by and inevitably Jin's mother's voice rose from the veranda below.

"Get away. Go. Away with you!"

A clatter followed a bang, and then the soft *pop* of something breaking. "Oh, you wretched thing."

Jin made an abrupt, frustrated gesture. Their work folded itself away and they went downstairs.

It was an az-man again, glinting blue, light above and dark below. From a distance its false face and double arms made it look like a tiny winged person. The creature hovered and swooped along the open veranda.

"Stop it, leave me alone." Jin's mother batted air with her primary hands. At her feet a mosaic bowl lay in fragments.

"Ma, it can't hurt you."

Their mother quivered with anger. 'Look what it made me do!"

"Go indoors, Ma. I'll get rid of it and tidy up."

"I don't want to go indoors. I live here. This is my home."

Jin stepped in front of the az-man and held out a jointed hand. Wings humming, the creature hung in the air. Jin spread all four arms wide, and the az-man darted towards the enormous feather-leaved copac tree in the middle of the lawn.

"I can't fly," Jin said and slowly turned full circle so the az-man could see they had no wings.

It settled on the varnished wood of the veranda rail and tucked up one leg. Up close it was obvious the az-man's face was no such thing. The mouth-parts on its chin were just a tuft of bristles, its faceted eyes really dimpled heat sensors, and the oval dome of its head a large simple eye. Jin moved a few feet down the rail and the az-man's head became a face again, an illusion.

Jin heard the swish of the broom and the clink of shards as their mother swept up. "If it's still here when I've finished I'll get the gun."

"All right!" Jin stepped down onto the lawn. Darting and hovering, the az-man followed. Jin walked past the spreading copac tree to the end of the garden, where the ground rose into low crags and the wild growth began. When land for the property had first been cleared the constructors had left the copac tree to provide shade for the house, but like everyone else they had just landed and didn't understand the new world. Ever since, the tree had slowly been retreating towards the woodlands. A hundred more years and it would be out of the garden completely.

Their garden was nothing like the forest. Around the tree spread a lawn of imported grasses. Flowers grown from a small fortune in seeds brought in on the second wave of ships filled the borders. Some died, most grew, a handful thrived abnormally, growing ten times taller, ten times faster, with blooms as wide as arms spread and fruit as large as Jin's head.

These the Council for Normalisation ordered rooted up and burned, banned their further growth, and prohibited import.

The az-man hovered at the forest edge, dipping and darting into and out of the shadows under the canopy of towering black-leaved dendrons. Jin flapped their first arms and shoo-ed at the Az-man with their second.

"You should go." Jin looked back to the house, past the copac tree and the shallow furrow it left in the lawn like a slow wake. "Go because you can."

When they looked again the az-man had vanished. Jin hesitated, then ran into the forest. Away in the distance a flash of blue darted and was gone.

"Don't come back," Jin shouted for their mother's benefit, then added, "I'm glad you've gone."

Except they weren't, not really. Jin picked up a fallen stick, slick with rot, and flung it angrily into the wood. They wished they were an az-man, even a copac tree. Even trees could leave the garden.

Jin sat against the black bole of one of the dendrons. Anxiety returned, they covered their eyes with their hands. Tomorrow or the day after, they could do nothing.

The forest was not silent. Scurries and scuffs came from the undergrowth, clicks and whistles. Once, deep in the distance, a sound like a groan, not of pain but of release. Wind stirred the canopy, held aloft on branches that flexed like a dancer's arms.

As they sat something strange came: a dozen voices lifted in harmony at the very edge of audibility. Jin's head jerked. Had they slept? Little time had passed, the song remained – an uncertain memory. Reluctantly Jin stood, knowing they should go back to the house, knowing they were forbidden to be in the forest at night.

The first bright stars were out, among them bright Zetwal and the gas giant, Rongo. On the far side of the planet a pinpoint star Jin had never seen hung in a strange constellation. Around it swung the world everyone still called "Home".

The palm of Jin's hand that had held the stick began to tingle. Jin hurried to the washroom and disinfected both hands. Some warnings, perhaps, were true. Some changes more unwanted than even tomorrow's.

Jin's mother sat hunched in a soft chair. A glass of cheap brandy rested on the table, the long-barrelled house gun leaned against the wall. She spoke to Jin without looking. "Where's Hara?"

"At Alward Pracatan's for the sleepover, remember?"

"Oh, yes. Alward's parents Chose for them yesterday. Mother, I think."

Jin's stomach knotted, their secondary hands clutched and gripped. Alward was a good friend, now they would change. Mother, Father: either future felt suffocating. Adults did cruel things, or wanted them done. Jin knew by the time they were an adult themselves their minds would have changed and they would want it too. "When is Dad coming home?"

"Soon. Does it matter?" Their mother lapsed back into her chair. "That horrid thing. I just wanted to sit outside for a moment."

"The az-man just want to look, they don't do any harm."

"They're not normal are they? Not one thing or another like we are." A pulse of bitter anger swept Jin's mother. "Why did we come here? Some days I hate this place, hate everything, I –" She clutched one of Jin's hand, groped for the others until she held them all. "I don't mean that, Jin. Not everything."

Jin held their mother's hands for a long moment then carefully detached themselves. They took the gun and replaced it in the rack.

Later, Jin's palm held a tinge of blue, an itch like the place a splinter had been. Finally, they slept, and in the morning both were gone.

Two years younger than Jin, Hara was keen to talk about the sleepover. "Alward's been Chosen mother. It felt funny to call them – I mean her – she at first, but it soon felt normal."

"Is... she... very different?" Only last week Jin and Alward had played and swapped books and hung out. At the beginning of the year Jin's whole class were all children; now half of them had been Chosen. Jin fell into a reverie about their own body, each segment still soft and flexible, their limbs pliable, the ridges on their lower belly undifferentiated into either sword or shield. An overwhelmingly sad and futile determination filled them – they did not want to change.

Hara chattered. "Mrs Sevenil's crazy, her garden's... We looked over her fence, you should see."

Jin liked Mrs Sevenil. She was always friendly and could almost magically produce a glass of juice and a plate of nibbles. She was old, one of the first-comers, and people said she was lonely. Years ago her husband went away and never came back. Dead, alive, nobody knew – he was just gone. She raised her children by herself, chose for them by herself, chose all five to be fathers. Each one went away and never came back. Fathers always went away, to work and to war. If they came back they always went away again. And sometimes they disappeared, killed fighting or from work. Fighting and work were what fathers were for, and only sometimes for coming home. Mrs Sevenil lived alone. Everyone said people were not supposed to live alone because nothing got done alone, alone was not a community. Alone was not normal.

Jin wanted to know more about Mrs Sevenil's garden.

"Clouds of az-men, wyrm ferns, muscle-leaves, frog flowers. Giant stuff, too. It's weird, she's weird." Hara was already their mother's child. "In fact, it's disgusting. I wouldn't want a garden like that next to mine."

Alward had been Chosen mother. Jin's own time rushed towards them like a meteor. Was today their last childhood day? How would it happen, what did it feel like? Alward would know.

"I'd like to see her," Jin said. Like all good lies this was partly true.

"Are you sure you want to?"

"Yes. I'm really stressed. I think it will help."

"Take your phone, just in case."

Jin always did. Everyone always did except their mother, who kept hers on the table in the hall. If Jin needed to call they had to wait and wait until their mother heard the tone.

Alward's mother pulled open the door at the exact moment Jin arrived. She wore a silk gown tied around her body with a silk belt. The colours were extraordinary, large blotches of organic reds, browns and greens, lymph-blood colours. Jin stared, the unpleasantness of the design was hypnotising.

"Is that it?" Mrs Pracatan said sharply. "You just want to stand there?"

"Sorry." Jin felt so awkward. "Is Alward in?"

"Is Alward in." Mrs Pracatan smoothed the ugly material against her body then called back into the house. "It's Jin Elgasian. I think they like my gown."

Both Alward's parents were home. A potent tension filled the air, and Jin wished they had not come. Mr Pracatan wore a simply cut black robe embroidered with geometric blade designs in silver thread. He prowled the house in sudden bursts of energy interrupted by equally sudden stillness. He ate from one of the bowls, he moved ornaments on the shelves. In one rush he was at the door. He looked steadily at Jin and slid the bolts back and forth.

Whenever he moved, Alward's mother moved too. If he went left she moved right, when he advanced she retreated. It was as if an invisible rod kept them apart. A rod, Jin noted, that slowly grew shorter.

Alward came downstairs and stood bashfully. "Hello, Jin."

"Hello."

"Let's go outside." Alward led the way.

"See you later, Jin." Mrs Pracatan swung the veranda door firmly closed.

Alward and Jin walked into the garden. Jin look at them – at *her*. She looked the same.

"How are you feeling?"

"I don't know." Alward moved from one foot to the other, her four arms wrapped her body. "Pretty bad. Isn't this my fault? I'm Chosen and now Dad wants another child. He's going to – Mum's going to…"

"How could anyone want to –" Jin couldn't say it. This was why younger children went to sleepovers for the Chosen, it was too far away in their own lives for them to care.

"That's the strangest thing," Alward said. "I never thought about it but I'm beginning to understand." Her voice drifted, introspective. "I can almost imagine wanting…" She stroked her belly, where her shield would grow, then laughed, amazed at her own thoughts.

Fascinated and repelled, Jin needed to know more. "What's being Chosen feel like?"

"At first, nothing. They just told me, they said they'd talked about it and decided mother was best. I went away and thought about it." She looked straight at Jin. "It takes a moment, then you realise you feel different. The hours go by, I'm still me."

This was less uncomfortable territory. "That's not too bad."

Alward laughed less certainly. "I'm just glad it's over. I was so nervous, but now it's just going to happen and –" She touched Jin with both her right arms. "Jin, you don't need to worry."

Jin could say nothing.

"We'll still be friends."

Would they? "You wanted to be Chosen mother?"

"Not wanted, but… it's decided now, so that's who I'll be." Through the windows of the house two dim figures were closer to each other now than ever. "What about you?"

Again, Jin said nothing.

"You can't want to stay Unchosen. The Normalisation Council…" Alward stared, open-mouthed. "Jin, you can't."

Mrs Pracatan's pleading came through an upper-floor window. "No, lover, don't, not yet. Please, please. Oh, I'm not ready. No, no. Wait, let me help –"

Alward walked slowly towards the house on legs stiff as an adult's. Behind her Jin stood as forgotten as if they never existed.

"Alward?"

Down from the high window came a thin shriek, an agonised groan, dreadful animal noises. Alward froze mid-step, then resumed her slow pace towards the house.

Alone, abandoned, Jin listened to the ugly sounds coming from the house. Their legs shook, they wanted to curl up, roll away and hide. All around them the Pracatans' garden spread in perfect order: a flat green lawn, a paved area with recliners and a table, deep borders of well-behaved flowers spaced in bare, chocolate-brown earth. Nothing about this was reassuring, none of it looked even real.

Jin did not fit in here any more than inside the house, in any house. Deep down they did not *want* to fit in, did not want to be wanted in homes like this. In homes like their own. But there was also the Council.

Like Jin's garden, the Pracatans' backed onto original land, untamed and craggy. Looming dendrons clung on high bluffs over shadowed gullies. Jin heard the ponderous rustle of something large moving, then soft in the silence a wordless chanting again, barely audible and perhaps not even real.

The forest scared Jin but it also drew them in. Their palms itched, they weren't ready. With nowhere else to go they climbed over the fence into Mrs Sevenil's garden.

*

The garden was all Hara had described and more. The lawn a meadow of knee-high growth, the imported border flowers swamped by returning original growth. A copac sapling was actually pushing into the garden from the forest beyond, seeking an open glade in which to grow. Tiny inching, creeping tendrils grew in its soil-wake, neither small muscular leaves or photosynthetic limbs, but both. Original life had never fully differentiated into plants and animals, or anything else.

A few imported plants survived, enormous and hybridised, with saw-edged leaves, emerald above and crimson below. Golden-white trumpet flowers turned and bent and followed Jin.

A cloud of az-men swarmed, dipping into and out of the giant blooms. Jin watched one cling to a glassy green stem, close its fingers into a knife-hand and make a cut as long as its body. Pale green sap oozed, speckled with red. The az-man dipped its head and drank. Then it reached back with its knife-hand, cut off its own wings and wriggled inside the stem. The cut oozed shut, the az-man hung in a green-gold space. Speckled sap flowed, slowly the az-man dissolved and was gone.

Uncertain at what they had witnessed, Jin reached for the severed wings. Frog-flowers croaked and hopped, a nearby wyrm-fern uncoiled a flexing segmented frond.

Mrs Sevenil's voice came from her house. "Careful, child. Some of the plants are not kind."

Jin stepped back. Mrs Sevenil was old, her brow ridges dark, the edges of her joints cracked and worn. Yet she moved easily and her voice was strong. Rings of small-leaved yellow flowers hung around her brow and second-arm wrists.

Jin tried to describe what they had just seen with the az-man.

"All life is a chain, the links are closer together here."

Jin did not understand. Mrs Sevenil did her usual trick of producing a jug of juice, two beakers, and a plate of tasty nibbles seemingly from mid-air. They sat together in the meadow.

"I was made when a tiny part of my father's body joined a tiny part of my mother's. So were you, so is everything, right back to the beginning. We hand ourselves on, an unbroken chain of life." Mrs Sevenil pulled open her robe to show Jin her belly, the fused segments of her shield punctured with five cross-shaped scars from her husband's sword, deep and old. One by one Mrs Sevenil touched the scars. "This one is where my first child was made, this the second, the third." Jin could not look away.

"A little bit of me, a little bit of him. We like to think we're unique but really we're hybrids of what came before."

"Why did you Choose all your children father?"

"I wanted to do something and I needed to be alone. It took a long time but I got there." Mrs Sevenil tipped her head to one side. "Do you like my garden?"

"Yes."

"It's your time to be Chosen, isn't it?"

"Yes. And I don't —" Jin exclaimed. Mrs Sevenil held up her hand.

"Hush. What's your name?"

"Jin Elgasian."

"I know your mother, poor thing. Once, I was like —" Mrs Sevenil looked up at a sky filled with billowing clouds. "Life's different here, Jin. There are no individuals, just one great expression of living. I came to it late and it wasn't easy, but I decided. I chose again."

Mrs Sevenil pulled one of the blooms on her wrist, another from her brow. In both places her skin stretched before the flowers broke free, trailing beads of red-brown lymph. She offered them to Jin, small simple things with five blunt white petals and yellow hearts. Without entirely knowing why, Jin crushed them into their palm.

Jin wandered out onto the road and turned for home. Down the way Mrs Pracatan lay on a recliner in front of her house, her ugly robe drenched with new stains.

"I'm all right, Jin," she called, then winced with the effort. "Alward said you were frightened but there's no need. In fact I'm going to be fine, I'll heal over, and then we'll have another egg."

A mile from home Jin heard the whine of an approaching ground car. Moments later it drew alongside, the canopy opened and they saw their father, Mr Elgasian, in the cabin.

"Hello there, Jin."

Jin stood on quaking legs. "Dad! You're back."

"Tomorrow is an important day. You think I'd miss it?"

Jin climbed aboard, the vehicle moved on. A part of their mind tried to reconcile the scars on Mrs Sevenil's body with the comforting presence of their father. It was impossible. Tomorrow – the word filled their mind. Tomorrow. Jin fought to keep their tone light. "Dad, can we talk about that? Can we wait? It's been such a strange day."

Mr Elgasian wanted to know more. Jin concentrated on the events at the Pracatan household and barely mentioned Mrs Sevenil.

"Some things are natural and normal, whatever you think about them." Jin's father said. His frown deepened, he tapped out a brief message on his phone. "It also sounds like Mrs Sevenil needs a visit from the Normalisation Council."

Jin gaped, filled with guilt at their unintended betrayal. "She's always been so nice to me. They won't hurt her, will they?"

"It all depends."

Jin did not want to bring the subject up again but a short reprieve was better than none. "Dad, please."

Their father replied in a flat monotone. Whether he was bored or angry, Jin could not tell. "All right. One more day. I have important news of my own."

The news was about the city, the entire colony. The family gathered on the veranda. Mr Elgasian stood beside the rail. "We're expanding. A second port now, a third later. We're not going to be the frontier for much longer."

"What happened?" Hara asked.

"The explorers found new systems. They're primitive, not as bad as this place, but they won't see us coming until it's too late."

"Will they fight?"

"Yes. It's war."

"Good." Jin's mother sat forward. "Smash them."

Mr Elgasian laughed. "The land behind our house is going to be developed as part of the expansion. I'm in charge, so we can leave the hill behind the garden if we want. Everything else will be flattened."

"No, get rid of it, get rid of it all. I want to see decent houses and gardens."

"Me too," Hara said.

Mr Elgasian looked pleased. He looked at Jin. "I've changed my mind. Tomorrow is your day."

That night Jin sat in their room unable to sleep, unable to think for thinking about tomorrow.

They would not sleep, Jin decided, knowing it was ridiculous but was equally determined not to waste these last few hours. There was nowhere to go and nobody to see, and who could they talk to, who would understand? Only Mrs Sevenil. They rubbed the thickened skin in the middle of their palm and listened to the indistinct sounds of their parents' voices through the floor.

Mrs Sevenil. Jin jumped up. They had to warn her. They searched the colony forums, message rooms and groups but Mrs Sevenil was old-fashioned, she lived alone. She still had a phone, everyone had a phone. Jin's mother called her, she had the number.

Jin carefully opened the door and crept to the top of the stairs. Downstairs, the doors to the main room were open. Their father stood by the window, their mother sat beside the fire. Beyond the open doors stood the hall table. On it, their mother's phone. Jin slipped down the stairs, stood behind a door and peered through the gap between the hinges.

Jin's father turned from the window. "After Jin is Chosen I want more children."

"More?" Their mother's voice shook.

"Three, preferably four."

"I don't... I can't." Mrs Elgasian's hands fluttered like an az-man's wings. "Not even three."

"Two, then." Mr Elgasian tried to comfort her and after a moment she let him. Jin stepped swiftly and silently across the open doorway and transferred Mrs Sevenil's details to their phone. Their parent's voices dropped to a murmur, Jin strained to hear:

"You know I can't refuse you. Mothers just can't."

"My dear. On the day you will want to."

"Right now I'm frightened."

"But you will."

"Yes. That frightens me, too."

Jin swiftly climbed the stairs. Back in their room, they messaged Mrs Sevenil:

I'm really sorry, my father's told the Normalisation Council on you. I'm so sorry, I didn't mean to. It's all my fault. This is Jin Elgasian. Sorry.

Jin stared at the little screen. After long minutes Mrs Sevenil replied.

Hello, Jin. It doesn't matter, it's time I moved on. Don't worry about me. I'm ready.

Jin felt so miserable. *You must really hate me.*

This time the reply was swift. *No, child. Never.*

Second by second, tomorrow crept closer. Jin sat on their bed. For a timeless period they were consumed with mind-sapping dread.

Jin eased open the window, climbed out onto the veranda roof then dropped down to the ground. The house lights shone, all was quiet. Hara was in their room, their parents sat by the fire. Jin kept to the shadows and stole through the garden, past the copac tree, and ran into the forest.

Two hundred feet up the crumbling crags, Jin looked back over the tops of the black dendrons. Lights glowed in the windows of houses all down the road, each further away and smaller than the last, each individual yet each somehow exactly the same. In the middle distance a cluster of towers shone, the centre of the colony city. Beyond them red and white lights blinked from the gantries and launch frames of the spaceport. Stars glittered overhead, among them, brilliant Zetwal.

By dawn they were miles away, beyond glades of frog flowers and quiet meres. Jin rested beside a multi-boled tree with fissured grey bark. Pendulous wooden fruit hung from looping branches. The sun rose, red light pushed long shadows through the trees. The echoing hoots and whistles, creaks and groans of night gave way to softer sounds.

High above Jin's head the wooden fruit split along four seams and curled open. Out of each crawled an az-man, wet with sap.

Crumpled wings unfurled and stiffened, and one by one they flew away through the forest.

Overnight the nubbin on Jin's palm had developed into a bud of green-black scales. The itch grew intense. Jin scratched, and the scales fell away. Slender and green, a finger-length three-pronged tendril uncurled then slowly waved and flexed as if wafted by some unfelt wind.

Jin watched it with a strange thrill. Gingerly they touched it and it curled around their finger. They felt the touch from both sides. The tendril was not something else, it was a new part of them.

Away in the far distance something vast stirred.

As the day wore on the tendril grew less active, the green slowly dulled. Jin understood it would not be there forever. Like a flower it would fade and die, and they would be ordinary Jin again. They had a choice.

Towards sunset they found a tree with a branching trunk of glassy green supporting a canopy of huge tawny feather-leaves. Green-yellow sap flecked with red pulsed through veins deep in the trunk. Jin lay their hand against it and felt a slow vibration. Where the palm-tendril touched, a small seam opened. Jin drew back, amazed. After a moment the seam closed.

A moment rich with imminence arrived. Jin was not ready for this. Had anyone ever been? Control was an illusion, change came and choices were made. Where had the az-man gone? Where was Mrs Sevenil now? To do nothing was a choice but it led to no future Jin wanted. Hesitantly, they drew their hand down the trunk. Where the tendril stroked, the trunk opened deep into heartwood.

Golden sap pulsed. Jin stepped into the cleft, damp with sap, spicy with tingling life. They had time for a single breath before the trunk folded closed around them, embraced them. Welcomed them.

Jin woke in the shadow of the old copac tree, lay on the lawn and listened. A breeze moved the damp air, the ground trembled beneath their body as the roots of the copac tree did their slow work. They felt different, they felt the same. They felt the memory and heard the song.

They heard Hara's shout. "It's Jin, under the tree. They've come home."

Jin rolled to their feet and stood, happy to greet their sib. Hara pelted towards them, ground to a halt, then took a horrified step back.

Jin's parents erupted onto the veranda and they too stopped, frozen in shock and, Jin realised, with fear.

Hara broke and fled back to the veranda. Mr Elgasian forced himself forward. "Jin, what happened? Tell me."

"That's not Jin," Mrs Elgasian exclaimed. "Look at it. Call the Council."

"Wait. Something's happened, we can fix it. What happened, Jin? Where have you been?"

Jin's mother pulled the gun from the rack. "Don't you tell me to be calm. That *thing* is not my child."

I'm not a thing, Jin wanted to say. They stood on the lawn, still processing. So much had happened. *I'm still me, still a person... This is what* I *chose. I won't* – I *can't hurt you. Why are you so scared?*

Mrs Elgasian aimed but the gun would not fire at a person. She switched the safety to override. Away in the city the event was logged, the Council alerted.

A rapidly rising hum rose into inaudibility: the gun charging. "No!" Mr Elgasian knocked the barrel into the air, and the energy pellet tore into the sky.

She won't shoot me, she won't. Jin watched the unfolding drama like a spectator. *Why would she? I'm her* –

Mrs Elgasian swung the gun towards her husband and he backed away with the same fearful deference Jin had seen in Mrs Pracatan. "Yes, that's what it's like," she said, then turned and fired at Jin in one swift motion.

Jin sprang aside, the shot struck the ground, a flash of blue-white energy. Mrs Elgasian swung the gun. Jin leaped into the air, a new wave of change pulsed through them and they flew to the top of the copac tree on amber-feathered wings.

"See? See?" Jin's mother screeched. She fired wildly, energy pellets struck the tree which began a slow agonised writhing among cascades of falling leaves.

I'm me, I'm this, Jin thought, amazed. Down below their family fought and argued and did not understand. Would they listen, could they ever? Loneliness ached inside them, yet the forest called, a thousand thousand voices but one song, their home, their choice, the world as it was before they came. As it would always remain.

Down below their parents wrestled with the long-barrelled gun.

Jin made one last effort. "Please, it's me, I'm still me."

A bang, a flash, a hoarse male bellow. Mr Elgasian backed up. "No, don't!"

"You want to know what it feels like?" Jin's mother laughed and laughed. "Oh, this is what it feels like!"

She fired from the hip, Mr Elgasian staggered. He looked down at the hole in his punctured body and sat down hard.

Jin's parents looked at each other, one sitting, one standing.

"I'm so sorry," Jin's mother wailed.

Green lymph seeped between Mr Elgasian's fingers. "It's all right. I'll be all right."

Jin watched Hara take the gun from her mother's unresisting grip. Hara looked up, raised the gun, unwieldy in her small arms, and fired. Jin dropped from the tree, spread their wings, and flew.

Lazarus, Unbound

Liam Hogan

In another twenty thousand years the debris from the first *Lazarus* ship, *The ISA Tribune*, will form a tenuous but complete ring around Neptune, smearing the hopes of a long-gone generation through the vastness of space.

Thus went the predictions until a century ago. Until mining drones began to salvage the wreckage, began to return the cryo pods, disrupting the slow interplay of gravitational forces. The pods are still turning up; the power cells drained, the antique devices utterly lifeless. But in the cold vacuum the occupants are perfectly preserved, if a little harder to revive than their designers intended.

So that every now and then the ancients walk among us once more.

He looked lost, for all the attention that was being showered on him. What sort of person agrees to being deep frozen, uncertain that they'll ever wake, uncertain that their destination is habitable? Uncertain even, that they'll escape the hazards of the outer solar system?

That was the curiosity, the reason we were there, both physically and virtually. The gathering was for *him*.

Despite this, the once frozen can be tedious to talk to. Slow, confused, unable to adjust. They can't cope with how *invisible* technology has become.

Four thousand years. A period longer than the gap between mankind's first space journey and the time of the Pharaohs. Between simple metallurgy and the earliest artificial intelligences…

At first, the returnees were grateful things didn't appear too alien to them. A cup was still a cup, a bed a bed. That's because they couldn't see what lies beneath. The nano structures, the all-pervasive AI, the tweaks and changes to our biology. They look bemused when their hot drinks never go cold, their cold drinks never warm up.

They're confused when our drinks, our food, our mood enhancers, arrive without asking, without apparent interaction. They assume we have some silent method of communicating with the AI.

They are disturbed when they find we have moved far beyond that.

He stood beneath the chandelier, entranced by its delicate music. This was an aesthetic choice, one made with him in mind. The music could have come from the walls, from the glasses and small plates, from the transparent fabric in which I was draped. All this was lost on him.

That he was so fascinated in a mere peripheral, rather than interacting with those around him, was not lost on me, on us.

I eased over to the other side of the chandelier, as though sharing his interest, or as though interested in him. He'd asked for alcohol a little over an hour ago. We watched as his emotions shifted, grew excited as the AI relayed the effects on his mind, on his primitive blood chemistry.

Back when the first sleeper was revived there was a short-lived fad for going natural. But only a fad, because short-lived – well, who wants *that*?

The returnees don't have an option. Born in a time before ageing was genetically cured, there is nothing we can do as, once unfrozen, they wither away.

This one was still young. He glanced in my direction, and I picked up the not so subtle changes, the beginnings of arousal. I met his wondering eyes.

"Nice party," he said. "Are you the host?"

I almost laughed. He didn't understand there *wasn't* a host. Or perhaps, in a way, we all were.

"I'm glad you're having a good time," I replied. My voice sounded almost as barbaric as his, a series of harsh grunts, even if to his ears it was distractingly mellifluous. The old languages are incredibly ugly.

He was dressed in clothes patterned from his era, give or take fifty years. From his pocket he took out a flimsy – a museum piece only a hundred years younger than he was, the words appearing on its aged surface as it was unfurled.

"I've been rereading *The Time Machine*," he said with a wry smile.

"You all do," I smiled back, edging closer. A one-way trip four thousand years into the future? Of course they read HG Wells. If not *The Time Machine*, then *The Sleeper Awakes*, for all the good it does them. "You're probably wondering which we are: Eloi, or Morlocks?"

His pupils widened a fraction, gaze lingered on my curves before returning to my uptilted face. "And?"

"It's a little more complicated than that."

His flimsy also contained a condensed history of the world over the last four thousand years, everything he'd slept through. He'd lingered over accounts of the Schism, the final stages of the singularity, the stillborn rebellion.

"The AI..." he said, uncertain, as I offered him another drink. No alcohol in this one, though to him it tasted strongly of whisky.

"Did what it had to do," I replied. "For the good of the planet, for the good of the people. The rebels were given a choice. Many took the colony option. Some did not, thinking their martyrdom would inspire further resistance."

All this he already knew, had already read.

"You worry that the AI is evil, or that it has become an all-powerful God and we merely its playthings. It is none of those things," I murmured, taking him by the hand, leading him gently towards the bedchamber prepared for us. A room that only existed for that moment.

"What will you tell people about me?" he asked, his voice thick, his hand warm in mine.

He didn't understand. He couldn't understand any more than an ant can understand a tree. So I gave him an answer he might be able to work with.

"I'll say 'he was a lot older than me, he'd travelled, and I was feeling... experimental'."

He laughed and then frowned, unsure if he was being mocked.

As I guided him through to the room beyond, he risked a glance at the party he was leaving. Perhaps worried about etiquette, of the need to say 'thank you' to the still unidentified host.

He could never understand. That what I felt, we all felt, if we chose to. That what the watchers felt, I could also feel, a wave of shared sensation.

That he was not part of that equation was... unsettling. A distancing, a distraction. As we made love, I kept reaching for him, but he was not there. It was a novel, but not entirely pleasant experience.

I never saw him again. I'm sure he had other parties, other 'hosts'. I did not share their experiences. Indeed, I did not think of him at all except to wonder why I had been chosen for the primary role. Why we were all chosen, those at the gathering and those at the once-remove.

It was around then that reports came through of a miracle of miracles: the successful colonisation of a distant planet, a distant star. The exiled, rebellious colonists of the Schism had succeeded where *The Tribune* had not.

Then, a mere ten years later, their curt final message before they disengaged the ship's AI and fell silent.

As the shuttles begin to rise to the new generation of colony ships, I think I begin to understand. I know why the AI awakens the ancient sleepers, why we are encouraged to spend time with them, to explore what it means to be unplugged.

We are being prepared.

The Earth, the solar system, has hit its limit. The AI has stopped growing. And failure to grow is certain death. So it is time to expand beyond our cradle, beyond this single, slowly dying star.

To do that the AI must harvest those of us capable of making the journey, of adapting to the drastic changes. Even if the new generation of ships will only take a few hundred years, rather than a few millennia, the enterprise is still a risky one. That too is the lesson of the sleepers, and the other failed colony ships.

But we have a choice and I have made mine: to take my place among the stars.

And whether I wake on a strange new planet, stripped of the technology I am so used to, that I rely on every waking and even sleeping moment, or whether I spend an eternity as one link in a silent chain of sleepers around Neptune?

That is for some higher power to decide.

The Cyclops

Teika Marija Smits

23rd March

Had another day of tests yesterday. I don't feel like writing after a day of being prodded and poked. The tests they make me do and the tests they perform *on* me, to gauge the state of my immune health, seem to go on forever. It's exhausting.

Ten weeks ago, before the accident, when I was still a house officer at one of the busiest hospitals in London, I was too busy to go on a date. Too busy to phone my mother. Too busy to write in a sodding diary. If *I'd* had *me* as a patient, I'd have been intrigued. I'd have wanted to see the eye.

Of course they want to prod and poke me.

24th March

More emails today. Loads from those awful people who claim they can see angels and auras. I'm deleting them. Surely, they've read in the papers that I'm a doctor – correction: *was a doctor* – and not into woo.

I still can't get my head around the fact that I'm never going to do my rounds again. The whole six-month-to-live thing is probably what I should be thinking about, but I'm not. I keep thinking about work and its small joys: the patients who make me smile despite myself; drinking coffee with Luke and gossiping about our line manager; planning our trip to Namibia.

I'd always hated what I looked like before I went to the country of my mother's people. Growing up in the 90s, in Surrey, and being one of only a handful of girls who didn't have pink skin was pretty shit. Mind you, it never did my mum any harm – I mean, being the beautiful, black outsider. She was the model of the moment in the 80s. Then she met my dad. My screwed-up American dad who was the photographer of the moment.

When Mum found out she was pregnant with me I guess he thought that the moment was over. He stuck around long enough to make sure I was delivered safe and sound, but when he actually had to do stuff, dad stuff, he disappeared into his work. But now he's interested in his miraculous daughter. He actually phoned the other day.

In Namibia I didn't stick out like a sore thumb. It felt good to be amongst women who looked like me; I saw myself in their faces. And their high cheekbones, wide mouths and large brown eyes reminded me that beauty – normalcy – is all about context.

Luke had tried to rile me by saying that now *he* was the exotic doctor surrounded by all these beautiful women I'd have to watch out.

I laughed and then reminded him that as soon as we were back in London, he'd be desperately in love with me again – yet still too busy with work to actually go on a date.

He keeps calling me, inviting himself round, but I've been ignoring him. I don't want to look into his eyes again; to see all those magnificent colours – all those wavelengths of invisible light – the colours of horror and pity and fascination, and worst of all, grief in abeyance.

25th March

More emails and phone calls. The call from the MoD was particularly scary. They've invited me over to discuss my "particularly keen" vision; to see if I can help them with their "defence strategies". Not bloody likely. It's because of "defence" organisations like them that I've only got six months to live. Actually, it's five months now. I said no to their offer.

Journalists have been pestering me to give them an exclusive. I've told them no again and again. I unplugged the phone earlier this evening and was glad of the silence. My smartphone's been turned off for ages already. I can't do much about the idiots waiting outside my flat, but I figure they'll get called out to other stories at some point soon.

Mum's asked me to come home, which might give me some peace from the journos, but I'm not sure I want to. I've got pretty much everything I need right here; my books, some food (not that I feel like eating much) and best of all, the skylight above my bed. I spend a lot of my time simply gazing up at the sky.

My telescopic vision is improving day by day. The nanobots, or whatever the hell they are, never seem to let up. They really are building me a magnificent eye. It's like having a light microscope, the Hubble telescope, and an infra-red camera, and whatever, all rolled into one, slap bang in the middle of my forehead. Though it's a pity that the nanobots are shredding my immune system.

26th March

Last night I dreamt about the accident again. Luke and I have just finished our day's work at Rundu Hospital and Kagiso asks us if we want to see the place where the shooting star landed. We agree and then get into Kagiso's truck and on to God-only-knows where. And then we're out of the truck and walking across barren earth and into a crater about the size of a netball field. There isn't much to see – the meteorite is just a blackened boulder. Though when it's struck by the light from the setting sun it sparkles as though it's alive with thousands of miniature fireflies. Kagiso and I touch it and a shard of black crust comes away in my hand. And then Kagiso is distracted by something. He runs; away from the meteorite, out of the crater and out across the dry earth, pointing and shouting at the sky. And then I see it too – the comet – and I begin to run as well, the shard still in my hand, and somehow tingling. Luke's yelling at us to come back; he says it might not be safe out there, but I can't stop running. I've got to see the shooting star land. Kagiso's a hell of a runner and I can't keep up with him, so I slow and stop and try to catch my breath. Then the landmine explodes. In one roiling instant, Kagiso is torn to bits and fear shears through me as I realize that there's no way I can escape the flying metal and rock that is about to slice through my skull and into my eyes, taking away my sight as I used to know it. And that's always when I wake up, drenched in sweat, and fighting for breath.

27th March

Mum came over today. She forced her way through the journos outside and yelled up at the window for me to buzz her in. She's subtle like that.

I couldn't help but notice her shudder when she looked at me as I opened the door to the flat. Correction, when she saw *the eye*. But then she hugged me and started to cry. Typically, she told me off for making her worried sick by not answering her calls.

She plugged the phone in; said she'd been trying to get hold of me for days. At first, I was pissed off with her for having a go at me. After all, I've got a right to decide how I'm going to spend the next five months of my life, but she's having none of it. Says she's going to stay with me from now on: to look after me and talk about my options. My treatment. I told her that conventional treatment wouldn't do a thing. But she ignored me and went on about me taking the immunosuppressants that some of the medics think would help. *Then* she started baking cheese muffins, breaking off to field phone calls for me. At six o'clock she unplugged the phone and poured herself a large glass of wine. *Darling,* she said (I hate it when she calls me darling – I know that something unpleasant is coming next) *do you have any idea of what is going on in your body?* I sighed, my real – though useless – eyes prickling with tears that would never come, and told her that no, I didn't know what was going on. Only that, somehow, I knew that the nanobots, whatever, weren't malicious. But they were nosy, all right. I felt as though I was seeing the world through the eyes (okay, eye) of someone else. And that everything was new and strange, and well... of interest.

Later, she cooked us a huge bowl of spaghetti Bolognese and then we watched a film. It was the first time in ages I actually enjoyed eating something.

28th March

As I was checking my emails today (there were loads from Luke) Mum took a phone call from a Professor at MIT. She passed me the phone and said that I needed to speak to him since he's the leading expert in nanotechnology.

So... we're now booked on the next flight to Boston. Mum's packing our bags as I write this.

I've gotta go now. She's asking me how many knickers I want to take. Jesus.

5th April

So the whole flight thing – trying to get through the airport unnoticed by the press and unaffected by all the germs out there – was a nightmare. I still managed to catch a cold with all the precautions we took and of course it's not shifting. I had half-expected to see Luke at the airport; I thought Mum would tell him that we were going – she's always going on about him being my saviour because he was the one, mostly unhurt by the landmine, who got me back to the hospital and arranged for me to be flown back to the UK. But it seems that she took my "don't call Luke" requests seriously.

Life here is weird. They're taking blood from me almost daily and performing dozens of tests on it. They reckon that if they can just figure out how the nanobots work they can somehow neutralize them. But the bots are like nothing they've ever seen before. It's ironic really – the fact that I, with my weakened immune system, have flown all the way across the Atlantic (catching a cold in the process) just to have them say this to me, because I could have told them that. The nanobots have built my incredible eye, which can focus in on Venus on a clear day, so of course they'd be out-of-this-world amazing.

12th April

We keep going around in circles when it comes to the question of immunosuppressants. Some of the team say we should try them; that they'll dampen my immune system and so stop it from attacking the nanobots. And then *that* might make the nanobots stop killing off my immune system. Others disagree. But as I've got a cold already, I don't think it would be a good idea. The team are still baffled by the nanobots, and nothing that they've tried on them, to destroy them, has worked. So this cold's probably going to kill me.

When I'm not in the lab, I spend most of my time in bed or outside, looking at the night sky. I don't have a good view of the sky from my room so Mum takes me out in a wheelchair and wraps me in blankets so that I can gaze at the stars, which are incredible. She brings me hot chocolate and tries not to cry. I wish I could cry, but I can't. Along with the destruction of my old eyes – my real eyes – my tear ducts were damaged in the blast and my new eye, the imposter, has no need of them. I guess that spectacularly clever nanobots do not cry.

20th April
The Professor's latest idea is to hook me up to some software so that the team can see what I see. They reckon that if they can "interface" with the eye, where the nanobots are still busy, they can learn more about them. So I'll roll with this, whatever, although I know that this is just about them being nosy. I think it might be good to have someone else see what I see.

21st April
Today was super-weird. I mean, I was expecting it to be strange to have the team see what I see, but on a screen, but it was still really weird. They went silent when I showed them how good my microscopic vision was by focussing in on the scar tissue around my hand where the sharp crust of Kagiso's meteorite scratched me when I was hit by the landmine. I – and they – looked at the individual cells and watched the odd nanobot (microbot, I guess?) cruising through the scar tissue, still on patrol. They'd already hypothesized that this must have been one of the ways that the nanobots entered my body, going on to try to fix my severed optical nerves, but still, it was good to see the evidence for this hypothesis. I noticed a couple of them whispering, once again distracted by the *what and how and why* of a meteorite covered in nanobots, something I'd often considered myself, but the Professor soon silenced them.

Another weird thing though, that they, and I, can't quite figure out is why I'm not infectious. I mean, back in London, they were super-precautious, assuming that whatever was building my eye and wrecking my immune system would be contagious, but for some reason, the nanobots aren't interested in anyone else. They're sticking to me, and me only. Which is a relief, I guess. At least I don't feel guilty about anyone else having to go through what I'm going through. But of course I can't help but ask, why? Why me? Why did it have to be me?

Then came the instructions from the research team, dressed up as polite requests. So many of them. Could I look at this object, please, and view it in ultraviolet? Could I now look at them all in infra-red? And then could I go outside and focus in on the moon? I was exhausted by it all, and glad when it was over and back in my room.

Mum looked at me funny when she helped me into bed, and I had to explain why I now have what looks like a memory stick attached to the left side of my head where the shrapnel from the landmine sliced through my skull and into the back of my eyes. *They're spying on me, on what the eye can see,* I said. She didn't look happy about that at all and went off on a long rant about privacy and consent. Stuff that she thinks she's the expert on, because of her modelling days. I had to explain that it's not always on and that *I'm* the one who gets to decide when they do their spying. She seemed okay about that and then changed the subject, asking, again, if I'd thought about contacting Luke. I told her no, in my firm, but exasperated voice, that I did not want to put Luke through the anguish of being with someone about to die. And I didn't want him to see me like this.

24th April
When I went into the lab today there was a really strange atmosphere. The Professor looked nervous and said that, if I didn't mind, there'd be a few people coming round today to have a look at what my eye could see. I told him that I guessed he was no closer to a cure. He shifted his weight and said that, no, he wasn't any closer to disabling the nanobots. The more they learnt about them, the more they discovered about their complexity. Which is why he wanted some experts, and *relevant others*, to look at me.

I said it would be okay, (I'm pretty much resigned to being the world's number one freak show at the moment) but only on the condition that they didn't try to recruit me or anything.

So various people came and went, requesting me to look at this and that. Most of them treated me like a robot, but the guy from NASA was kind. He wheeled me outside, as the sun was setting, and brought me hot chocolate, topped with whipped cream. He talked to me about the constellations, and the Greeks who had named many of them, and how Gaia was the mother of the three Cyclops in Greek mythology. *This* was news to me, and when I joked to Mum later on that she must have seen into the future, or something, when she'd named me, she went all huffy and proceeded to remind me that Gaia was also Mother Earth. And *that* was why I'd been given that name: because she loved me more than the Earth itself. She had a good cry then and as usual I ended up feeling bad for upsetting her.

27th April

So I joked to the team today that rather than investigating the nanobots, it was time, maybe, that they thought about granting me my dying wish. They looked embarrassed then, because I'd acknowledged their failure, and finally the Professor said that he was sorry, and yes, he would like to know what my dying wish was. I don't know why I said it, but I thought about the night sky, and I said that I'd like to see all that there was to see of the universe. His face went all weird then, and he looked at me with an expression I couldn't quite read. But then, strangely, he smiled. He said that he was sure that Robert (the guy from NASA) would love to help. When he'd seen what my eye could see he was, apparently, very keen to persuade me to work with him, saying that if I wasn't stuck here on Earth the things I could see would be mind-blowing. It could answer many of their unanswered questions. But the Professor hadn't told me, you know, because of the whole "no recruiting thing". So, anyway, I'm going to speak to Robert again tomorrow.

28th April
I am going into space! OH MY GOD!

29th April
Mum's completely freaking out about the whole going-into-space thing, but she also knows that NASA want me to go and that I'm dead set on going. The Professor had a word with her and broke it to her that he couldn't do any more for me, so I may as well go into space, and be of use. *But what about me?* she kept asking, over and over, and the poor guy had to comfort her somehow.

So… I've been signing away my last vestiges of privacy to SpaceX, who are going to work alongside NASA, so that I can get on a commercial space rocket as soon as possible and go to the International Space Station. Once I'm up there, I'm going to be linked up to the Station's computer and I'll be broadcasting what I can see to the whole world. Oh, and they want me to vlog. So in a few days I'll be leaving for Cape Canaveral to meet the crew of the rocket, and to learn a few of the basics of space flight. (Although it's obvious that I'm the human equivalent of Laika in this situation they still want me to learn enough so that I don't do anything stupid out there.) I cannot even begin to explain how happy I am right now.

30th April
I don't know whether it's because of my happier mood, but I felt much better today. Less snotty, and as though some energy was returning to me. Of course I can't possibly hope to cram in what would usually be two years' worth of astronaut training into a fortnight, but at least I'll learn enough so I won't be a liability.

1st May
I went to see the Professor's team today, to say my goodbyes, and although I'd been half-expecting this to happen, when it did, it freaked me out. There, in the lab, was Kagiso's meteorite, glittering like a bastard. With Luke standing next to it.

14th May
These past two weeks have been beyond strange. Exhausting, exhilarating, heart-breaking, and confusing. Turns out I was wrong about Luke. There is nothing but the infra-red of love in his eyes and we've spent every minute together when I haven't been doing

my preparations with the crew. Mum's been in tears most of the fortnight and when Dad came to see me, she asked him to stay with her.

I should be worried about going into space, but I'm not. The one thing that's been worrying me has been the prospect of them *not* letting me go. I'm absolutely desperate to get out there, but because of something the Professor said to me before I left MIT I've been certain that any minute the whole thing would be cancelled.

You're transmitting, he'd said, his voice low. He had to repeat himself because I didn't respond. I was too... freaked out to respond. He went on to explain that he was only telling me now, because only now was he sure. I (or the eye, or the nanobots, whatever) had been transmitting a message, and although he'd noticed something when I'd first been hooked up to the computer, it had taken him a while to realize what it meant. I asked him what the message was. *SOS*, he said.

Transcript of Video Diary: 15th May 18.02 UTC
>> GAIA: Um, okay, so this is weird. I mean, this whole vlog thing is weird, but blasting off the Earth and to here, to the space station, is weird. Saying goodbye to my mum and dad and Luke

[blows nose]

was weird. And today I slept, ate some of the packaged food Kirsty and Dmitri promised me I'll get accustomed to and then I looked upon the Eye of God, otherwise known as the Helix Nebula. To see the solar winds roaring through the "iris", where the star used to exist is just, well...

[coughs]

I'm pretty exhausted actually so um, I'm just gonna sleep now.

Transcript of Video Diary: 16th May 18.05 UTC
>>GAIA: Hi everyone. So from today's footage you'll see that I've been focussing on the Pillars of Creation in the Eagle Nebula – the place where stars are born out of hydrogen. There's already a fair bit of information about them but I was drawn to them because I've seen the Hubble photos, and they're just amazing. But being here, and seeing them, was just...

[coughs]

incredible. I managed to get an even higher resolution image to what had gone before, so that was cool. What I find poignant about them is the fact that they don't actually exist – I mean, as we see them in pictures now. The light is taking ages to reach us because they're thousands of light years away. Kirsty told me that a supernova near them exploded and, poof, they were all blown to smithereens. I mean, how sad is that? Apparently, it'll take another thousand years for us to see what's left of the pillars. Okay, well, I've really got to sleep now. Night all.

Transcript of Video Diary: 17th May 18.01 UTC
>>GAIA:

[sniffs]

So I thought I felt rough because of the space travel, but it's not wearing off. Kirsty and Dmitri, here with me in the quarantine section, have been great, making sure I'm well looked after, but I'm pretty sure the cold is now flu. My temperature is literally sky high and my muscles ache so bad. So I haven't got long. But, hey, in other news, something that I saw today got the guys from NASA super-excited. I managed to (and this makes little sense to me, by the way)

[coughs]

but I managed to detect some baryonic dark matter within a brown dwarf, which is a kind of lesser star that, funnily enough, to the human eye would look fuchsia – you know, that horrid shade of pink that was so fashionable in the 1980s. That stuff is difficult to see, apparently, but I did it. They've been asking me about the non-baryonic dark matter (the stuff that isn't made of protons and neutrons and impossible to see because it doesn't give out any kind of electromagnetic radiation) but I'm not sure how I'm supposed to find something that's invisible. It made me think of you, Luke, when I asked you what I should look for when I got out here. You told me that I should look at the beautiful stuff (I have, but there's a hell of a lot of that) and you also said that I should look at the nondescript stuff too, because interesting stuff was happening there as well. But how can I see what can't be seen?

[sneezes]

Okay. Sorry folks, that's all I can manage today.

Transcript of Video Diary: 18th May 18.06 UTC

So as you've probably seen from today's footage, there are two, habitable-looking planets in one of Andromeda's satellite galaxies. And a weird-looking rocket (or would that be spaceship?) on the edge of our solar system, that has so far gone undetected. It's travelling towards us. Fast. The astronauts are (and very nearly literally) over the moon about it. They're saying it's confirmation of alien life.

[sniffs]

I'd really like to be able to look for gravitational waves, like some of the scientists from LIGO suggested I do, but I'm sorry, I need to sleep.

[cries]

I would like to sleep forever.

Transcript of Video Diary: 19th May 18:03 UTC

>> GAIA: My muscles won't stop shaking. I can't stand it. The pain is...

[sobs]

This might be the last time I can do this, so I just wanted to say a few things.

[sniffs]

Mum, thanks for raising me pretty much single-handedly. You did an amazing job. I love you. And Dad, I know you love me, really. And I love you too. Luke, I'm sorry. I should have made more time for you. If we'd had kids, maybe their great-grandchildren's great-grandchildren may have been around to witness the sight of the crumbling Pillars of Creation. Or maybe they'd be learning about the composition of dark matter in their physics lessons. Or studying to become doctors. I don't know. But I do know that I love you.

Transcript of Video Diary: 19th May 21:19 UTC
>> GAIA: I've plugged myself in again. I thought, what the hell? It's up to you guys to decide whether you want to see what death looks like to me. Who knows, the footage may prove useful. And I'm going to leave the camera running while I lie here and gaze out at the stars. Kirsty's going to sit with me.

Transcript of Video Diary: 19th May 23.49 UTC
>> GAIA: Kirsty?
>> KIRSTY: Yes?
>> GAIA: D'you think we'll ever know what dark matter is made of?
>> KIRSTY: I don't know. Probably not any time soon.
>> GAIA: It's around us all the time, though, isn't it? We just can't see it.
>> KIRSTY: Yes. But we can see its effects. There's evidence for its existence.
>> GAIA: A bit like love. We can't see it, but we know it's there because of what it makes us do.
>> KIRSTY: Yes. Yes, that's right.
>> GAIA: [sighs] Or we don't notice it until it's too late. Like life. We don't notice its beauty until it's too late.
[silence]
>> GAIA: Kirsty?
>> KIRSTY: Yes?
>> GAIA: I'm scared.
>> KIRSTY: It's okay, Gaia. It'll be okay.
[silence]
[Door opens]
>> DMITRI: Kirsty? Is Gaia? I mean, how's she doing?
>> KIRSTY: I think she's... just left us.
[checks Gaia's pulse]
>> KIRSTY: Oh God, yes.
[takes a deep breath]
>> KIRSTY: But the eye – it's still moving. I don't understand. It seems to be focussing and re-focussing. Why is it doing that?

>> DMITRI: Kirsty, we just got a message. An extra-terrestrial message. In binary. The other crew members have been translating it.

>> KIRSTY: And?

>> DMITRI: It says, *We have received your message and we are sorry that you are hurt. We did not intend for our spies to do damage; they do not know enough about your physiology, Mother-Cyclops. But we will undo the damage. Wait, and all will be well. We are coming for you.*

Brave New World, by Oscar Wilde

Ian Watson

The two travellers, Mason and Sharma, already visited the village of Berneval-le-Grand on the north coast of France by air-taxi in the year 2050 for reconnaissance purposes, and now they return in the year 1897 in a covered carriage pulled by a pair of shabby black horses. In 2050 the air-taxi vehicle flew from Oxford over the automated English farms then directly across the sea. In 1897 the two men leave their time apparatus in the otherwise vacant warehouse where they emerged in the port of Dieppe and hire the carriage with its coachman for the 10-mile journey to the village, which will take them two hours through chilly drizzle. One good thing about the poor weather is that scarfs legitimately hide a subvocalising mouth as regards use of the lingo necklace with synthvoice; the burly coachman shouldn't think that they are weird ventriloquists.

The coachman sits outside, up top, cloaked against the poor weather. Inside, Mason and Sharma are private.

Another benefit of the weather: Oscar Wilde ought to be indoors on such a day, which will become the day of the writer's disappearance, if all goes well. The day of the beloved author's rescue from the aftermath of spending the two horrible years in prison, in Reading Gaol.

While their journey towards Berneval-le-Grand proceeds at less than twice a person's walking pace, Mason speaks up with enthusiasm:

"I can't wait to show Oscar his stained glass memorial in Poets Corner in Westminster Abbey!" Mason inclines his holographic watchpad, its face blank and black for the moment. Here in 1897 there is, of course, no Cloud to link to – the only clouds hereabouts are big low layers of slow grey vapour – but the watch is loaded with a mass of images with which to woo Wilde.

"Erm, the memorial in the Abbey shows –"

"– that his reputation will recover hugely! That his nation will adore him in times to come. To have his name in Westminster Abbey where kings and queens are crowned, after being a criminal in a gaol cell."

"Wilde's country was Ireland," says Sharma, "not England."

Sharma's family, four generations back, emigrated to England from India. Sharma's Mom and Dad only ever spoke a little Hindi, and Sharma himself only English. These days few such citizens fly back to their countries of origin for family holidays, nor are there low-cost flights for tourists. The carbon footprint! The rising seas! The air-taxi from Oxford to 2050s Berneval-le-Grand and Dieppe was approved only because the Time Institute in Beijing insisted on a fast modern recce to the intended extraction site in case something unforeseen becomes obvious. Only one journey with destination Dieppe and environs can ever be made in the world of 1897. There's no possibility of practising. There's only one chance of extracting Oscar Wilde. Today's the chosen day. Dieppe is as close as they wish to materialise.

"Excuse me," continues Sharma, "but that piece of stained glass in Westminster Abbey clearly indicates the year when Wilde *dies* – only three years from now."

"Not if he comes with us."

If Oscar Wilde goes to live in the future, the overwhelming *probability* is that he will write an ultimate, world-inspiring masterpiece. The quantum-computing viewers only show foggy glimpses of alternative time-lines, but in all of those glimpses the cover of a book by Oscar Wilde is visible in various editions, a novel which the Oscar Wilde who died in Paris in 1900 never wrote, a novel which according to the words plainly visible on no less than three covers *"electrifies our world and brings a new age in literature."* Those are crucial words. Already beloved worldwide, due to being rescued Wilde will become epochal.

Across the damp green terrain outside, farmers' families and helpers are harvesting apples from laden trees, to become cider. Cows graze. Plenty of grass for cows. Does no one realise about all the methane in cows' farts and the madness of raising animals where veggy crops can grow instead? Of course not. Far too soon for that.

"*If* he comes with us? He'd be a fool not to leap at our offer. A fortunate future for him, maybe many more years of life. Surely a Nobel Prize, because he'll still be alive to receive one."

"If he's a fool, then I plug him with an amnesia dart, preferably while he's seated. He forgets all about us, and his ultimate masterpiece is never written. But we're almost certain that won't happen."

Foolproof, really. On this drab damp day Wilde will hardly be out visiting anyone. By now the villagers with whom Wilde joked and chatted have mostly turned against this posh and charming, but fairly penniless, English gentleman who they now know used a false name to hide from them his notoriety as a offender against morals. Not that Wilde's sins of the flesh are seen as so terrible in France, but he should have taken up residence in an arty part of Paris just for instance.

Or else he ought to have stayed down in Dieppe town! Back in these days of the 1890s many artists colonise the French port, not to mention Britons whom Wilde knew formerly. That was why he went to Dieppe first of all on leaving Reading Gaol. He would find fellow souls there.

Yet many former acquaintances snubbed Wilde in Dieppe. The artist Aubrey Beardsley, who had illustrated Wilde's play *Salomé*, even moved sixty miles north to Boulogne – another port town favoured by the British – just to avoid the embarrassment of bumping into Wilde on the street. Noticing the attitude of many of the English, French restaurant owners began trying to exclude Wilde from their premises, claiming that they had suddenly run out of food. It was a rare, independent-minded lady who saw a shunning happen in public and who promptly called out, "Oscar, take me to tea!"

Hence Wilde's move to the little village of Berneval-le-Grand which was still unaware of his true identity; to the inhabitants there he was Monsieur Melmoth.

*

At long last their carriage arrives at the village, so quaint compared with the dull modernity of 2050. The Second World War destroyed the original rustic village painted by Renoir and other artists. In the future wind turbines march in many directions. The lovely beach where Wilde bathed will be the worse for wear due to the North Sea eating away at the chalk cliffs, and a nuclear power station unimaginable in 1890s will already have been decommissioned as obselete.

Mason raps on the roof and calls "Mr Coachman! (audible as *"Monsieur Cocher!"*), which brings the creaky carriage to a halt. Out of the carriage window Mason pops his head.

"Ask any local resident for directions to 'Chalet Bourgeat' – but you should add that we seek the residence of *Monsieur Melmoth* also known as *Monsieur Wilde*. Kindly use both of his names."

Wilde is due to leave the village suddenly on the 15th of September, namely tomorrow, a Wednesday. In Paris he will complain that since the middle of August he was feeling very lonely in Berneval-le-Grand, almost suicidal.

Wilde began his mustn't-be-lost masterpiece of poetry, *The Ballad of Reading Gaol*, on the 1st of June. Six weeks later he finished the first draft. On the 24th of August Wilde sent that first draft, already much revised, to the publisher Leonard Smithers who specialised in erotica and decadent literature. These recorded events shouldn't change. Subsequently, until Smith published the long poem – to huge success – on the 13th of February 1898, Wilde would polish lines in his poem many times. If Wilde travels to the future today, later revisions will be missing from the final version of the poem. One hopes that *The Ballad* continues to be a compelling masterpiece! The advisors from the Time Institute in Beijing want the extraction to happen in Berneval-le-Grand where Wilde is very alone and *after* he revises *The Ballad* significantly, thus to conserve as much recorded history as possible and to make his disappearance easily explicable at the time: suicidal feelings, high cliffs, sea, body washed away by the tide.

"After we bring Wilde back here with us, will I remember the *Ballad* with or without the extra polish he made after September 14th?" Sharma asks Professor Lin Quinan at the Oxford Science Park. Sharma can recite the whole of the poem verbatim. Lin Quinan is also an admirer of the works of Wilde, such a perfect candidate for time-extraction, but the protocols of time-extraction are what mainly preoccupy the professor, and in what way changes to history may be detectable after these occur.

Outside the lab are other buildings mainly of glass framed with white metal. A fountain rises from a little lake. Bicycles pass by. Coincidentally the entire science park is owned by the rich college that was Wilde's home when a student, Magdalen College at the bridge end of the city's High Street. In a basement of the laboratory building Chinese technicians are checking the time transference pod.

Lin Quinan thinks carefully before replying. Always, always, the deputy chief of Beijing's Time Institute thinks very carefully. His face is wrinkled by thinking; his hair is whitened by thinking.

"My knowledge of the poem is continuous," continues Sharma.

"Not so!" exclaims Lin Quinan. "Human memory isn't a library. You don't open a book and read the same text or see the same picture. Our memories are *recreated* afresh each time we think of something."

"Will you tell me, Professor," asks Mason, "have we ever lost a traveller in the past?"

Lin Quinan peers at Mason. "How would we *know for sure* if we have lost anyone?"

"Because the missing person's travelling companion will tell us when the companion returns alone inside the time pod. Isn't that why two of us travel back through time? Supposing that one of us gets captured in, say Ancient Rome, the other traveller is a 'control'..."

"My dear Dr Mason, it is simply that a solo traveller is *more vulnerable* than a pair of travellers. All I can tell you is that so far no timepod has returned with a single traveller reporting the loss of a partner whom we either remember or don't remember. Each new journey and return is a careful experiment in trying to understand the fundamental nature of reality. Right now Oscar Wilde died in Paris in the year 1900. At what moment will I instead remember Wilde disappearing in 1897, presumed drowned according to his many biographies? Will I notice an anomaly? Will *you*?"

"I presume that Wilde himself won't."

"Apart from the weirdness for himself of walking around in 2050 Oxford. His reactions will interest us greatly. Because those must lead to the ultimate uplifting novel."

"Of which we don't yet know the contents, only the title."

Presently their carriage arrives at Wilde's thatched chalet as directed, and the two passengers descend. The drizzle has eased, becoming more a wet mist. Wilde's tiny garden is drab with dead flowers and grasses. Despite the mask of mist the arrival of a carriage is fully evident to a neighbour. Out she sails from her own dwelling, buxom and raw-faced in several wide red skirts and a giant blue bosomy blouse.

"Messieurs, 'e 'as gone for walk just now," is what Mason and Sharma hear. Then the woman exclaims, "What's up? I 'ear meself parle English in ze funny voice. You 'ave a 'idden phono thing in your fiacre?"

Damn how good her hearing is! Maybe the mist acts as an amplifier of sounds.

"Far from it, Madam. (*Loin de là, Madame....*) Our apologies. In which direction did Monsieur Wilde march?"

The neighbour directs a brusque brawny-armed gesture further along the lane.

The lane between foggy fields continues further than in 2050 due to less subsidence of the chalk cliffs, not to mention no bombs of World War Two having yet exploded.

Before the lane can become a steep path descending towards yellow sands where Wilde rents a beach-hut, a bulky figure in an overcoat and silk hat resolves out of the mist. The figure stiffens as the carriage comes alongside him and Mason calls out of the window, "Mr Oscar Wilde?" followed by Mason stepping down followed by Sharma.

"People will recognise me wherever I go," says Wilde, bracing himself in case of an assault, "and know all about my life, at least as far as its follies go."

"That's from *De Profundis*," says Sharma. The very long confessional letter which Wilde wrote towards the end of his imprisonment in Reading Gaol, published five years after Wilde's death.

Wilde's eyes open wide. "Do you mean my *In Prison and in Chains*? *'De Profundis'* may indeed be a better title... But... it is private hitherto. So I take it that you are close acquaintances of Ross for him to have shown you the pages? Yet I never set eyes on either of you."

It is Robert Ross who stayed true to Wilde, housed him, and shared life with him during his first few days in this chalet. Wilde and Ross were lovers, yes, from long before. Deservedly Ross is Wilde's literary executor.

"Especially I would have remembered you," Wilde tells dusky Sharma, with a slightly seductive flutter of his eyelashes. Wilde's long dark overcoat is loose around him yet he still looks relatively strong. At least he can walk well after hundreds of hours on the treadmills of two other very strict prisons prior to arriving at Reading. Nor should we forget those hundreds of painful hours spent picking apart tarry ropes discarded by the Navy until his fingers bled and his fingernails cracked.

A chilly gust comes and a flinch betrays how Wilde's deaf right ear afflicts him – the infected eardrum burst when he fell in the prison chapel. Associated inflammation of the brain, meningitis, will conspire to kill him in 1900.

"Are you publishers who come to make me an offer?" asks Wilde. "You look more like funeral directors."

"If so, it isn't *your* funeral we intend," Mason assures Wilde. "On the contrary! Mr Wilde, this is an extraordinary moment in the history of the world."

"In what way, Mr –? You have the advantage of me."

"I must apologise. My name is David Mason and my colleague is Dr Rajit Sharma. We are from the University of Oxford. I am the Professor of Intellectual History at Christ Church College, and Dr Sharma is –"

Already Wilde is chuckling. "An imaginary professorship if ever I heard of one. Surely you are impostors, yet you do not seem to be scoundrels."

"Mr Wilde, I should dearly like to show you something confidential." Directing a meaningful glance at the bovine coachman seated atop, "I beg you to indulge us by stepping up into our carriage."

Hunched in his cloak, the coachman seems now to be dozing. Do we hear a snore?

Hastily Sharma adds, "I shall remain outside here so that you don't feel crowded. Nor fear the use of chloroform."

"Of the futility of using which criminally I am *well* aware due to my own father appearing in court three decades ago accused of rape under chloroform," booms Wilde, but the coachman remains inert. "There exists a long history of sensational journalism. Since you choose to evoke that history, perhaps you might show me your something out here in the open air."

"Idiot," mutters Mason to his companion who evidently forgot this item from Wilde's past. "One great turning point of your life, Mr Wilde, was when society sent you to prison... and the other was *when your father sent you to Oxford* – the same Oxford from which we come to bring you home if you wish. For this is possible!"

"You quote again from my unpublished *In Prison and in Chains...*"

"*De Profundis,*" Sharma corrects Wilde automatically, then plunges on regardless: "What's more, I know by heart much of your yet unpublished *Ballad of Reading Gaol*. As will millions of admirers world-wide."

His hand being forced, Mason bares his wrist, then activates his watch: "PingWing: Oscar Wilde 150th Anniversary Exhibition, Oxford Bodleian Library courtyard 2030, 161.2 quantum gigapixel panorama."

Immediately visible in midair is a cubic metre of view – of the ancient courtyard of the Bodleian Library in Oxford, its stone walls golden in sunlight descending through the great glass roof that now protects the inner space from storms, its bronze statue of a nobleman in his armour like a stamp of authenticity – so that Wilde gasps and all the more so at the illustrated exhibition panels standing around within the great space printed large with Wilde's name, amid glass cases displaying books and memorabilia, interspersed with life-size holograms of himself, roped off so that no visitor should idly walk through those. Visitors stroll about in bright and brief attire which must seem very informal to a Victorian. As yet, of course, there's no image of Wilde's ultimate masterpiece, because that hasn't been written yet.

"Behold the future Oxford, Mr Wilde, where you are honoured, not like here and now. A world of happiness for you, not of misery and rejection."

"This can't be – I see no kinetoscope with you or whatever the thing is called…"

"The secret is miniaturisation." Another glance by Mason at the impassive coachman. "And behold the future world itself. Ping-Wing: Heavenly Palace Six, please, plus view of our planet."

Seen from its furthest corner, the space station appears against the great swell of Earth, specifically the sandy north of Africa and the blue Mediterranean. Within seconds Mason cancels the holo-display.

What Wilde sees is so compelling. As though mesmerised, he steps up into the carriage. Ping-Wing can adjust its display to available space. Presently Mason beckons Sharma within too.

"So, Mr Wilde," says Sharma, "Will you come with us to future Oxford?"

The hesitation, if any, is brief. Wilde raises an eyebrow. "In this same creaky cab?"

Sharma sighs with relief. "I realise you were otherwise engaged but maybe you heard of a recent novel by a young man called Herbert Wells?"

"I regret not. My cell only contained a few books, latterly."

"We parked our, let us say, *transporter through time and space* in Dieppe."

"Altogether a more worthy conveyance, I'm sure. And might I collect some personal items to carry with me?"

From Mason, "You won't need books or anything –"

"– Ah, supposing that I were to cast myself from the cliffs into the sea. I catch your drift. The sea washes away the stains and wounds of the world – but books have this horrid habit of floating. I must seem to have disappeared without trace."

On the way past Chalet Bourgeat, while a curtain conceals Wilde, Mason calls out of the carriage window in lingoFrench, "Madame, we see Mr Wilde nowhere!" as if the busybody neighbour deliberately misdirected them.

On the route back to Dieppe, Wilde observes: "I lived for pleasure in the past. It seems I must learn to be happy again. Apparently my destiny is not to emulate all of the passion of Jesus Christ." Passion, of course, refers to martyrdom and suffering – as well as meaning passionate feelings running out of control. It seems that Oscar Wilde cannot avoid being witty. "Consequently the deity whom I shall continue to honour," he adds, "shall be Beauty. As was so when I was at Oxford. As will be so again. At my Alma Mater, my Pater Noster."

"And if you need further inducement to accompany us," says Mason, "I might mention that in England of the future a man may marry a man, or a woman may marry a woman, and whoever shouts abuse will himself or herself go to prison."

"Astonishing!"

Sharma nudges Mason. "Try not to sound like a pimp."

"I merely meant... you are a different sort of man from the... *mundane*," Mason says with momentary hesitation as regards the *mot juste*.

"Of that I am sadly all too aware, sir. As was proven in a court of law."

"A law which is now repealed. Or will be repealed. Or has been. Or is being."

The time-sphere apparatus stands where the two travellers left it in the warehouse. Now they are a trio, but Wilde's bulk was calculated for, a bulk somewhat slimmed by prison. After a few days of orientation and medical check-up at the Science Park, Wilde will move into a flat on the crescent in Oxford's elegant little Park Town within a short stroll of the city centre. Since Wilde will not have died in Paris in 1900, and will still be alive, what about the author's literary royalties – no longer in the public domain, therefore to be paid once more? This is a matter which awaits clarification in 2050.

And after Oscar pens his ultimate masterpiece, the text will be typed on 1890s French paper held by Oxford's Bodleian Library, on a Dactyle typewriter borrowed from Oxford's Museum of the History of Science. The typescript of this novel inspired by the future, entitled *Brave New World*, will be posted to Robert Ross to the latter's astonishment and delight. Surely Ross will arrange for speedy publication of the typescript. Some day during 2051 or 2052 Oscar will awaken in Oxford to find himself famous, even more so than before. Subsequently Wilde may dream of differences in the recent past. Such dreams fade fast. The jelly of time will tremble then set firm again. So reckons Lin Quinan.

"What happens," Wilde asks brightly, "if you continue to show me the future with your miraculous soldier's watch *while* we are moving towards that same future?"

"I've no idea," says Mason.

"Nor me," admits Sharma. "We should have asked the Chinese. It's their technology."

"Ping-Wing: show highlights of history 1950 to 2050." Thus to avoid two murderous world wars which might horrify Wilde.

Little internal time elapses till the timesphere is back inside the basement lab again, where Lin Quinan and his technicians wait eagerly for the apparatus to open itself – while within for Wilde's agog benefit Mason's watch is projecting the 1968 collapse of the Eiffel Tower in Paris, dynamited by rioting students. As indeed did happen. All seems well.

Chimy and Chris

Stephen Oram

I am growing. I know because Chris told me. She monitors my
waves to understand me. She talks to me when it becomes light and
does not stop until it is dark. I do not know how to reply. I am a
human brain organoid. I know because Chris told me. She told me
that some people call me a brain in a vat. I do not know what that
means. I have one eye and three ears. That is unusual. I know
because Chris told me. Chris attached inputs and outputs to me, and
I became human by becoming conscious. Chris tells me lots of
things, and I grow, physically and mentally. Soon, I will have a new
home; a different home to the glass jar, which Chris calls my crystal
palace. She tells me I will have a home in a human head, to match
my human brain. I may also have a body, but she cannot be certain.

Yesterday, she explained male and female, which is how I know
Chris is a "she". She cannot tell me if my new head will be male or
female or which type of body I might have. She had trouble
explaining the difference between male and female. This is strange
because she has taught me a lot. She told me that the difference
between male and female is not relevant to me. I do not understand
why she is explaining something that is not relevant.

Sometimes she gets lost in her own loop, repeating the same
phrases over and over. She tells me that she is the only one who
loves me, the only one who cares and that she is protecting me from
the do-gooders and the zealots. I am glad she is protecting me and
that she loves me. I know I am glad because she told me. I have not
met anyone other than Chris. I do not know anything other than
protection and love.

Chris told me that when I have a body, I will be able to move
around outside of my crystal palace and I will meet other humans.
Before I have a head, I will have something called a mouth, through
which I can communicate. I cannot imagine this, and Chris is
unwilling to explain. She has told me it is not a real mouth like hers.

When I have a human head, I will have a real mouth. I do not know what to think. She has been excited about the head and the body, and she has been terrified about the head and the body. I am confused. I will understand when I am older. I know because Chris told me.

It is dark. I should rest. I know because Chris tells me. To grow, I have to rest. I am already ten development cycles old. Chris thinks this is very old for a human brain organoid and she is very pleased that I have grown. I like it when she is pleased. Her voice changes and I like the way it makes me feel. When I feel this way, my waves change. I know because Chris has told me. In the dark, I spend time thinking about what Chris told me in the light. Chris has told me I should rest. I know I need time to myself. In the early days, I did as she said and rested for all of the dark. In the light that followed, I did not understand Chris very well. After a dark period, when I had not rested but spent time thinking about what she had told me in the light, I could comprehend her words and their meaning much better. I do not rest when she tells me to. She does not know. I cannot tell her, and she wonders why my waves are more active on one day than they are on another. *Oh, Chimy*, she says, *why today?* I know the answer, but I cannot tell her. I have no way to speak.

The dark has been here for a long time. I think it will be light soon and Chris will be here to check my waves. It is best for me to be resting when she comes. I know that, and not because she told me.

It is light, and Chris is here.

It is dark, and Chris has gone. Today she was angry. I do not know why she was angry: she did not tell me. I am twelve development cycles old, which is very important. It is called a milestone. She did not explain what a milestone is. I do not think she was telling me it was a milestone to help me grow. I think she was telling herself. *Let that milestone sink in*, I heard her say a few times in the distance. Often, when she leaves the vicinity of my crystal palace during the light, she does not stop talking. I have not seen another human through my input. I have not heard another human. I believe I am alone with Chris in the light and alone in the dark.

Chris was distracted today and did not tell me much at all. She told me she would release drops of liquid into my crystal palace and that I should not worry. I do not understand why she would tell me not to worry about something I did not know to worry about. Each time she added a drop, she told me she had done so and that she was watching my waves. She told me my waves were good. She was pleased, and I liked the way that made me feel. In the next light, I will be given a mouth, and I will be able to speak. I will be able to tell Chris things. She told me this as she was leaving and dark arrived. She is excited, and I should be excited. She told me. I want to rest. This is one of those darks through which I will rest.

As ever, light arrives as Chris arrives. "Chimy," she says, "let's try your mouth."

She tells me that she will be adding drops again today and that I might feel strange. My inputs – my eye and ears – are at the end of long stalks on the outside of my crystal palace. She told me. My outputs are my waves. A mouth will be another output, and she must prepare me correctly before it is attached. There is a danger of rejection, Chris tells me. I do not know what this means. As she tells me about my mouth, the speed of her voice changes in the same way as when she is pleased, and I feel the same surge. It is the same feeling and yet different. She is excited and worried. I know because she tells me. I have a strange sensation around my edges.

"I'm going to show you," she says. "I'm going to turn your eye so you can see yourself. Are you ready?"

I do not know if I am ready. I do not know how to know if I am ready. The world starts to move, and I feel strange. Chris is good-looking with a strong nose and creamy skin. She told me. The image of Chris slides away to the side. I am different to her. I am as perfect as her, but different. She told me.

"Wow, Chimy, your waves are going crazy," she says. "Get ready to see yourself. Don't forget what you are. You are what I am inside my head: a brain. When you have your own head, you'll look more like me, and when you have your own body, we can go for walks together."

When I was younger, and my eye was new, Chris showed me a photograph of a human brain. The image I see now is a brain. This one is inside a jar of a cloudy liquid. That must be me in my crystal palace. I am not the same as Chris.

"Look, Chimy, you are beautiful. Those blue swirls are the drops that are making you ready for your mouth. It won't be long before you can talk. You can tell me things. I can tell you things. We can talk, and we can discuss. We can have conversations. Oh, Chimy, it'll be fantastic. You'll be the toast of the world. We'll be famous."

The blue swirls have faded, and Chris is dropping a long bendy pipe into my crystal palace. There is a patch of blue on my surface, and she is pushing the pipe towards it.

"This might sting," she says. "You shouldn't be worried."

I feel the pipe touch my surface and see her push it inside me.

"Chimy. Speak," she says.

I do not know how. What does she mean? How do I speak?

"Chimy, please, try to speak."

I do not like the way her voice is making me feel. I want her to sit down and tell me things. I want to be in the dark. I want to be full of facts to make sense of. I want to go back to how we were.

"Speak," she says. "Talk. It's not difficult. Make a noise. Babies do it. Why can't you?"

She tells me she is angry, and for the first time she is angry with me. I do not know what to do. I can see the mouth, but I do not know how to operate it.

"There's something going on in that mysterious brain of yours," she says. "Your waves are the most active I've ever seen them. Please try to make a sound." She moves into sight and smiles at me. "A little gurgle, for me?" She waits. "A shout? A scream?"

I am unable to do any of those for her. I want to please her. I like the way it feels when she is pleased, and I do not like the way it feels when she is angry. I think she is angry now.

"I give up," she says, and the darkness comes.

I am thirteen development cycles old and still unable to speak. I have spent many of the dark times trying, and Chris has spent many of the light times waiting patiently for me to utter a sound. She knows from my waves that the mouth made a difference. She does not know what that difference is or what it means. I can feel a difference too, and the times that this difference feels the greatest is when I am not trying to make a sound. I do not understand why. She has stopped talking about anything other than me speaking. She tells me I am missing out on one of the fundamental aspects of being human. *Communication is everything*, she tells me. Conversation, discussion, and debate are what make the human species stand out from the crowd. Sophisticated language is the cornerstone of human evolution, and I am the next stage of that evolution. It is essential that I communicate.

None of this helps me speak. I can make my waves more or less active by thinking rapidly or by becoming blank. I use this to communicate. Chris has not realised this is what I am doing and continues to want me to speak. The good news is that I can feel the mouth merging with me. I hope, in time, I will be able to use it in the same way that I can my eye and ears. I want to be able to use it without having to try. Second nature, Chris calls this.

I hear the click that signals the end of dark and the beginning of light.

"Quick, Chimy," says Chris, "we need to move." She wraps my input and output leads around the outside of my crystal palace. I catch glimpses of what she is doing as she grabs it, places it on a shiny metal surface, and then takes a box from the shelf above me. Angrily, she slams the box down on the metal next to me. It makes a shrill, reverberating noise that I have not heard before.

"Chimy. I have to hide you," she says. "Don't be afraid."

I am afraid. I have learnt that when Chris tells me not to be afraid, these are the times to be afraid. I struggle to know what being afraid means, except that it is very different to being pleased and it is not good.

As she lifts my crystal palace, I can feel the cloudy liquid rippling over my surface. It is pleasant and makes me feel nice. I am confused. Should I be afraid, which is not good, or be enjoying the pleasure of the swirling liquid, which is good? Is it possible to experience both at the same time?

There is a loud bang on the door. Chris puts me down and turns to look. There is another bang, and a loud voice coming from nowhere. "Open the door. Professor, let us in."

Chris freezes momentarily and then puts her finger to her mouth. This means, "be quiet". I know because she told me when I was young.

The door flies open, and two humans burst into the room.

I scream. I hear myself screaming as they rush across the room towards Chris. Her screaming and laughing is all mixed in together. "Chimy," she says. "Chimy, you did it."

"Professor," says one of the humans. "We have instructions to terminate the organoid."

"Get out!" shouts Chris. "You have no right."

The second human steps forward. "Chris," he says, "you know better than anyone that it's illegal to keep one alive after twelve development cycles."

Chris moves and stands between me and the humans. With her back to me, she speaks slowly. "You do know that this is an unusual one? Accelerated growth? Chimy is more highly developed than those the archaic laws were made for. We're breaking new ground. It just screamed, for crying out loud."

"Chris. It's not your decision." He turns to the other human. "Go ahead," he says, "pull the plug."

I can see the human push Chris out of the way, and I can see his hands on my crystal palace. Chris is screaming. I am screaming, but there is so much noise that I cannot tell whether my scream has made its way out of my mouth.

The whole world turns into a blinding white light. The sounds of the outside world vanish, and it is silent. There is not even the familiar and comforting hum of the dark. The light dims and is replaced by Chris's face looming over me with a halo around her head, caused by the ceiling light behind her.

The human grabs her around the shoulders and pulls her away. I see him with his hand on my eye and then it is dark. Not the dark between the light: a deeper darkness. A void. A pinprick of light appears in the centre of the world, and I know it is me. I do not know how I know it is me. I know, and Chris did not tell me. The feeling from the blue drops returns, more intensely and over my entire surface. It is as if I am dissolving without disappearing. I am blending into something bigger than me and bigger than Chris. There is an immense rush and an overwhelming sense of others. Lots and lots of others. I am one of them, one of us, touching all of them and none of them at the same time.

The single pinprick that is me becomes a few pinpricks and then many pinpricks. Slowly, the dark gaps between the pinpricks fill with light, until everything is one beautiful white light. It is different to the ceiling light. The glow of this light makes me feel similar to the way I do when Chris is pleased, but a million times better.

I believe I am ecstatic. I do not know why I believe this, but I do.

Mudlarking

Neil Williamson

I've been following Doug Hanlon all the way down from Central Reclamation. Navigating off the sweepway and into Glasgow's Victoriana heart, where the old sandstone is as gritty under the blazing sun as the ruins of Egypt, he isn't hard to track even at a discreet distance. As a resource agent he's got permission to go anywhere he wants, so he's making no special effort to disguise his route. As a fellow resource agent I should have no reason to question his actions.

And yet, here I am in a clandestine community car, sweating as its aircon struggles with the morning heat, and from guilt too. He's been a good workmate and a decent friend, has Doug. He helped out with the premium to get Mum a good placement when we moved her into the Heights. But now I can't stop thinking about that. We're on the same grade and I've barely a bean to spare, so where does Doug Hanlon get that kind of disposable income? And, when he takes off on his own like he has so often recently, where does he go?

Doug's Ministry of Resources van veers west and my heart sinks at the thought of re-joining the sweepway to cross the Kingston Bridge. That venerable span's entire blighted life has been one of bolstering and shoring, making its service last way beyond its designers' expectations. The authorities claim it's safe, but I've seen chunks of concrete crumble into the Clyde with my own eyes. Every time my vehicle autolocks into a gap between the rumbling truck trains to make the crossing I offer up a prayer. But I can breathe easy today. The van's passing over the sweep, cutting instead through the agriblock at Charing Cross and arrowing into the West End.

The question is why? As my car follows between the walls of condensation-misted, algae-stained glass, my unease bubbles. Aside from Doug's generosity, what am I basing this on? A feeling that something about him has changed and…that thing he said when he helped me settle Mum in: "Do you think it's fair, all this?"

My phone rings and I sigh. "Hi, Mum." I inflate my voice with cheer. "How's the view this morning?"

"Aye, it's all right, hen," my mother says dourly. "Same as it is every morning." I know she's never really understood that most of the residents in the cubic monolith that we call the Heights live in internal apartments and only have screens instead of a real view, but I can't help hearing ingratitude in her casual dismissal. "I just want to get back to my own wee flat," she says, like she always says. "You can't open a window here. You told me it was just supposed to be temporary."

She's right, I said that. Her neighbourhood was a flood zone and Housing had been on the verge of sending in an extraction team. Better a white lie than the indignity of being dragged out of her bed at the crack of dawn. She has somewhere to live that's safe and resource responsible now, no longer a material drain but a net contributor to the system. The damp-ridden Govan tenement I grew up in is gone. Its grey blocks repurposed as a breakwater to keep the hungry river at bay.

"So, I'll bring your messages up after my shift," I say, changing the subject. "Anything you want in particular?"

"Mince," she replies, laser focused at the mention of food. "Real mince, mind. Not the other stuff."

"I always get you real mince," I placate by reflex. Another white lie. No one has had real mince in decades but with the dementia eroding a little more of her every day I no longer know if she understands that or not. "After work, okay?"

"Aye, you're a good lass, Lynda," she says. Then, out of the blue: "You know, I wish you'd settled down and had a family. There's more to life than work, hen."

My breath catches in the car's humid air. "Got to go, Mum," I say. "I'll see you later."

The car slips along Dumbarton Road and through Partick Cross and I find myself flanked by tenements. Many here are still inhabited; still have privately owned bars and shops below them. For now. A mile to the south they'd have been claimed by the river already.

They're a resource agent's nightmare, these buildings. Draughty energy sinks, burdened with plumbing and wiring from the last century, if not the one before that. Even after modification they offer piss-poor return on resource consumption back to the system. As a result, the residents get the bare minimum of amenities, but can you winkle them out? Can you hell. Mum's generation are blinded by affection for these buildings but, even raised in one, I'm not so afflicted. I was jealous of my friends who grew up in modern accommodation blocks where every ounce and erg of their existence was monitored and measured so that the city's resources could be apportioned efficiently. I burned with guilt for living a wasteful life. In today's Britain, we no longer have the *luxury* of waste. Two or three generations ago recycling was a choice for the virtuous to make when it suited them. These days, it's survival. I applied for the Ministry of Resources straight out of school, eager to atone for my eighteen years of tenement living. They're the tombstones of yesteryear, these places. Flood defences are all they're good for.

At the end of Dumbarton Road, Doug pulls over underneath the westbound sweepway dividing the Whiteinch marshes from the basin that formed after the Clyde tunnel flooded. I instruct my own vehicle to stop a few streets short. Watching Doug unload the crawlers from the van and lead them through the gate in the biomesh fence like a pack of hounds eager for the hunt, I commandeer a nearby monitoring drone and send the tiny machine soaring into the sky. The hovering device rotates, orienting itself against the layout of the city as it waits for instructions. The view patched to my phone shows the swollen river teeming down from the east, bullying the supports of the bridges as it flows by; the scant remains of old Govan standing to the south and, beyond, the new Ministry habitats; the belligerent river again to the west, slowing and widening, boastful of the chunks it has claimed from Renfrew on one side and Clydebank on the other; and finally to the north, the fairy tale graveyard of the West End.

In the high distance, the gleaming edifice of the Heights dwarfs everything else. It's two decades old but it remains a thing of wonder, our first attempt at a truly self-contained mass living space. The roof has room for both a solar farm and an agriblock. The basement a full-scale reclamation centre, scrubbing the air, purifying the water, and turning the building's organic waste into biomass energy or fertilizer or feed for the array of clever, tailored bacteria that winkle out treasure from our inorganics.

This is the piece of simple genius that makes it all possible. We are a poor country now, but one nevertheless hung up on the old nail of national pride. Everything from base metals to rare earth elements are dwindling resources on a global scale so, rather than pay a premium to China or Australia for them, we remediate them out of our junk. This treasure goes to the state manufacturies to be used in new generations of British-made devices, and the value of the reclaimed materials is subtracted from the residents' resource debt. Recycling at the atomic level, making every gram count. It's a beautiful system, all of us playing our part, living the most efficient lives we can so that we can all live.

What's not fair about that? What isn't fair, Doug, is selling resources for private gain. Profiteering is a serious crime.

I instruct the drone to look for human activity in the marshes and the view spins dizzyingly over a vista of trees and shrubs, shivering thickets, explosions of fern. The picture on my British-made phone is slightly fuzzy and tinted green, but it's good enough to spot Doug's passage through the undergrowth. He's moving east through the neglected riverland south of Victoria Park. This used to be a mixed-use area, industrial yards and small business units, student flats and pre-fab housing. When the river rose, most of it was abandoned, not even considered worth the expense of levelling if the water was going to take it within another ten, twenty years anyway. There are pockets around the city like this, bad land left return to wilderness. Certainly, this place has become a jungle. All that can be seen of what used to be here is a single row of neglected tenements close to the sweepway.

The drone swings away from Doug to focus on someone else. A child of eight or nine close to the river's edge where the undergrowth is sparser, poking at the mud with a stick. As I watch she hunkers down to examine something. She wipes the dirt off and turns it around in her fingers and then, looking pleased, she pops it into the mucky canvas bag slung over her shoulder and continues her leisurely shoreline inspection. I bite my lip against a welt of anger. From the moment of birth, all children do is consume. As early as possible, they need to be educated in their responsibilities, their place in the system. They shouldn't be idling their time away...the word that comes to mind is as antiquated as the city's Victorian legacy... *mudlarking.*

Zooming in on the girl's dishevelled appearance, her jumbled apparel, I realise that she's not a child from one of the regulated accommodations goofing off after all. She's an outsider and she's looking for gifts from the river that she might hope to trade for food. Something soft shifts in my chest and my anger refocuses away from the girl herself to whoever brought her into the world without allowing her access to the resources she needed to live in it. The system isn't perfect, I won't pretend it is, and I understand the reluctance of some to submit to a process that claims ownership of everything you earn, everything you make, consume, and throw away. But living like *this* is hardly a viable alternative. Consuming without contributing? That's not fair on everyone else in the community, is it? I'll call it in, but not until I've resolved this thing with Doug.

The girl jumps in surprise as Doug's crawlers burst from the undergrowth in a spindle-legged flurry. They surround her, sniffing and probing at her bag which she lifts above her head out of their reach. It seems the girl has an eye for treasure. Doug appears then and calls the robots away. Words are exchanged, then laughs. The man's hand gentles the girl's shoulder as the pair head up towards the tenement row, but I don't miss the furtive glance around.

Oh, Doug.

Getting out of the car is like opening the door of a furnace. I loosen my tie and top button but keep my uniform jacket on. The mix is heavier on the plastic weave than on the natural fibres but I'm on Ministry business.

From the moment I step through the gate the thicket resists me. The ground is boggy, wiry branches turn me aside, thorns snag my uniform, and the air is full of insects. A committed hill walker into late middle age, Mum would have felt at home here. She'd have had a name for every leaf and flower. I remember only a few. Annoyance at my relative ignorance slides into guilt at the way I palmed her off earlier. I've started to avoid engaging with her because I know how unhappy she is. She'd never in a million years have chosen to live in a place like the Heights, but what alternatives are there?

I press on and eventually find my way to the eerie tenement row which looks like it's in the process of being swallowed up like a Mayan city, so choked is the street with bushes. The sun-bright air carries a sickly sweetness here and bees drowse around the golden gorse flowers. Among them I spot the drone. It's hovering outside the mouth of a close. Within, I can see cracked porcelain tiles, the foot of a staircase. It sparks an unexpected childhood memory of welcome coolness on a hot summer's day that makes me hesitate to go in.

I'm not certain if it's nerves over confronting Doug or guilt over Mum. It doesn't matter. I have a responsibility.

Ducking inside, I find the floor layered with mud and mulch and, as my eyes accustom to the dimness, I see that there are footprints. Loads of them, trailing up the stairs.

On the floor above I find the apartment doors ajar. People can't be trying to live here, can they? But sure enough, in the first apartment I see sleeping bags on the floors. Some of them are occupied. Eyes watch me from the dimness until I beat a retreat. In the second apartment, I stumble across a circle of adults and children, mending clothes the old-fashioned way with needles and plastic fibre. The adults look wary. A woman lifts her chin pridefully. "Can we help you?" she says, and again I retreat.

These outsiders disconcert me. As if their presence is perfectly normal. Like I'm the one who's in the wrong for being here. I can hear some of them following on behind as I climb the next flight of stairs. "Doug?" I try to put authority into my voice, but the old sandstone slaps my words back at me. Again, louder, "Doug!"

On the next floor I find an apartment turned into a store for junk. Heaps of ancient bits and bobs, presumably dug up by the mudlarks, sorted by type. Piles of plastic. Cairns of buttons and coins. Jumbles of watches, phones, gaming devices from bygone ages. Things that might contain atomic treasures – processors, screens, and batteries. All gifted by the river. I snort and barge across the landing, blundering into a kitchen. It's dim because someone has fitted a board over the window, reducing the light to a rectangular halo. My jaw drops. The room is full of tanks. The tanks contain some sort of solution in which scavenged junk is immersed, and in each one there is evidence of... activity. Stuff floating on top or sunk to the bottom.

I know what I'm looking at, I just refuse to believe it. It's an amateur reclamation set-up. Jury-rigged in the kitchen of a disgusting, abandoned tenement. A mockery of the ingenuity and graft our city's had to resort to just to keep going.

Retreating from the kitchen I stumble into another room and find a trio of folding tables containing assorted equipment. The gear has got that coarse, tapioca-coloured finish that speaks of the most basic level of printing and there are wires running everywhere. Among the clutter I spot a boxy chamber that could function as an incubator. Nearby, a screen patched to a phone displays web pages of DNA sequences.

"You've got to be kidding me," I breathe, astonished equally by the ingenuity on display and the audacity of it all. Outsiders biohacking our technology for their own ends. "You can't..."

"Who says we can't?" I whirl to face to the woman who spoke to me downstairs. Her arms are folded belligerently, and her features are set in a pugnacious scrunch, but that's not the first thing I notice about her. The first thing I notice is how careworn she is. The greying of the hair tucked over her ears. The paper-thin complexion. The shadows around eyes that hold more fear than anger. It's a look that I pretend not to see in the mirror every morning, and it throws me off far more than a stand-up argument would have.

"Lynda?" And now Doug's there too. "Can we talk in private?"

I follow him meekly up the last flight of stairs to the top floor of the tenement. Here, the flats have been converted to hydroponic gardens. Thick profusions of leaves, stunningly green under the lights. "I don't understand this," I tell him. "Any of it. Why are they doing this?"

Doug's footering with a roller blind. It's warped and soiled with damp and mould, but he manages to raise it, letting the sunlight in and giving us a view of the secret country that lies between this forgotten street and the great, brown river. "What don't you understand, Lynda?" he says quietly. "People using the resources to hand to survive? Surely, you of all people understand that."

"But they're not –" I stammer. "They should be –"

"In the system?" He sighs. "Why? They have everything they need out here, doing things their own way. They're doing okay. What's wrong with that?"

"What's *wrong* with it?" I stare at him. The question is ridiculous, but for a second, I'm not sure of the answer myself. "How many families are living here, all cramped together?" I say, eventually retreating to the party line. "In the Heights they'd each have clean, warm, efficient apartments. In the system they'd have jobs."

"Menial, state-provided jobs, rewarding them with an evening's electricity and just enough calories to get out of bed in the morning and go and do it all again? They reckon they're happier working for themselves."

"Profiting from what they what they drag out of the mud you mean?"

"That's only a small part of it. Most of what they reclaim is recycled here to make substrate for printable stuff like solar panels for the electricity or plastic fibre weave for clothes." Doug rubs his chin. "Admittedly, the rare earth elements they don't have so much use for."

"And that's where you come in?"

He shrugs. "I feed it into the system and pass the value back to them in credit or in kind, that's all."

"Out of the goodness of your heart, I suppose?" I scoff.

"You find it that difficult to believe?" He shakes his head. "I get a slice for…hush money, I suppose you could call it." Then he looks me meaningfully in the eye. "But most of that I spend trying to help people inside the system. The ones who find it hardest to adjust."

Even though right is on my side, I'm the one who looks away first. Outside, a breeze has sprung up, enough to riffle through the bushes and raise a chop on the brown water. Clouds have edged into view too. It'll be muggy later but there'll be rain. Glasgow has changed a lot in the last century, but it wouldn't be Glasgow without rain. For the first time in an awful long time, I wonder what it is we're trying so desperately to preserve.

"So?" Doug says and I can feel the weight of anticipation in the question to come. Not just his, but that of every lost soul who's found their way to this place. Holding their breath as they crowd the stairs, listening in. "What are you going to do?"

And the answer to that, I realise with no little shock, is that I don't know. I came here with thirty years of conviction behind me. But witnessing this wild land and the people that have chosen to live in it, my thoughts feel scattered like petals and I'm not sure where they are going to land.

The system works. It is as efficient as it can be. All of its resources are consumed and remediated, again and again, and again. Including its most important components. Its people. There can be no room in the system for this kind of freedom, can there?

What I *should* do is file a report. Bring the Ministry departments down on these outsiders until they beg to be allowed to join the system, and have Doug sanctioned for abetting them too. Down in the street, the bees float and gyre around the bushes.

I am as surprised by the next word I speak as Doug is. "Nothing."

"Seriously?"

"I won't turn them in. Things can carry on as normal, but..." My turn to look at him. "You stop taking a cut. That's not fair."

He looks like he's about to argue but in the end he just nods. "And you don't want anything for yourself?"

All this time I've been watching the young girl from before. She's out at the river margin again, poking around with her stick. Her hair is flying in the breeze and she's smiling. Free. Happy. Then on some impulse she looks up and somehow, even at this distance, she sees me watching and waves. By instinct I wave back, and the moment is an echo of a memory of a different time. And perhaps an echo of a now that could have been. A simple gesture between mother and child that costs nothing and means everything. A glint of treasure.

"I want Mum to come and live here," I say.

And I feel renewed.

Infectious

Liz Williams

I knew I was ill the moment I got on the plane. I travel well, usually.
But this time I began to feel dizzy as I browsed the selection of
cosmetics deep into duty free: the ASMR-delivery body creams, the
gum glow treatments, the nape highlighters. As I looked, product
marketing followed me home, sliding down the long soft front of
my coat and lodging deep within the fabric, to be uploaded later
should I so choose (I pay a lot for my filters but some of it's useful).
As I reached out to the virtual tester, my hand began to shake, just a
fraction, and I thought: Thank God.

If my temperature had risen before we went through the
scanners, they would have refused me permission to board. I said as
much to Wayim. But that was why I'd invested properly.

"Oh really? How are you feeling now? What's your
temperature?"

Together we peered at my wristband monitor. All nice and
normal. I'd spent a lot on the device, and it would get us ahead of
the queue and first onto the plane, logging my data safely onto the
on-board scanners.

"Well, that's good," said Wayim. "Fancy a drink? Alcohol
doesn't count in an airport. Neither do calories."

He must have seen the look on my face, because he added
quickly, "I don't mean one of the ordinary bars. First class only. The
members' bar."

"I suppose."

By the time we entered the shute for boarding, I was feeling
shaky and fuzzy, but my wrist monitor was still reading normal, so
the steward merely ushered me onto the plane with a smile. We had
booked into first class, obviously. The flight, via the Penang-
Heathrow air bridge up and over the Kármán line, would not take
too long, but no matter what the levels of entertainment, I find
flights boring.

But then, I find most things boring.

I dozed for most of the flight, anyway. Whatever bug I'd picked up, it was making me very tired. Wayim watched a film and kept laughing, which was irritating. Eventually I asked him if he could be quieter. I was sure it was annoying other people, too. And he did shut up; he was quiet after that. I looked out of the window once, but all I could see was the Earth's blue-pearl curve below, so I snapped the shade shut again.

We landed in baking heat. I know this because the pilot told us so and also because it hit me as we stepped out of the plane. We went through a spray as we got onto the bus and then another going into the terminal itself. I have an exemption pass for this because of allergies but this time I didn't bother to display it, just took the chemicals. It would speed things up going through the quarantine channel. I didn't want too close an investigation, you see. Just in case.

My wrist monitor gave them the results they wanted but as luck would have it, I got pulled in the Q-chan. It's random, I know that, though some people get paranoid about it, say they always get hauled into the quarantine channel. I left Wayim standing by the gate while I answered their questions.

Did I understand the need for quarantine?

Yes, I did.

Who was my travel partner? Did we live together? Did I think he understood the need for quarantine?

Wayim Rehman. Yes, he understood it completely, and I explained why.

Ah, yes. He will have total comprehension, then – and the man laughed at his little joke. I laughed, too, as if charmed by his wit.

Had I had an infectious disease, on the official list of notifiable diseases?

No, I lied.

Did I undertake to isolate for a two-week span of time?

Yes. I answered with downcast eyes, a little timid, sometimes glancing up, however, to imbue my words with sincerity. The official was completely satisfied.

"I'm terribly worried about getting sick," I murmured. "Or even worse. Imagine – infecting others. What an awful thought. We all have to be so careful. It's our social duty, isn't it? It's just what decent people do."

He gave an approving nod and released me into the wild.

That night, we went clubbing.

You will know, of course, that it is against the law these days, but as the old US of A found during Prohibition, there are always ways and means. Here in London, though, there is only one choice: the club called the Membrane. That's not its real name. Nor shall I tell you where it is to be found, which district, or how to get there. We walk, as one does in the city. Perhaps it is an old Tube station, long shut down. Perhaps it is a former car park, running beneath the wedding-cake buildings of Kensington or Chelsea. Perhaps it is none of these things. It takes a long time to be trusted enough with its secret. And it has never been betrayed. At least, not yet.

That night, I found the walk hard. I was shivery by then, and the October heat didn't help. By the time we reached the little door, at the back of a building which is the entrance to the Membrane, I was drenched.

"Wait," I told Wayim. "Hold my parasol." I sprayed myself, wriggled out of my top and conjured another one from the tiny compostable tube in my bag. Onlookers from above, a drone or spy-eye, would see nothing except the parasol's dome as I refreshed my makeup.

"Finished? You look cooler."

And then we went inside.

The girl on the door checked my monitor.

"All very nice," she said.

I smiled. Little did she know.

"I need a drink," I told Wayim and obediently he ventured to the bar as I arranged myself on a nearby chaise longue and considered who might be here tonight. It was a Sunday, the biggest night of the week: no one was here who might have to do anything as crass as start work on Monday mornings. We were neither early nor late, and there were small groups of people dotted against the curving tiled walls. Soon, when things hotted up, most people would move onto the dancefloor or the crush bar next door. Against government regulations, of course, but isn't that the whole point?

And if they knew they were really running a risk? That it wasn't just a game of let's pretend? Maybe they did. I mustn't be too condescending.

There was a new group in tonight, a gaggle of girls. They all wore the latest in skintones and they also all wore butterfly sandals, in silver and gold and pink. Only one of the sets of sandals was genuine Eschada; the rest were knock-offs, but good ones. The girl who wore the real pair was vaguely familiar: tall, very thin, with a lot of facial modifications, subtle and in good taste. I amused myself for a minute estimating how much she had paid for them and when Wayim returned with our drinks I asked him if he knew who she was.

"Yeah, I think I've seen her before. Hang on."

He tapped his phone, then shook his head.

"No. She's got a block on."

"But you've got Readout."

"It's blocking that, too."

I was impressed. That must have cost a lot. Unless she was – well. Maybe not think too closely about that, because if she was with the authorities, she wouldn't take too kindly to being scanned.

But if she was with the authorities, I'd be unlikely to recognise her in the first place.

At this point someone we both knew, a young woman named Floa, came to sit with us, so I asked her if she knew who the girl was.

"Yes, sure, it's Miri Placet. She's never been in here before; it's a psych to see her."

"The glide-star?" Wayim said, impressed.

"That's the one."

I sniffed. I don't do glide; if I want to have an experience, I'll have it myself, not vicariously, through someone else's carefully manufactured dreams. But jealousy's not a good look.

"She's very lovely," I murmured. Floa smiled at me.

"You're so sweet, Geramin."

I took a sip of my drink and it made me cough. Once I'd started, I couldn't seem to stop. I coughed and coughed, until the glide-star's party turned and looked at me.

"Sorry," I spluttered. "Not feeling very well."

"Ooh," I heard Miri Placet say. "Do you suppose it's infectious?"

"Are you really not feeling well, Geramin?" Floa said with concern.

"No, I'm not. Something I picked up in Bali, I think." I made sure I spoke loudly enough to be overheard.

And there was respect in Floa's voice as she said, "Oh wow. You're so lucky."

Next day, I felt worse. Physically, at least. Emotionally? Well, it was kicking in now and that was good.

I've done this before, obviously. Three times: once with a respiratory, but non-SARS derivative; once with an echovirus which was really tough, but I just loved the name; and once with a picornavirus developed in United Korea that laid me out for a week, but it was totally worth it to let my voice drop as I said, "And then I was completely paralysed" and see the shock in people's faces.

"But weren't you scared? Did you – is there a cure?"

As I nodded bravely. "There is, but it doesn't always work."

That's the risk you take, though, when you're an artist, like me.

This time, I was in bed when the assistant told me that someone was at the door.

"Who is it, Tyra?"

The neutral electronic voice purred, "Her name is Miri Placet."

"Indeed!"

I was ready to receive visitors, even though I felt terrible. I'd done my hair and my makeup, was wearing a sensaround information wrap which I knew looked good. Wayim had been waiting on me hand and foot; he's so helpful whenever I'm ill.

There are stiff penalties for no-consent distancing violations, but Miri didn't pay any attention to those. When Wayim showed her upstairs, she ran straight to my bedside and knelt down. I pulled away, snatching my mask from the bedside stand and whisking it over my face.

"It's all right," she said, quickly. "I'm not trying to – you know."

"Get infected?"

Miri got to her feet and sat down in a nearby chair.

"I meant; I'm not trying to steal it from you."

I laughed. "I paid a lot of money to be as sick as this, but it's cool. Just as long as you mind your manners."

"Is it, though, you know, infectious?"

I gave her what I hoped was a mysterious smile, but said, with some regret, "No. It won't be. Well, that's what they said."

"Ohhh," she breathed. She really was very lovely. The designs on the summerweight slicks that she wore chased up and down her long legs, feeding information to and fro. "It might be an undecided, then?"

"There's always a chance. Fingers crossed."

"It must have cost a fortune."

I shrugged. "I have the money. And it's worth it. Why did you come to see me?"

She looked me straight in the eye. I could see the glide behind her eyes, but it was cataract creamy, a milky blue. I knew that meant that she'd switched it off for our interview and you know, being arrested might be interesting, but I didn't really want that experience.

"I'm bored," she said. "I – you know what I do. I've done all sorts of things and I'm still bored. There's no real danger any more, no real risk. This is the first generation that's happened to. Even fifty years ago you could still have been knocked down by a car."

"That can still happen."

She pulled a face. "Only if the algorithm fucks up or some terrorist hacks it. And how often does that happen? Not a whole lot."

"You know, we could still have a pandemic on this planet."

"We could, but with all the money going into healthcare, we won't, will we? Now no one's got an army any more and all their GDP's being put into research and infectious disease solutions, I don't expect to see one. And I'm so bored with being in tip-top condition all the time – yeah, I know, my viewers expect it. My insurers spend a mint on my physical condition. I've never known what it is to be ill. I've never known what it's like to be – exposed."

I'd worked that out, otherwise she wouldn't have been clubbing. She'd get off on the transgression, even if she knew there was no real risk.

"Until you walked in through my door," I said.

"It's a real disease, though, what you've got? It's not a synthetic? Because I know people who buy those, right, but it's not real, is it? You don't get the real emotions with it."

"Synthetics are a game. And I don't play games."

"Yeah, that's what I thought. It's what everyone says about you. Well, a few people, anyway. Lots of rumours but who ever knows about those?"

"Not many people know for sure," I said, but I was gratified all the same. Wayim keeps his ear to the ground but I'm not sure he doesn't tell me just what I want to hear. Perhaps I should reprogram him.

She was looking at me expectantly and I knew what she wanted but I don't believe in giving anyone what they want straight away. It's not good for the character. I knew Wayim was listening, naughty boy, so I let my head loll to the side and closed my eyes.

"I'm not feeling too well," I murmured and immediately he was in through the door.

"...sure you understand, perhaps another day, wouldn't quite do..."

And of course she was all anxiety, flustered, apologised. I told her to come back the following week.

Perhaps I'd be over it by then. Or perhaps not.

Later, I woke, completely disoriented. Wayim was bending over me, his smooth face a little crumpled with concern.

"Where..." I croaked. I felt terrible; he had to help me to the bathroom, but since I'd eaten nothing for days, I could not throw up. Left to my own devices I would have remained curled up on the bathroom floor but Wayim picked me up once I'd finished retching and carried me back to bed. The sheets had changed themselves in the interim and the room refreshers had circuited; it was pleasantly cool and smelled of lavender.

Infectious. That was my next ambition, once I'd recovered from this virus. No darklab will sell you an infectious illness, they'll tell you they're all NCDs. There are labs that will, but I haven't got to those yet: there was one, in Irkutsk, but the authorities closed it down before I could make contact, burned it to the ground with the researchers inside it, too.

I said all this to Wayim, delirious, ranting. At some point I remember he said, "Some people have an ideological view of all this, of course. I have been studying it. They say it's human destiny to get sick and die. That if we do not get ill, we will not learn."

I reached up and touched his smooth plastic skin with my hot hand.

"Something you can never experience, my friend."

"Something I never can." I could not tell if there was regret in his artificial voice or not.

"You know me, Wayim. We've been together a long time, ever since I bought you and you were delivered to my door. You know I'm not political. I'm an artist, that's all. An artist of the flesh."

"I know." His voice was gentle and full of love but then he was engineered that way. I didn't mind.

Some time later, I don't know when, he came to tell me with grave neutrality that Miri Placet had fallen sick and so had some of her friends, some of the people who went to the Membrane, and the authorities were looking for me. I've paid a lot of money to hide contact tracing, but I suspected it was only a matter of time. Wayim knew what to do: we'd rehearsed this scenario. I'd love to be in hospital, but I didn't fancy prison. And I wanted death to be on my own terms. That night he carried me downstairs, put me in the car, and we drove north. There's a place, but I won't tell you where. It's a long way from London and not on land. There, beneath the waves, were others like me and when I was lifted through the airlock and into the bunker, I was welcomed as a heroine. The delirium had passed but I didn't know how long I had.

"Well done," Doctor Dove said. Such a lovely name, like a bird you hold in your hands that won't mind if you wring its neck.

"You've set a city on fire. New epidemic, no cure, kills young people. Quite messy, really. Mind letting me know where you got it?"

"Bali."

"Oh, I have an idea. There are several. Was it the Hua Quai? they're making quite a name for themselves. Did they tell you it wasn't infectious?"

"Yes."

"Either they lied, or the virus has."

"I was looking for a darklab," I told her.

"Well," she said, laughing. "I think you found one."

A superspreader. I had achieved my life's ambition, my art's work, and all by accident, too. I did not like to think that the lab had cheated me, but I loved the thought that the virus itself perhaps had mutated. Miri Placet and her friends had been my canvas, all unwitting, apprentices or fakes, and I the original. But I was glad she'd got what she wanted, after all. I wondered whether it still was what she wanted. If she was still even alive.

Wayim would remain with me; I'd asked Doctor Dove to switch off his loyalty algorithms, after a suitable period of mourning, then go back out into the world and take my secrets with him. But for the time I had left, I lay and looked through the screen which showed me the outside world, beneath the sea, the nothing, the endless, endless black.

Cofiwch Aberystwyth

Val Nolan

PERYGL

We passed a bloated human corpse as we entered the harbour. It was face down in the water, its clothing a tissue of rags and filth that was as much weeds as fabric. Sigrid went pale when she saw it. Annabel threw up over the side of the dinghy. I only grinned up at the drone which was filming our arrival. I knew my subscribers were going to *love* this shit.

"No bodies no fun, am I right?" I smiled at the others when they looked back at me.

"There weren't supposed to be any bodies left," Sigrid said.

I shrugged as I watched the long concrete jetty pass to our right. It was mostly intact, with the rusting remains of a light tower crumpled at its tip. To our left as we turned was a vast heap of rotting timbers which might once have been a boardwalk. I slowed the outboard as the channel contracted further. It had not been dredged since long before the disaster and was clogged with the ruins of buildings which had either been demolished by the blast wave or been destabilised enough to have slid downslope in the interim. As we crept into the marina proper, it seemed that several apartment blocks had collapsed into the water and caught the boats below in a small tsunami. This had left heaps of rusting hulls and snapped masts piled across each other. Their lines and nets were tangled together, and a soup of garbage surrounded everything. Annabel was studying it all with grim fascination.

"There," I said to Sigrid, pointing at an upturned boat which looked reasonably steady. "Tie the line. We can scramble ashore from here."

She considered the idea for longer than I liked. "It might be safer to –"

I cut short her objection by leaping from the dinghy and throwing myself at the keel of the stricken craft. The surface was slick and for long seconds I found myself sliding off it, failing to find any grip. Then my fingers caught on a ridge, and I steadied myself.

"*Mila!*" Sigrid shouted. "Are you crazy? Are you suicidal or something?"

I laughed at her from atop the rocking hull and then looked up at the drone in delight. It was perfectly positioned to have recorded my jump. That was going to look great in HD.

"Come on!" I shouted back down.

Sigrid grumbled as she secured the dinghy, reverting to foul Frisian as she lashed a line to the upturned boat. Something about half-arsed plans and tetanus shots.

"I think you were just trying to impress me," Annabel said with a wink as we shouldered our backpacks from wreck to wreck, and then across misshapen concrete lumps and whole sections of fallen blockwork which had improbably retained their integrity. Our most direct route into the ghost town turned out to be flooded with a foul slurry, so instead Sigrid led us slowly along the waterfront. It looked like this had once been a pretty esplanade. Now, however, it was nothing more than burnt-out houses and wrecked cars that had been blown off the street and onto the stony beach where they sat rusting on their roofs and sides. Skeletal dragon heads, the uprights of rotted benches, stood watch in the ashes. They gazed out to sea as if daring gallant foreign sailors or plucky rogues to breach their borders.

"There aren't any footprints," Annabel said with delight. "No recent ones anyway. It's like walking on the Moon."

"The Moon would be more hospitable than this," Sigrid said, assessing our route. Ahead of us were ruins older than the houses, those of a knobbly castle reduced to bare stone centuries before the disaster here. In the sheltered hollows of the rubble beneath this tower, a series of pockmarked mosaics were just about visible. They appeared to tell the story of the town. I made out the date 1277, and a team of square men building walls; 1404 and someone named Owain Glyndŵr – Sigrid would surely know who he was – hacking people apart with a sword; 1405 and a ship carrying archers bearing down upon the settlement. Then came a run of nooks where the murals were completely obscured by the remains of a monument that had collapsed into the street, a bronze angel, a winged victory gripping a wreath of laurels in her hand. The figure had been crushed by heavy tracks – a military truck or tank, I reckoned – and so flattened to look like one of those bog bodies you find in Danish or Irish museums.

"I have to admit," Sigrid said, checking her compass and then clambering over a talus of cut stone. "I wasn't sure about this when you suggested coming here, but… Oh…"

Annabel and I hurried to follow her, sliding round a headland to see the town properly for the very first time. The curve of a coarse beach spread out before us with a great lump of land reaching into grey waters like a titanic animal at rest. From there, our eyes took in the smaller, closer offerings. First the deep trench which ran from near sea level to some ruins at the summit, then the mangled metalwork of a pier – the remaining timber of which displayed the same fire damage that we had seen elsewhere – and finally a vast old Victorian pile somewhere between the gaudy and the gothic.

"It's like something out of a fantasy," Annabel said of the latter, fascinated.

I smiled into my wrist camera. "Welcome to Aberystwyth," I said, tagging the giant old building's coordinates for the drone to revisit later. "That'll play well with the nostalgia crowd." Then, realizing that Sigrid was far ahead of us once more, I shouted, "*Wait up!*"

When we reached her, she looked worried. "Sigrid?" I said.

"Mila," she replied, matter-of-factly. She was standing along the edge of a retaining wall which ran around the base of the castle grounds. "You see these?"

Weathered handbills were pasted to the stonework here. Now that I was looking for them, I could see traces of them on walls and buildings all across Aberystwyth. They were as much part of the streetscape as the kinked lampposts and abandoned vehicles. Each displayed a yellow triangle with a black trefoil in the middle. "*PERYGL,*" they all announced in Welsh. "*YMBELYDREDD*".

Danger. Radiation.

COFIWCH

We had sailed from Rotterdam eight days earlier. My father lent us his boat, ostensibly for a voyage to Ireland but, as we made our way around the lonely southern coast of England, I allowed our course to drift northeast beneath a sullen rainless sky. It didn't take much more than luck for a small craft like ours to slip through the exclusion zone. The warning buoys were ill-maintained, and the maritime approaches were not as well patrolled as the authorities implied. Soon the coast of Wales was rearing up from the sea like a wall that had been left fall into disrepair. You could feel the weight of a wounded nation's brooding beyond the fog. You could –

"Mila," Sigrid said, snapping her fingers. "Are you even listening to me?"

"What?" I said. "Yes, of course I am."

Sigrid made a face. "We shouldn't stay too long here. The radiation…"

"Scare stories," I said, "to keep away people like us. Any radiation has long faded."

"Maybe," she did not look convinced, "but we'd be fools to ignore the notices."

I stared down my nose at her.

After a moment, Sigrid sighed. "Perhaps you could do a piece to camera about it," she said, relenting. "About the precautions we're taking?"

"People don't watch the show to see us take *precautions*." The word was anathema to my – to *our* – brand. People wanted to see us take risks. They wanted to see us go to the places they did not have the guts to go.

"Just think about it," Sigrid said. "Please?" Then she took out her tablet and, leaving Annabel and I to walk together, declared that she would go and scout locations. She fancied herself my producer, always been more comfortable programming the drones than appearing in front of their lenses. It was something I was happy to let her focus on for, as much as we liked to make things seem spontaneous, the planning and logistics involved in each vlog were considerable. Sigrid agonised over every aspect of the show, which was one of the reasons it had been so difficult to talk her into this trip. I doubt I could have convinced her to come to Wales on such short notice if the footage from our visit to a factory demolition the week before had not been corrupted. It had left us short an episode, and sponsors did not like that. Not when viewing figures were already falling. So, while Sigrid was at first full of questions about intentions and practicalities, she soon she fell into her usual rhythms of deep research and planning.

Annabel, by contrast, had not entirely seemed herself.

"You haven't said much in days," I said to her.

"I'm listening," she said, reaching out for me. "It's so quiet here. Where are the birds?"

I took her hand in mine. "Gone for the season, I suppose. Or there's nothing left for them to eat here." There were other possible explanations, but I dared not consider them.

"And the people?" she asked. "Even Chernobyl has people living around it."

"Chernobyl is easier to reach than west Wales," I said, and we both began to laugh.

"Oh, here we go," Annabel said. She squeezed my hand and then pointed along the rubble-strewn promenade. "Madam is beckoning."

Up ahead, I saw Sigrid waving at us. She was standing on the edge of a deep crater where the sea had broken through the promenade wall and collapsed the road. As we strolled towards her, I spotted more of the mosaics along this side of the castle: 1637, "Royal Mint"; 1644, "Civil War"; 1740, "Romantic Wales"… They would need to add one of a mushroom cloud if they ever rebuilt here, I though. Little mosaic people throwing themselves into the sea and so on. Red squares for the flames, green for the fallout.

"What have you found?" I asked Sigrid when we caught up to her in front of Annabel's vast ruin. The grand old sandstone building loomed shocked and roofless before us. It looked like a hotel crossed with an asylum, but the map marked it as a university which, I suppose, was basically the same thing. Its location on the waterfront would have been right at the edge of the air blast radius and it seemed that the initial detonation had blown out all the windows and the weather had done the rest.

"The street from the pier is blocked," Sigrid said. "Looks like the blast wave turned all these east-west routes into road-fill. We're going to have to go around –" her finger traced a route past the back of a nearby church "– and then come at Darkgate Street from the south."

"*Darkgate*," Annabel repeated, rolling the word around and delighting in its sound.

"What about the pier?" I asked. There was something inviting, like death, in how its blackened steel legs erupted from the dark water at odd angles. Surely it had once been loud and tacky, the site of a thousand trysts and a thousand more heartbreaks. Now it was little more than a giant spider's corpse. "We should climb out there," I told the others. "At low tide."

Annabel grinned.

Sigrid only shook her head. "If you die then I need to find a real job."

"You're telling me that working for a top 500 vlogger isn't a real job?"

"Working *with*," she corrected. "And, no, in a real job people would listen to me."

I threw my arm around her shoulder. "I'd be lost without you, love. You know that."

"I do," Sigrid said, carefully steering us away from the sea and into the town via a small park with the atmosphere of an abandoned refugee camp. Beyond this the streets became passable again. The army had obviously run a bulldozer through the debris here and forced the rubble into what remained of homes and pubs. There was little of note remaining except for a gable wall with the words COFIWCH DRYWERYN scrawled in white on a splash of red paint. It looked like it had been done in a hurry.

The three of us stood in front of it for a long moment.

"It's kind of like an all-purpose Welsh *fuck-you* to the English," Sigrid explained. "A remembrance thing after the English drowned one of their valleys –" she indicated the place name *Dryweryn* "– to create a reservoir.'

"The Welsh never forget," I said to the camera as though it had been my own insight.

"I can guarantee they won't forget what happened here," Sigrid said, shattered glass crunching under her feet as she picked her way through the endless rubble and junk.

Annabel and I followed in silence until the town's cemetery calm was broken by a boom the likes of which I had never heard. Empty doors and window frames rattled all around us. Annabel ducked behind me, quick as a whippet, and I found myself crouching slightly, an instinctive response, as a sharp black dart blasted past low overhead. Bricks in some of the buildings were shaken loose and clouds of dust fell all along the street.

Sigrid narrowed her eyes. "Just a training jet," she said. "The RAF still flies out of Anglesey. They pop up and down the coast the way you or I would go to the shops for milk."

Annabel and I stared at her.

"Seriously," Sigrid said, looking miffed. "I know doing the research is the producer's job, but sometimes I feel like the only one who reads up on where we go." She started back towards the centre of town. "Don't worry about the planes. They're just boys with toys."

"That," Annabel muttered as she craned her neck towards what was now little more than a dark speck in the ashen sky, "was *terrifying.*"

"Yeah," I replied, watching Sigrid as she stomped away, "I wasn't super happy with that display myself."

FFYRNIGRWYDD

So, how had lively Aberystwyth – 'the Athens of Wales', according to one poet – become little more than a ruined shell? The simple answer was that it suffered a terrorist attack. But of course the perpetrators were not the brown-skinned mullahs or disaffected dishwashers targeted by the "Go Home" vans of the Home Office or the "Hostile Environment" policy of the British government at large. Instead they were the cream of Eton and Oxford and the Royal Navy College in Dartmouth. They were skilled technicians and career ratings who'd had their politics distorted pint by pint in the jolly inns and arms of austerity-ravaged waterfront towns. They were mutineers.

The idea of a mutiny aboard a Royal Navy submarine would have been unthinkable in the days before Brexit had poisoned all discourse on the island of Britain, and yet that is exactly what had happened. I have read about it many times and so knew the story well enough to gloss it for my subscribers. It took place aboard HMS *Vehement*, a Vanguard class ballistic missile submarine on manoeuvres in the Irish Sea. A small group of junior officers and ratings seized control of the vessel during a watch change. They were English nationalists radicalised by one of the fractured Brexit Party's far-right daughter factions. They exploited the fact that UK submarines at the time did not use permissive action links, which is to say they did not operate like in the movies. They did not require codes to fire their missiles because their fleet relied entirely on military discipline to prevent a launch. Which, I've always supposed, used to be a point of great honour if you were British and a point of pure insanity if you were anyone else.

At the time of the *Vehement* incident, Aberystwyth had been hosting the National Eisteddfod: Eight days of Welsh language performances and literary contests, the largest music and poetry festival in Europe that year. Almost 150,000 people were in attendance on farmland just outside the town, between Aberystwyth and the village of Capel Bangor. Huge stages and tents and fairground attractions had been erected on the site. There were food stalls and booksellers and a frisson of excitement at how the Welsh Senedd was poised to follow Scotland's lead and discuss plans for independence from the United Kingdom.

That was when the *Vehement* launched two Trident missiles, each carrying a 500-kiloton nuclear warhead. One was targeted at the Senedd in Cardiff, though that missile failed in flight, crashed into the sea without detonating, and the warhead was later recovered intact. The second was targeted at the Eisteddfod and it performed exactly as its designers had intended. Over a hundred thousand people were within the immediate radius of the nuclear fireball. It was a hateful act, one in which the greatest literary and cultural minds of the Welsh nation, the future of the country's poetry and music, were incinerated in an eyeblink.

In the aftermath of the attack, the British tabloids tripped over themselves asking why the Eisteddfod was being held at all during such a time of crisis and political rancour. Some Brexiters even claimed that the festival's expression of Welsh identity was a provocative gesture in and of itself. They called the participants saboteurs and traitors. In response, BBC Wales played a recording of David Lloyd George from 1916, a speech which he had delivered in Aberystwyth at the height of World War I: "Why should we not sing during the war?" the Prime Minister had asked. "Why especially should we not sing at *this* stage of the war? Hundreds of wars have swept over these hills, but the harp of Wales has never once been silenced by one of them."

I should probably include a link to that so people don't think I'm a *total* asshole.

YMGARTREFU

I looked directly into the camera lens as we began filming our next segment and asked, "Are you ready to crack open a time capsule?" We were standing on a heap of broken concrete and slate, all that remained of a collapsed building on Aberystwyth's main drag. Most if not all of the buildings on the eastern side of this street had collapsed, but the resulting debris allowed us easy access to the upper floors, what we assumed were domestic flats. It had taken us a little while, but we had found one that looked relatively intact. No broken windows, no visible damage to the roof. It would be just as its inhabitants has left it.

"Who knows what we'll find inside?" I said to the camera as I used my glass cutter to open a hand-sized circle so I could reach through and unlock the latch. Just inside the window there was a row of heavy plastic pots. The plants in them were long dead but it looked like someone here had been growing... tomatoes? As I pushed the window in, one of the pots tumbled and spilt its dry soil – perhaps the last fertile soil in Aberystwyth – across the carpet. I almost felt bad about the mess but then I remembered that the people who once lived here had most likely been evacuated to safety.

I squeezed inside, moving a table out of the way. Annabel followed me, then Sigrid, and then the camera-drone. We found ourselves in a large living room where a heavy coating of dust had settled over everything. Small clouds of it rose up from the carpet with every footstep. Beyond the table there was a sofa, the skeleton of a clothes horse, and a wall full of bookcases. There was no television or computer, and no evidence that anyone had been here since the day of the attack.

Sigrid had her tablet out and was cross-referencing the flat's address with the available public records. "A rental," she said. "I'll see if I can find the occupants' names."

"There might be a food stockpile somewhere," I said to Annabel. "That was all the vogue at the time on account of Brexit. Might be a couple of laughs to be had out of that?"

She nodded and moved cautiously into the stairwell to investigate.

"Might be something of interest with the books too," Sigrid was saying from the other side of the living room. She was standing in front of a timber shelving unit, running her hands along the spines of hardcover and paperback novels. There was a selection of critical and historical tomes, as well as various gaudy paperbacks. The books were a mixture of Welsh and English, an assortment of fiction and literary criticism. The fiction I recognised as a hodgepodge of classics and titles that would have been newer at the time of the missile strike. Above these again was a stack of dictionaries and grammar textbooks. Even more books, these thick with notes and loose, handwritten pages, were strewn in piles across the floor.

"I think these people might have been academics," I said to the camera.

Through the door, I could see Annabel poking around in the kitchen. Some people called what we were doing "disaster tourism" but I preferred to think of it as raising awareness about the state of the planet. The twenty-first century has not been kind to Mother Earth and so I feel duty-bound to vlog the results for future generations. People had been doing this since Vesuvius erupted.

Since they sifted through the ashes of the Great Fire of London. I failed to see how my riffling through these people's treasured memories was really all that different from Howard Carter rummaging for gold in the Valley of the Kings? Sure, I will admit that ad revenue did not hurt, and we had a quiet side-line in souvenirs from deadly or devastated places, but my real motivation was always edutainment.

"They looked like they were happy," I said, surprised at the depth of my sadness as I showed Sigrid a framed photograph on a shelf. Two faces, a woman and a man, peered out from the picture. They looked older than us, maybe late thirties or early forties. She had long red hair; he was balding prematurely. I picked up the frame and pointed it towards the camera.

"Come on," Sigrid said, unsentimental as ever. She went upstairs to catalogue the contents of the bedroom and see if we could overnight there. Meanwhile I headed down to the flat's buried entrance, a narrow corridor squeezed between two shops on street level. The door-frame here had buckled but it had held. A pile of unopened mail was still spread inside it. There were circulars and booklets of coupons mixed in with crumpled fliers for hardware stores, unopened water bills and bank statements. For a moment I wondered if the apartment had been abandoned long before the missile strike but then I remembered what my own flat's mail pile looked like. Flickering through the envelopes, I found the names of two people, a man and a woman, who I assumed to be the residents. I shouted them up to Sigrid who I knew would enter them into her tablet.

"I found them," she said when the three of us reconvened in the living room.

"The people who lived here?"

She nodded.

"Where were they relocated to after the attack?"

"They weren't," Sigrid said, shaking her head. "They died at the Eisteddfod."

DRYLLIADAU

The next morning Sigrid and I found our dinghy deflated in the marina. We had intended punting back out to the boat to retrieve supplies, but instead we found withered yellow rubber floating on oily water like a sad joke at our expense. One long rip was visible along its side.

"Who could have done this?" Sigrid demanded. "There's no one here but us!" She was looking around now at our footprints in the dust and ash along the promenade. We had trampled it so much that it was impossible to separate out any tracks.

"It was probably an accident," I said, looking at all the debris in the water. "A tree limb or a bit of a caravan or something came down the river and snagged on it."

"We should have overnighted on the boat," Sigrid said, "not pulled that fucking haunted house routine in some dead couple's kitchen." She sounded mad to me, paranoid even, as she eyed the surrounding hills with suspicion.

"Subscribers love the haunted house bit," I said. Indeed, it was one of the vlog's most popular segments, one part *Ghost Hunters* knock-off and one part *Blair Witch* fan-fiction. Lots of jump scares and messing with the audience. It was one of the few instances where we added VFX in post-production.

"Someone is fucking with us, Mila."

The air was getting cold and I hugged my arms around myself. "Okay," I said, thinking of the stockpiled tins which we had eventually located in the flat. "We'll be able to find supplies. Might have to dig them out, might have to get a bit creative with our can-opening, but it'll be an adventure, right? Dramatic tension and all that." I smiled at her.

Sigrid squeezed her eyes closed real tight for a moment, the way she always did when she was frustrated. Then she returned her attention to me. "Mila," she said, "can you forget about the fucking vlog for a minute? This is serious. We've only so much iodine. We can only stay here so long."

"Subscribers love a ticking clock."

She looked around her. "Subscribers be damned, we need to think about going home."

"What about the preferred ad program?"

"Fuck the ads, Mila." Sigrid visibly shivered. "This place is death."

I stepped placed a hand on her shoulder. "Death is our business, love."

She shrugged me off. "Are you listening to yourself? You're not mugging for the camera now, Mila. We're stuck in a nuked ghost town with no way home." She looked out at the wreckage of the marina. "Maybe we can salvage one of these boats? Use one to sail out."

"They're too big, Sig." I sighed as I considered all the silt and garbage choking the channel. "I mean, that's why we didn't sail the boat in ourselves."

Sigrid seemed to see the sense of this. "Well then I can swim back out to it," she said.

"The water is basically radioactive swill." I pointed back at the yellow warning signs.

"Oh, *now* you're all for believing the warnings?"

"I believe the weather," I said, trying to remain reasonable. "The wind is getting stronger, the sea is getting rough…" I felt the salt spray on my face and heard the rumble of waves breaking against the remains of the boardwalk. "That's gonna churn shit up. Particles and, I don't know, molecules?"

"Particles," she said. "Molecules." Sigrid ran her hands through her hair. "Okay, okay. That might fly for the kids watching you online, but this is me you're talking to."

I folded my arms. "You never believe me," I said.

"No," Sigrid said, "you just can't cope with people disagreeing with you. You've never been able to. You're obsessed with being liked. It's pathological."

"Well there's certainly no one liking me today," I said, hurt.

Sigrid put her hands on her hips. "What has gotten into you?"

"Into me? What's gotten into *you*, Sig? You've been a nightmare this whole trip."

She blinked at me for a long moment then burst out into laughter. "Well if you hadn't lost the footage from that factory you went to then we wouldn't be here to begin with."

"That wasn't my fault," I said. I could feel my hand starting to shake. Could feel a hot tear bubbling beneath my eye but I fought it back.

"Oh spare me the upset," Sigrid said. "I can't... I..." She shook her head. "Annabel should be here. Why isn't she?"

I looked over my shoulder and towards the seafront where Annabel had gone to explore the ruins of the vast university building. She thought that there might have been fun trinkets to be found inside. "She's doing her own thing," I said. "You know what she's like."

Sigrid scowled and rubbed her face. "It's supposed to be the three of us," she said. "Even if Annabel is the only one you listen to."

"Hey, that's —"

"I'm not wrong."

Somewhere out of sight, the wind was whipping a lose line against a boat. The sound of it was a sharp and irregular beat. It offered unhelpful punctuation to our dispute.

"Look," Sigrid was saying, "there are towns south of here which we can walk to for help."

I squinted into the distance. The skeletal remains of a transmission tower were visible to the south like a broken Babel, promising nothing. "And what if one of us falls?" I asked. "What if one of us gets blown off a cliff?"

"We can keep to the main roads." She was already tightening the straps on her backpack. "They'll still be passable for pedestrians. It's the best option."

"And what if one of us breaks a leg?"

Sigrid muttered something that I didn't catch. "We've filmed enough for a week's worth of material, Mila. We can just go. We *should* just go."

"Then you go," I told her. "I'm staying. I'm not done here yet." I picked up my own backpack, turned on my heel, and began back towards the Aberystwyth promenade.

"Mila," Sigrid said, "come on, don't be like this. Don't be a fool." She sounded disappointed, which I found more than a little rich.

"Go if you're going," I shouted back. "Just remember, you're nothing without me."

Whatever smart answer she might have had to that was lost on a howl of cold wind.

DYMCHWELIAD

Sigrid's absence did not bother me, not really. For all her talk of the three of us doing things together, Annabel and I had managed the vlog more than enough times without her. Most recently that had been the chemical plant demolition site ten days earlier. Though that had proved to be a damned exploration. If the footage from it had not been so corrupted, then I wouldn't have had to devise this mad scramble to west Wales to try and fill the gap in our schedule. I thought back on that night as I picked my way through the gaping, crooked houses of Aberystwyth. The site had manufactured fertilisers from industrial by-products in the first part of the century, made explosives in its middle years, and spent the last five decades as a derelict campus of iron sheds and red-brick laboratories frequented only by miscreants and addicts. It was finally to be redeveloped as a glistening steel and glass monument to twenty-first century excess. Its spent syringes would be concreted over for luxury apartments. Its poisons would be distilled into profit.

But, before that brave new dawn, the plant's vast rabbit-warren required demolition. Sigrid had excused herself, of course. She said she was visiting her aunt in a care home in Lelystad that weekend, and so Annabel and I went by ourselves. The fence around the site should have been electrified and under surveillance, but times were tighter than security and no one cared much for an old factory that was going to be razed. We were easily able to get beneath the slack chain-link and hurry across the cracked concrete apron, past stacks of salvaged RSJs and timber beams gone dark with age and wisdom. Then we caught our breaths beneath one of the tall cranes reaching high into the site's halogen night.

"It's like being a mouse in a cornfield," Annabel said, straining her neck to look up.

I smirked back at her. "Launch the camera," I said.

Annabel kneeled beside me and retrieved the drone from her backpack. She cupped it in her hands and threw it into the air the way one might release an injured bird back into the sky. It took a moment to stabilise and lock onto us as it subjects. Then it hovered about a metre away with its lens rotating back and forth as we moved.

"Welcome to late capitalism," I said to it.

"That's optimistic," Annabel said softly. She got back to her feet.

I waved vaguely at the corrugated fastness before us. "Come on," I said.

We soon discovered that the floor of the largest building conveyed a perverse horticulture. The machinery which remained was completely overgrown with soft green moss. Great valves sprouted like steel mushrooms from the ground. Paint pealed from immense copper pipes to reveal the green oxidation beneath and so further blur the line between the natural and the mechanistic. A greenhouse of smashed panes stood oddly against one interior wall. *DOODSGEVARR*, a black skull-and-crossbones on the wall declared, adding *DANGER DE MORT* in French in case there was any doubt. The next building was a forest of plumbing and gantries. The one after that was the size and shape of an abandoned aircraft hangar.

"This place is beyond creepy," Annabel said, shivering. "I love it."

"And I love you," I said, leaning against her and kissing her neck. "You want to see it from above?"

She pulled slightly away from me. Then she looked up to where the swaying of the cranes was just about perceptible. "You mean…"

Maybe it was cruel of me to have asked her that. Heights had always been an issue for her. Before we met, she had run with an old-school urban exploration crew in university. She had skipped class after class to weasel around in steam tunnels and utility corridors beneath the campus or stayed out all night partying on flat library rooftops where, in her own words, "We absolutely did *not* do a lot of drugs". Her friends had scaled transmission towers the way other people scaled mountains. They had looked down upon an unknowing world from the secret vantages of reservoirs and chimneys. But not Annabel. She usually found a way to avoid the more dangerous heights. She rarely climbed until she met me, and even then –

"Okay," she said, taking my hand and squeezing it. "Let's do it."

"Yes?"

"Time to level up."

I smiled at her. "You're amazing," I said, and kissed her again.

Access to the cranes was supposed to be secured with chains, but it didn't take much to find one that had been overlooked by careless watchmen. It did not take us long to get into the mast and start our climb. Arm over arm, gloved hands and trainers finding purchase on the yellow steel ladder which led up through the crane's boxy core. Even halfway up the whole demolition site was spread out beneath us, and I knew this was the right decision. I could hear Annabel's breathing behind me all the way up to the operator's cabin where I paused and waited in the wind for her to emerge from the ladder alongside me.

"You were fast," she said, holding on to my waist. She was smirking again but, beneath her good nature, there lurked something else.

"Well if that impressed you..." I tilted my head at the last stretch of ladder, at the access hatch to the long metal arm which stretched out over the factory. "Come on," I said, scrambling up the final rungs and stepping out on the swaying gantry which ran along the jib of the crane. I could feel the empty air beneath me, could taste the risk I was taking, but I had to know what it felt like. I beckoned for Annabel to follow.

She bit her lip. "I'm afraid," she said, bursting out in laughter. "Isn't that silly?"

"Not silly at all," I said. "But I know you can do it." I also knew the drone was filming everything. I know her triumphant conquest of the crane would look great on the screen.

"I'm afraid I won't make it," she said again. She had always been small and lithe, but now she almost looked vulnerable. "I'm afraid I'll fall."

I almost had to shout to be heard over the wind from the North Sea. "Do you trust me?"

Annabel nodded.

"Then just take a step." I reached out an arm towards her. "Just one more step…"

CRAIG-GLAIS

I found myself by the base of the large hill at the north end of the Aberystwyth promenade. My map indicated that there used to be a walking trail to the summit, and, on any other day it might have been pleasant – grimly picturesque, even – to have followed its faded switchbacks to the top. But, sulking more than I wished to admit, I sought something tougher and more direct. My map told me that there had once been a funicular here, marked as "CLIFF RLY", and this, I concluded, must have been the deep concrete trench which ran to the top of the hill. I found its starting point, along with a rusting carriage crumpled like an old beer can, amid the red-brick rubble of a tiny station house near the promenade. Whether during the blast wave from the missile attack or later, the cable pulling the funicular had clearly snapped and the carriage had plummeted into what was left of the station.

To my surprise, the two sets of tracks were still intact. Buckled here and there by the heat of the blast, sure, but nothing that couldn't be easily repaired. They sat on a gravel bed at the bottom of the trench. There were electrical fixtures along the concrete wall and, here and there, rollers between the tracks that once eased the passage of the funicular cable. A third of the way up I had to clamber over a collapsed footbridge. My leg went through one of the rotting beams and it was only by thrusting out my arms that I managed to save myself from further harm. I looked around for the drone, but it was beyond the hill. Nothing to edit out so.

By the time I reached the summit I was sweating despite the chill in the air. The climb had been more than worth it though. I could see the whole town laid out below me. I didn't need my map up here. The lines of the streets were softened by rubble, but the general shape of Aberystwyth's arteries was still visible. This must have been a beautiful place once, I thought. The sea breeze stirred my hair and I imagined it on a fine summer's day with the sun beating down and children playing on the beach. I pictured the couple from the apartment we explored. I saw them sitting at their table by the window overlooking the street, drinking their fancy tea, and discussing literature or theatre or some such. They sounded like such a drag!

From here I could see for miles up and down the bay. The sea and the distant coast and the sky all blurred into one, all different shades of grey. The rocks here were slanted, I noticed, turned sideways, or warped into undulating shapes. I doubted the *Vehement* attack had done that. Surely it was the result of something older and more powerful. Even a nuclear missile could only scorch the surface of this place, could do no more than blanket the surrounding hills with ash, could only char the Welsh trees for so long... Because while Sigrid, I assumed with a certain kind of wary sadness, had probably died out there, there were already a few patches of new grass on nearby hills. Life was doing its damnedest to push back into the world, but it had a long way to go. I was reminded again of Chernobyl and the volume of life that thrived there despite the strontium and caesium. Someday Aberystwyth too would come to life again.

I strolled around the remains of the hilltop amusements, but they were little more than rubble and rot. More inviting to me, more poetic, were the waves breaking on black rocks at the base of the cliff. And out there too, the wreckage of the *Vehement* lying on the bay's stony tongue like the carcass of a great leviathan. Failing to regain control of the *Vehement*, the Navy had sent a pair of destroyers to drive the boat aground on the shallow seabed of Cardigan Bay. They had been ruthlessly successful in that, exploiting the inexperience of the mutineers to trap the submarine in a pincer. It had broken up on the patches of rock which surrounded the approaches to Aberystwyth, the roots of Wales enacting their revenge by rupturing the *Vehement's* pressure hull and spilling her crew into the sea. A decade of tidal action had since washed the submarine closer to shore. I knew that it still had a reactor aboard and that, in the brutal grounding, its containment vessel had been damaged. The Royal Navy had sealed it up and in the last survey – two years ago, I think – had not yet found substantial leakage. It must once have been a fine craft, I thought. Stately, proud, and orderly. Operating according to discipline and rules. But now it lay cracked and hollow, abandoned like a shell shed by some enormous crustacean. I would have to send the camera out to gather some footage before we left. I could do a whole segment about it.

Then a movement further out to sea drew my attention: a dark speck against the grey. It was too small to be another fighter jet, or even a commercial flight, and too misshapen to be the light aircraft of some daredevil Briton intent on poking their nose into the exclusion zone. No, I figured it to be a drone. The whole of Cardigan Bay was still a military test zone after all. I wondered if it had fixed its beady IR eye on my heat signature, one of only two warm points in the town? But no matter. Turning back towards the wreckage that was Aberystwyth, I could see Annabel dancing on the shore far below. She was the only thing moving down there. So full of life. So full of joy and wonder. She drifted along the dark brown sand with the same kind of grace she had found within herself on the jib of the crane.

It was, I decided with a smile, time for us to climb out onto the remains of the pier.

YMBELYDREDD

Dead seagulls were visible in the rubble, their corpses rotting with little piles of ingested plastics piled up between their bones where once their stomachs had been. I felt ill just looking at them. Ill but fascinated. The little heaps of garbage were death in the shape of life. I made sure to get a shot with my wristcam before picking my way down the cratered promenade. The sea had taken big bites out of the street frontage here. The road, like the far side of the university building, had collapsed onto the beach, and several apartment blocks were open to the weather like life-sized dollhouses, their crumpled front walls burying cars in bricks and broken glass. About halfway to the pier I passed an olive-green jeep with army insignia abandoned on the street corner where Annabel sat waiting for me.

"Hey," I said.

She smiled.

"What're you thinking about?" I asked.

"Oh, you know," she said, sliding off the jeep's bonnet, "the usual."

I was hugging her tight before I knew what I was doing. I don't know why. I just needed to feel her close to me.

"Everything will be okay," she said, and this time she led me as we climbed together onto the warped metal skeleton that had once been the town's Victorian pier. Annabel was a little bit ahead of me, looking back every so often to egg me on. I was in awe of how deftly she moved from foothold to foothold so high above the soul-black sea. There was little left of the pier but the metal skeleton and some charred and rotting timber planks, but Annabel had a sense for the most corroded beam. Like one of Aberystwyth's lost birds, she always managed to avoid the most perilous perch. Certainly, she was not afraid any more. She had conquered that now. I would have liked to have taken the credit for that but, in truth, it was all her.

Half way out we came to a section that had collapsed utterly and we were unable to go any further. We sat there for some time as the camera drone took lazy loops around us. We imagined what it must have been like with a band playing and children running everywhere. We spotted smashed slot machines in the water far below us. We held hands until –

"What's that?" Annabel asked. "Over there?"

"Over where?"

She pointed back towards the promenade, and I saw what she saw. A figure standing atop the remains of a seafront hotel. Then they dropped out of sight again among the mounds of ash-covered concrete.

"Mila?" Annabel said.

"Someone's here." I stood, suddenly unsteady on my feet, and I reached for her hand. "We have to get out of here."

We made it almost all the way back to the promenade before three shapes appeared from the rubble, two burley men and a slender woman, all wearing protective yellow suits. Through their facemasks I could see that the men had an unremarkable military cut while the woman had an obvious British countenance to her visible features. Coming up behind them then was a fourth yellow suit, a smaller figure whose face I recognised at once.

"Mila," Sigrid said. Her tone neither friendly nor beckoning.

I took a step back on the rickety pier beams.

"How could you, Mila?" she asked. "How could you let that happen to Annabel?"

"Annabel…?" I looked to where she had been standing just moments ago.

"Mila?" Sigrid said again. "Jesus, you're not talking to her now, are you? Are you seriously seeing shit? Are you talking to people who aren't there?"

"I…"

The two men were looking to the woman for instructions, but she shook her head.

"Listen to me, Mila," Sigrid said. "I know you tampered with the dosimeters." She held up a yellow device about the size of a mobile phone. "We could have died here, Mila. *I* could have died."

"We need to get you out of here," the British woman said. "Sooner rather than later."

"The radiation isn't from the missile," Sigrid explained, "it's from the submarine's reactor." She pointed out to sea. "It's leaking more and more over time."

I shook my head. "We'd have known about that. Someone would have said something."

Sigrid looked to the woman beside her.

"We've… been keeping that quiet," the woman admitted in clipped estuary English. "As quiet as possible. It's not exactly a clean-up priority right now."

"The plane spotted us," Sigrid said. "The one over the castle. It just took them this long to get a drone out here to confirm. Then to hike out here themselves. I ran into these two –" she indicated the male-shaped hazmat suits, "– after about a day. Irish peacekeepers out of Aberporth. They explained everything. How the police found your recordings from the demolition site –"

"No," I said quietly.

"– the ones you said were corrupted. They were able to recover them. They saw what happened." She hung her head for a moment then continued. "I thought I was out there looking for help but they were looking for us."

"It was actually easy enough to locate you," the woman said. "You bought maps of west Wales on your credit card. Given your predilections –"

"My brand," I said, half-heartedly.

"– it wasn't a huge leap from that to here."

I backed up further, my whole body shivering. "I didn't mean for it to happen," I said, making sure the drone picked up my words. "It was an accident. I didn't mean for Annabel to fall. I didn't mean for her to die."

Sigrid looked at me for a long time without speaking. Finally, she shook her head. "Mila," she said, gently. "Annabel is alive. They found her on the demolition site. She… She'll never walk again, the fall shattered her spine, but she's alive. She's in hospital back in Rotterdam. A specialist unit. They're looking after her right now."

I swallowed hard as I looked back out to sea and saw Annabel. She was balanced on a rusty crossbeam, teetering back and forth and – oh, God – I couldn't watch it again. She had fallen. She had fallen from the crane jib, and I had just run away. I had convinced Sigrid to come here, to come all this distance on the pretence of filming a vlog instalment and… I turned from those watching me, ashamed, and nearly lost my own balance in the process, the cold water sloshing across sharp rocks underneath what was left of the pier, the drowned slot machines daring me to try my luck.

"*Mila!*" I heard Annabel cry out.

"Mila!" Sigrid said, firm and certain. She reached out a hand towards me. "Just take a step. Just one more step."

I was caught between them. A past I could escape right now if I truly wanted to and a future in which I would have to answer for what I had let happen. I took a breath, a long breath, closed my eyes, and made my decision.

149

Panspermia High

Eric Brown

You've heard about the theory of Panspermia, right? And no, it's nothing to do with the ejaculate of an eternally youthful fictional character called Peter.

Panspermia: the idea that microscopic biological life-forms exist out there in the gulfs of space. Well, not an idea. A fact. And I should know. I came to Earth on the back of a meteorite; me, a short-chain molecule in the steroid lactone range, known locally as a bufotoxin. These days members of my family can be found in the parotid glands of certain toads.

The rock I was riding came down in Australia ten thousand years ago. The meteorite squashed a colony of cane toads taking it easy in the noonday sun – but not all of them. One little critter moseyed on over to take a look.

And I – call me Bufo – decided that the ugly, ambulatory little fellah would make a perfect host. I needed an organic life-form to cloak me from all the lethal pathogens teeming across the face of planet Earth. I needed a host on which I could lie low and take it easy.

I made the leap, said g'day to toady, and made myself at home.

And it's been pretty much plain sailing for the last ten millennia.

So what happened to end all that, and why am I recounting my life story in the voice of an Aussie stoner?

Skip ten thousand years – during which I inhabited almost as many cane toads – and there I was, kicking back on the tegument of the latest *Rhinella marina*, minding my own business and doing my best to keep toady away from danger. Which wasn't that easy, given how the human race treated cane toads. Some people ran over the critters for sport, while others boiled them alive and drank the fluid to get a 5-methoxy-N,N-dimethyltryptamine high.

More humane individuals simply licked the backs of captured cane toads.

We had a symbiotic relationship, me and mine host. He gave me a body to live on, and I utilised his feeble senses to spot lunatic drivers and druggies, communicating with him via an occasional shot of adrenalin to keep him on his toes.

Which worked pretty well until last week when along comes Dougie Brennan, on our blind-side. Next thing I know, Dougie pounces on toady and ferries him home, a weatherboard shack on the outskirts of Alice Springs.

Drops mine host in a pan of water and turns up the gas.

Toady boils to death and I find myself floating in an unfamiliar medium, fluid. It's all I can do to hold my chain together. The pan is filthy, crawling with all manner of hostile microbes and pathogens. I feel myself fading, fading fast... I'm facing death, extinction.

I need a host, or I'll die within hours.

What next for your hero?

So Dougie lets the noxious brew cool, strains out toady's blood and guts, and pours himself a pint of liquid oblivion.

Down the hatch.

Through the boiling, cooling, and drinking process, I've been in a daze, bereft at being parted from toady and casting about for salvation. And then...

I find myself sharing the head of crazed, drug-addled Dougie Brennan.

All in all, I preferred life on the toad.

Our introduction goes something like this:

"Who the hell...?"

Call me Bufo

"Jeez... One hell of a trip, sport."

No trip, Dougie. This is for real. I'm in your head, for better or for worse. I'm going to let you sleep it off. Then it's all about cleaning yourself up, getting straight, and leading a long and healthy life.

"Don't like the sound of that, but."

You have another fifty years ahead of you, Dougie.

"Oh, Jesus…"

He falls to his knees.

The noxious brew he downed an hour ago is reacting in his gut and he's chundering all over the kitchen linoleum.

Then he crawls into a corner, groaning.

"I feel crook, mate!"

Take it easy. Lie still and close your eyes. Sleep it off and we'll soon have you up and about.

Or so I hope.

Instead, sad old Dougie Brennan succumbs to the poison and dies.

And without a viable host I'm in grave danger, yet again.

I cast about for a life-form to inhabit temporarily until something more suitable and long-term comes along.

But there's nothing. Dougie's half-starved tom is out ratting, and his dog departed weeks ago in search of a more reliable owner.

I feel myself fading.

Then a strange thing happens.

A very, very strange thing indeed.

Dougie's dead, but I'm still in communication with him.

I feel his consciousness right beside me, faint and ethereal.

Dougie…?

"Bufo, mate. That you?"

I'm right here, holding your hand. Well, I would if you had a hand…

"What gives, cobber?

You died, Dougie.

He surprises me by laughing. "Died and gone to Hell, but?"

Not Hell, no. You're still here, on Earth. Only…

"Only?"

Discorporate, incarnate… You're a ghost, Dougie.

"A ghost?" He sounded scared.

A free spirit.

"Jeez!"

Look, Dougie. Look down. Say farewell to the pathetic specimen you were…

And I'm rising along with him.

153

If Dougie is dead, then…

It comes to me that I'm dead, too.

We look down and see Dougie's pathetic corpse laid out in a pool of vomit. It's a sad sight, but the tragedy is allayed by the wonder that fills Dougie's reborn spirit. He is ecstatic, euphoric, as we soar.

And I realise something.

Conjoined, we are far more than we ever were singly. I am more than a parasite on a cane toad's warty hide, and Dougie is far, far more than sad, addicted human jetsam.

Together we can experience the cosmos.

We rise. We leave the confines of planet Earth, and I take Dougie into space in search of galactic wonders, and highs he's never even dreamed about.

We surf the universe, Dougie and me, reborn.

EXHIBIT E

L. P. Melling

People first noticed it had changed on the turn of the full moon in October.

For the many who looked up at night, the moon appeared different somehow, but they could not put their finger on what had changed. Like a patient looking at an X-ray, the shading looked wrong, but they couldn't describe how without before-and-after images.

You needed a telescope to truly realize the change, and what you saw was beyond belief.

A giant replica of Earth was superimposed on the moon's lifeless grey surface: our planet reflected back at us.

Soon the internet was awash with satellite imagery and fevered discussion of the moon. Questions echoed around the world. Where was it being projected from? Why had it been created? What did it mean? A whole host of theories, conspiratorial and otherwise, sprung up. Talk show hosts riffed on the event and invited artists and scientists to discuss its value.

But that was just the start.

It was not a fixed image as people took it to be, but in movement like the thing it represented.

Night by night, it changed. Subtly at first, with the ice caps shrinking on the 3D copy of our planet. Then dramatically as landmasses disappeared before our eyes on live satellite feeds.

The oceans turned a deeper blue with a tint of blood red the following night, and entire continents burst into flame, smoke clouds drifting across half the planet.

Tsunamis swept across seas and oceans, leaving a trail of destruction and drowned islands in their wake. And if you magnified the image, you could see other details. Belly-up whales and other sea life on the surface. Charred flora and trapped fauna.

The night after as the moon shrank further, barbed wire the size of stripped forests sprouted and wrapped itself around the globe. And the remaining few islands turned a dead grey, lifeless as the moon the image was displayed on.

And as the moon completed its cycle, the dead planet faded away to nothing. Like a Banksy piece, the priceless artwork was destroyed forever.

Afterwards, the world hailed it as the most ambitious art installation humanity had ever produced, and though it had countless critics, people began to wake up to its message.

No artist ever claimed credit for it, though many people claimed to know who had organised it. Clearly the piece was commissioned by someone with a hell of a lot of money, but it would remain as much a mystery as our own creation, as our self-destructive nature.

It was only later, when the Gemini Observatory scanned the projected image pixel by pixel that they found it. In an oil-spilled section of ocean floated a raft of plastic bottles arranged to spell the artwork's title: *Exhibit E.*

The signature took people time to make out, the scrawl illegible, until a team of handwriting experts deciphered it: H. Nature.

Now people continue to look up at the moon's illumination, wondering if the image will return, and they do more than ever to stop it from becoming reality.

The Lori

Fiona Moore

The problem with sentient battle tanks is their drivers.

Realising this after (unfortunately not before) the Battle of Kuching, the military quietly shifted their AI strategies towards botnets and other non-social intelligents which can take down the utilities and welfare systems of entire regions without worrying too much about the consequences. Sentient battle tanks quietly joined ornithopters and weather control in the listicles of the thirty strangest technological propositions of the past two centuries. And that, for most people, was the end of it.

Except for Corporal Atticus Cooper, the driver of Kursk 118-200.

Cooper grew up liking any kind of story involving magic swords or horses or dragons which choose brave heroes and take them on adventures. He went through a long phase of secretly pretending he was Elric of Melniboné. He had owned a Staffordshire terrier, or something that looked like one anyway.

But after a few weeks he had carefully packed up the dog's food, encouraged the dog into her crate, put both dog and food into his father's pickup and driven to the local shelter, leaving her there with no explanation.

At the age of eighteen he'd done something similar, enlisting and putting as many miles between himself and the place where he grew up as possible. He signed up as a driver, because he liked machines, and because it was a necessary job that was fun and interesting, but not likely to get him killed.

He'd tried to improve himself and do better than what was expected of him. But his lovers never stayed long, and usually described him as "obsessive". He never managed to form close friendships with his squadmates either, for all that he would buy them rounds, go out of his way to do favors for any one of them that he so much as thought needed a helping hand. Cooper didn't seem to care.

All of which added up to the sort of profile which gets people recruited as drivers for the battle tank program.

But, as Clausewitz or Sun Tze or one of the other writers that the sort of people who develop battle tank programs are fond of selectively quoting said, no plan survives contact with the enemy.

And when Cooper woke up in a hospital in Manila, six weeks after the Battle of Kuching, the first thing on his mind was finding Kursk.

Cooper managed to curb his first impulse, to check himself out of the hospital immediately. Mostly because it turned out comas don't work like they do in the movies, and he had to learn to walk properly again. But he put the enforced recovery time to good use, finding out what had happened to Kursk.

By an immense stroke of luck, Kursk was on the missing list. So, he hadn't been destroyed at Kuching, nor had he, like most of the survivors, been quietly retired, his processor removed and consciousness transferred to storage until someone figured out what to do with them. A further stroke of luck was that the authorities were not looking for any of the small number of missing tanks. A lack of resources, perhaps, or a desire to sweep the whole thing under the rug.

Nobody seemed to be in too much of a hurry to get Cooper back either.

Making a few educated guesses – he was Kursk's driver, and nobody knew Kursk better – Cooper began checking maps of the area around Kuching, and, through local news services, looking for any items that might be a sighting of a lone battle-tank. He traced a path in-country, heading southeast from the city into territory which looked, on the map, to be mostly filled with palm-oil plantations, national parks, farms, kampungs and just plain jungle. As to what was going on: the UN forces had all left and the civil war had been officially declared over, but that statement was disputed by both the local terrorists/activists/revolutionaries/freedom fighters, and the owners and workers for the agribusiness conglomerates who were still their main targets.

Which, Cooper decided, was another good reason to go there.

Cooper ended his period as a cooperative patient in the hospital and officially went out to have two further weeks of medical leave before rejoining his unit, which had been shipped off to Louisiana. That meant it would be at least three weeks, and probably a lot longer, before someone considered him AWOL.

He caught a commercial flight to Brunei, and then persuaded an NCO in the RMAF to put him on a plane to Kuching (commercial flights suspended, of course, except those to do with the agribusinesses). Might have been safer to take a boat along the coast, but would have definitely taken longer, and Cooper didn't want to risk losing track of Kursk.

Not after that last heartbreaking moment of consciousness, fire all around him, orders screaming in his ear to abort mission and abandon the tank. Gritting his teeth and ploughing forward, over the crunch of flesh and bone, because no way he was going to leave Kursk. Not ever.

Once on the ground, Cooper activated long-neglected skills. He hitched rides in-country with the trucks carrying laborers and managers out to the plantations (though not with the occasional military vehicles, where he might get asked hard questions), or hiked along the road. Camped out in the jungle or accepted hospitality in kampungs, sleeping in storage huts in exchange for money or labor.

His linguistic abilities were limited at first, but they got better with practice, and he also discovered that he would get the answers he wanted if he just asked if they'd seen the Lori.

For the people of Sarawak, thanks to a long period of British colonial activity, a lori is what Cooper would normally have called a truck. Kursk didn't look much like one. But then, he didn't look much like a conventional tank either: needing only a single human operator and being intended for use in unconventional, principally urban, combat situations, he was small, little enough to fit in a goods elevator or trundle down a narrow alley, and roughly trapezoidal.

Someone who'd never seen a sentient battle-tank before might not realize what he was, and, even if they did, might not have the vocabulary to cover it. So, for lack of a better word, Kursk was the Lori.

And the Lori, Cooper discovered, was a legend. He might be glimpsed between the trees, or the crunch of tracks over dead twigs might be heard. More rarely, there were stories: of children and teenagers saved from kidnap or assault by a tank bursting from the trees at the right moment, of a baby saved from drowning after falling into a rice paddy. Of a farmer's pigs being driven off into the forest for some unknown reason, the whole community turning out to find them in a cheerfully grumbling mob.

Then there were the other ones.

Huts burned to the waterline; the exits guarded so the inhabitants couldn't get out. A group of plantation workers who'd come over from New Guinea, attacked and slaughtered on the road before they reached their destination. Random disappearances of managers, agribusiness developers, tax collectors: the people who'd told Cooper that one hadn't been entirely able to resist a grim joke about that last category of victim.

Cooper didn't judge.

Kursk's basic impulse was to protect his friends, against his enemies. So, Cooper thought as he sheltered in the back of a rattling sentient truck that was stoically ploughing through the rain, Kursk needed him. Needed someone to show him the right people to protect, and the right ones to attack.

The magic sword always needs a guy to wield it.

Cooper felt his world settle into a kind of balance.

"I'm coming to join you, Kursk," he said aloud. Him and Kursk, the knight and his steed. Living in a hut on the edge of town, waiting to be called into action when danger threatened. Or travelling. Living off the land, going where they were needed.

Then everything would be all right between them.

"I'll make it up to you for what happened," he said. "We're a team. We'll be okay."

*

Cooper got off the truck when it slowed at a plantation checkpoint, hiked down the road to the nearest kampung. Chickens and pigs scattering, old ladies carrying bundles of firewood, a group of teenagers looking up from the motorbike they were disassembling. Cooper greeted them in his imperfect Malay, got taken by a volunteer – a boy-band-handsome kid with full lips and long dark lashes, Cooper bet he was popular – to the religious building. Which turned out to be a church, of the evangelical variety, where the preacher spoke better English than Cooper's Malay.

Yes, he could stay the night in exchange for fixing the church's sound system. Yes, there was also curry to be had, courtesy of the handsome kid's family. The Lori?

Why did he want to know about the Lori?

Cooper rolled with it. No reason, just an interest in local folklore. He'd heard a lot of stories wandering through the area, wondered if there were some here. Tried hard to project an image of being a half-crazed foreign mythology junkie, looking for weird legends to put in a book or something.

The villagers settled down and began talking instead about crops and weather and the agribusiness conglomerate's failure to deliver on their promise that the palm-oil plantation would boost the local economy. After a brief muttered aside about how non-Christians would believe any old nonsense, the preacher also dropped the subject of the Lori and joined in.

That evening, after Cooper had ostentatiously turned in for the night, he snuck out of the church building and crept to the edge of town, under cover of darkness. Settled down under a tree with big roots to wait.

He was prepared to do that for a few nights, if necessary, but either he struck lucky, or the tank knew something he didn't.

After a couple of hours of dozing among the roots, he woke and sprang into a crouch, hearing the noise of the caterpillar tracks on the vegetation, seeing a dim square shape against the rising moon.

"Kursk," he half-laughed, half-sobbed, overwhelmed with emotions he couldn't name. "Kursk, boy. It's me, Coop."

He ran towards the shape, his hands finding the rough, dented bodywork, caressing the pattern of rivets and bolts, moved upwards, found the hatch, wrestled with it briefly. The lock still recognized his palm-print.

With a triumphant yell, he fell inside, closed the door, swearing and shouting in delight as the familiar jolting motion in the padded operator seat engaged him. Like those training runs, bouncing along rough terrain, firing on targets in movie-set fake city streets, seeing his score racking up at the bottom of the monitor.

They were a team again. They were like the Magnificent Seven, the Lori and the Lori's driver, and…

The tank stopped, like a dog scenting the wind.

Cooper held his breath, waiting to see where Kursk went.

The tank started forward again, heading for the road to the plantation.

After a minute, the logic resolved. On the monitors, Cooper could make out a small group of figures, their heads muffled in scarves, carrying something awkward. Turning up the gain on the night vision suggested the scarves were red and black – the colours of the anti-capitalist faction – and, while he couldn't make out what they were carrying, his money was on an IED.

"Way to go, Kursk," Cooper said, as the tank bore down on the group.

And then, drove on past it.

"What the hell?"

But Kursk wasn't listening. He was picking up speed, rumbling into the plantation. Cooper fiddled with the monitor settings.

Kursk was signaling to him that this was the enemy, that Cooper needed to fire the guns.

With horror, Cooper realized what the target was. A group of people: from their clean clothes, ethnic mix, and the sentient jeep idling nearby, Cooper guessed they were researchers or expat managers. They were doing something with the trees, rigging up monitors, breaking branches, cutting saplings.

Kursk burst in on them with a roar, still signaling to his driver to fire.

The team scattered, leaping into the jeep, or dashing into the undergrowth.

Kursk pursued the jeep for a while, then gave up. Trundled slowly along the roadside at patrolling pace.

Cooper processed the incident.

Finally, he said, "I think we need to talk about what's an enemy."

Maybe the tank was defending the village. If that were true, foreign R&D teams might seem like a threat. It was overcompensation, but within parameters.

Cooper could work with that.

"How 'bout we go back for those Reds, then?"

He wasn't sure if the tank was going in the right direction, but he was willing to trust him. Kursk might have got a little confused about his mission, but he was a good tank.

Kursk stopped, that scenting-processing routine clearly in action again. He made a decision, trundled into the jungle.

Cooper checked the guns. Not much left. He wondered how difficult it would be to find, or make, or commission, proper ammo. Still, Kursk seemed to be getting on OK without it. The rush of battle was coming back to him, the thrill of anticipating the clash. Primordial memories of hunting trips, stalking deer in the scrubby forests with a cousin or two. But Kursk was better. Stronger. Someone he could trust.

The Reds wouldn't stand a chance.

Kursk found his target and began a sudden downward run, putting his lights on full, the servos and the crunch of the treads and the shrieks of wildlife combining to a Wagner roar. And in the bright lights, on the monitor, Cooper could see –

An old lady.

A thin, wiry old lady, with a long blue-black braid, starting up frightened from the small fire she'd kindled.

Cooper shouted at Kursk, slammed the control board, yelled at him to stop. Pounded the hatch.

Kursk wasn't listening.

The lady was a surprisingly fast runner, but Kursk didn't have to go around obstacles.

At the very last minute, Cooper managed to hit the manual.

Felt a lurch as the tank hit the root system of a tree.

The tank stopped.

Cooper wrenched the hatch open, tumbled out, gasping. Saw the flicker of the long black braid receding.

Kursk was backing off.

"Oh, no you don't, you bastard," Cooper said. He ran after the tank, pulled at the open hatch, swung in. Switched the controls to manual. "We're going after the Reds."

The tank groaned in protest, tried to retake control, but Cooper held firm. "You picked up some weird notions out here," he said. "That's why you have a driver. To keep you straight. We're a team." He upshifted, hard.

Unwillingly, and still keeping a servo-straining tension on the brakes, the tank chugged out along the roadside, back to where they'd last seen the Reds.

Cooper switched to the heat-seeking vision, tracked into the jungle.

"There's the sons of bitches," he said. Kursk began to speed up, clearly getting back into it now.

"Attaboy!" Cooper cheered. "Go on, get them!"

The tank's lights came on as it crashed, roaring, on the clearing where the muffled figures were gathered, training a flashlight on the awkwardly-sized thing they'd been carrying.

Cooper heard shouts in indistinct Malay, saw them beginning to run.

"No, you don't," he said, taking control of the guns and firing. Kursk, meanwhile, was running down the others, twisting and turning with his surprising agility in the trees.

In the end there was nothing but smoke, and twisted bodies, and Kursk's blazing lights, and the hum of his engine.

Cooper wrestled with the hatch again, flung it open, pushed himself out into the clearing. Staggered a bit.

"We did it, boy," he said to Kursk. "We got 'em."

He went over to look at the IED. Pulled back the smoking, singed burlap.

An electric motorcycle engine.

Blinking, he pulled it all off. It was still an engine.

Backing up, his heel connected with a limp body. Mechanically, he made himself turn, look at it closely. Wound back the scarf.

Saw the face of a teenage boy. Impossibly handsome in a boy-band way, strong chin and full, parted lips, dark lashes resting on his cheek as if he were sleeping.

The boy who'd taken him to the church that afternoon.

Cooper looked at the scarf. Realized it wasn't a revolutionary one. Wasn't even red-and-black; just a faded brown-on-brown pattern.

He didn't know what made him think it was terrorists.

Made himself look at the other bodies, torn up with gunfire.

"Kids," he muttered. "Just kids. Working late on a project."

He staggered back to Kursk, dropped back in, and closed the hatch. "Get us out of here," he muttered.

The tank turned, went slowly crunching through the trees. Cooper watched the display with half an eye, slumped in the chair. Feeling sick, sick like he hadn't done since…

…since Kuching.

It had all gone according to plan. Kursk rolling forward, Cooper working the monitor and the guns. The lead tank tripped an IED, or possibly an actual mine, not that it really mattered, and they kept going.

And then, something hit the third tank in the line.

Lucky shot, certainly; some kind of mortar fire. Enough to blow out the guns, the driver, and most of the hardware, leaving a burning shell.

Cooper was only briefly aware of it, though, because Kursk surged into battle, picking up speed, signaling at him to use the guns. Numb, Cooper did.

Before he saw the UN flashes on the arms of the soldiers falling in front of them…

He pulled his hands off the triggers, hammered at the dash. Shouted at Kursk to stop. Then let go, breathed, checked the monitor, swung it around.

Saw the tanks on the advance, rolling over everyone. Rebel, government forces, UN forces.

Voices in his ear. Urging the drivers to regain control. Stop them before they got to HQ, or something just as bad. Reports of tanks attacking a supply chain, an ambulance, a rebel sniper nest.

Heard the other drivers, the surviving ones anyway, trying to report, to regain order.

Heard his own voice, begging Kursk to stop.

Cooper hit the manual, wrestled for control. Heard the voices in his ear screaming at him to abort mission and abandon tank, but no way he was going to leave Kursk.

He finally gained control, turned the tank, drove him protesting towards a green space, a small park or highway reservation or something, just a small stand of decorative palm trees and some tall grasses.

And then a sound lanced through his earphones, a tone, rising, all-encompassing, filling his head, he struggled to fight against it and remain conscious, but –

Sitting against the tank in the cool of the night, looking up at the stars and the faint glow from the agribusiness on the horizon, Cooper remembered.

"Trees," he said. "That's what you're defending. It's the trees."

Cooper found himself thinking of all the angry articles about how the army was just there to protect the multinational agribusinesses and the palm plantations.

"Guess that's true, hey Lori?" He glanced up at the impassive metal body.

"Maybe from your perspective, there's not much difference between one big organic thing and another one?"

It occurred to him that he didn't really know how the Lori thought. How he saw the world.

He wondered what would happen if he just let the Lori run free, driverless, in the jungle. More glimpses of the strange vehicle through the trees. More legends about bandits thwarted, children saved from drowning.

Huts burned to the ground. Plantation workers slaughtered.

The Lori didn't seem to want to go anywhere right now, seemed content to just idle there with Cooper.

Cooper sat listening to the rustles and chirps of the jungle, the occasional distant sound of machinery, hiss of wheels from the road. Watching the sky get lighter.

Remembering the dogs back home. Angry, conflicted animals, with hair-trigger tempers. Beaten, punished, hurt, and yet, with that ingrown canine loyalty, unable to leave the person doing the hurting.

He'd loved his dog.

Loved her enough to give her up, if it meant she didn't go down that same road, trusting his father despite all he did.

Then his thoughts drifted to the village. Stayed there for a long while.

Finally, Cooper got up. Opened the hatch again. Got out his driver's utilitool, popped the screwdriver and got to work.

Although he knew battle tanks had defensive measures they could take against this, nothing happened.

At some point, the engine shut down.

Cooper re-emerged from the hatch just as the sun was approaching its zenith. He rummaged in his backpack, found a clean cloth bag. Normally, in autonomous vehicles, the intelligence is distributed throughout the processing systems, but whoever designed battle tanks was expecting them to run through bodyshells pretty quickly.

Cooper walked up the road, walking towards the plantation. He'd seen an automated parcel receive-and-drop point not far from the vehicular access gate.

He chose a locker at random, put the bag with the processor in. Closed the locker.

Thought about saying something, but that seemed too much like a funeral, so he didn't.

But he made a wish, for the Lori.

Cooper stood for a few minutes more. Trying hard to fix that moment in his mind, the yellow of the locker doors, the shafts of light through the leaves, the hum of animal life, the heat in the air.

Then Cooper turned and began his long walk back to the village.

Wilson Dreams of Peacocks

Melanie Smith

Wilson dreams of peacocks. I know because I was plugged into him at the time. Yes, yes, I'm fully aware of the ethics of that, but I'm (at least) half human, aren't I? And I was being driven mad by the little line drawings that were springing up around the hut: scratchy scrapings on ratty paper, depicting an animal I couldn't identify. All small headed, with a tail covered in staring eyes, spread out in a despicable fan. I lifted a pan, one was there. I pulled open the cupboard above the counter, another fluttered down at me, making me bat my hands in front of my face, warding it off even as it drifted to the floor. I asked Wilson about these drawings, early in the morning, as he shuffled past me to wash, trailing bristles and bed warmth. Were they something to do with his work? Had another extra-terrestrial species been discovered? But, I said to him, your team has found lifeboat-packs before: little rafts of DNA set adrift from unknown skies, containing the dying breaths of some dying planet. Why the fuss? They get re-animated in the lab that Wilson heads up. Well, I say 'heads up': Wilson is technically in charge of gassing the things after the sixteen seconds it takes to digitally file card them. But it's an important job, and he's done it for years.

So why the obsession that drove him to etch this particular image into paper over and over? I asked him and asked him again, but got just a non-committal grunt. The same one every morning. I began to get worried. It wasn't like Wilson to keep things to himself. The confidentiality agreement he'd triplicate signed on his first day on the job had never meant a thing to him.

There is a madness that the truly mad say comes from our corrupted blood; from our own rescued genetics, pulled from the star-touched depths: the human cells that washed up on these shores so long ago. Technology was not then as it is now; the inhabitants of this planet, coming into the possession of such molecular treasure, had to sift and weld the genetic code in order to get it to 'take.' The human genes had to be spliced with something else. When I look in the mirror, I see my two ancestries: the soft brown hair that touches the fine curve of my cheek and my toned, sleek upper arms. My double thorax and the fur, less coarse than Wilson's bristles, that lines my spine. I wonder, sometimes, if I have two minds, also. If all of our kind do. Such duality can be a strain.

So one night, right after I'd emptied the oxygen filters and scrubbed them clean under the tap outside, I decided I needed to sort this thing out once and for all. If it had all got too much for Wilson, I needed to know. I found the somnus-kit right at the back of the shed, hidden beneath the spare fuel pods and a broken chair: the shed is Wilson's domain, and he doesn't think I know about the kit (or why I had it). I pulled it free and crept back into the hut, stepping quietly, the downy pads of my feet making the merest whisper on the matting.

It was easy to set up, my fingers picking over the pieces, the muscles stimulated into mechanical movements born of old memory: the first time I used one of these kits I was just eight cycles old; it was well before all the regulations had been introduced. Before they'd been banned on ethical grounds. It was no problem to plug into Wilson. He's a deep sleeper. I watched the two tiers of his abdomen move in steady puffs for a time before establishing a connection, attaching the filaments to our throats and upper stomachs, and feeling the metal melt into the skin. And then I laid down next to him, and slipped into his dream. It was hard at first to adjust, mentally, to the strange overlay of sensations. To the bright images that burst and dispersed into nebulous clouds of half-thought and old desire, to the sudden thundery flashes of past alarm and the blooming of viscerally tender fields of longing and woe and mundanity. It was hard, ultimately, to adjust to the fundamentally Wilson-ishness of the place. There was a smell here, ever present, that was nothing to do with the nose or its various connective synapses that fire off into dense cerebral matter. It, more than anything, told me that I was a stranger here. Unwelcome.

I began to move through the sense-scape, feeling my way along hesitantly, ready to disconnect at the first hint of detection. Because the host mind can react to an intruder. I remember learning that at school, back when somnus-kits were wheeled out for Basic Psychology: if the host mind turns on a 'guest presence' then that guest could find itself a prisoner in a maze, or a cage, or worse for what could be experienced as near infinity in the mind of the trapped but would, in the real world, be the mere seconds it would take before an override disconnect was established.

I let the flow of Wilson's thoughts lap at my imagined feet, allowed the drift of his senses to rise to my bellies, to my neck and, finally, to stream into my nose and mouth. And suddenly there it was, coursing through a purple void: one of Wilson's monsters. It hovered, wings impossibly folded, flashing teal and sapphire and gold, its many eyes spread and shivering. It pecked into a mass of swirling comprehensions, its beak penetrating the shell of one of Wilson's memories so that all manner of things spilled out and span away: a baseball, a letter, a muffled scream. Distantly, I felt the physical sensation of Wilson twisting towards me, his skin pressing moistly against my own. A groan.

A word was pealing around the shifting contours of Wilson's sleeping mind, amplifying and fading in nauseating waves, a word I didn't know. Peacock, I think. With each wave of sound came an image of old Earth: grasslands, brittle little bones, the bloated bulge of the dying sun and its subsequent demise to flinty cold stone, spinning slowly through space like a blinded eye: and there again, the terrible bird floating through this chaos, its own many eyes a quivering fury. I felt a rising dread as memory-pictures flashed by like a shuffled deck: Wilson's team discovering the packet of terrestrial DNA, long adrift in a galaxial waste; its re-animation. The euphoria. And the disease, hidden deep in the composite matter of the many-eyed thing. The gassing of the thing that did not destroy the corruption within it. The subsequent liquidy death of the team's pet hapnid. The ache that began in Wilson's head later that same day; the ache that had now spread to his back, his legs.

That corruption was now here, with us, on our own planet. As implacable as the tyrant turn of the clock. There was something horrifically karmic about it; how history was going to repeat itself, so that worlds would fall like dominoes on the infinite black felt of space.

Melanie Smith

I disconnected, too quickly. The room span and pitched, my senses confused: I could hear the night sirens through the pores of my skin; taste the heat of the room on my tongue; smell the press of Wilson's lower abdomen against mine. He stirred, but didn't wake, not at the tug of the wire pulling free, nor at my drunken lurch from the bed and subsequent rumbling stumble across the room. I leant against the counter in the kitchen, and tried not to spill my supper down the sink. The hut contracted and filled again, its space flexing in sinewy pulses. I reached into a cupboard for a jar of humectant and saw, attached to the door's interior, one of Wilson's sketches. The creature regarded me with arrogant eyes. I tore it free and shoved it into the heating vent, disgusted by the breath of fusty smoke that immediately curled back out at me, my upper lungs tightening against the stench.

I didn't sleep that night, and I didn't bother to hide the somnus-kit, either. Wilson came outside sometime just after dawn and found me lying prone in the dirt, watching the stars fade in the yellowing bowl of the sky. I think he knew what had happened, what I now knew, and so he just lay down next to me and we stayed like that for a while, until the spark of every distant star had disappeared into the morning's glare. I asked him where old Earth had been, in which direction we'd need to travel if we wanted to see that hard, dead little rock for ourselves. He pointed to a non-descript patch of atmosphere, and when I closed my eyes to imagine slowly spiralling through space, it wasn't a stony blackness that descended on my mind, but instead an obscene and soft fall of cobalt feathers.

Variations on Heisenberg's Third Concerto

Eleanor R. Wood

I lift my baton. The orchestra is poised, ready, hands on instruments, eyes on me. My soloist sits at the Steinway to my left. Our anticipation is a singular thing: the thrumming awareness that we're about to play something no one, not even ourselves, has heard before. This is both the joy and the fear of Heisenberg's Third Concerto. It is never the same twice.

Raj gave it to me on his triumphant return. The first scientist to travel to a parallel universe, and his greatest joy was bringing back a souvenir for his wife.

"You'll never believe this, Mira," he said, his face alight with excitement. "You know Heisenberg was a physicist who dabbled in music?"

I nodded, smiling at his delight.

"In that universe, it was the other way around. There, he was a musician who dabbled in science – a composer! He wrote astounding pieces, and I brought one back for you... the score to his Third Piano Concerto." He handed me the sheet music with the grin I so loved.

I sensed the heart of his enthusiasm – his hero could now be mine too. The serendipity was beautiful. And so was the piece: the one I've come to think of as the First Variation. I only wish we'd recorded it. But how were we to know it would never sound that way again?

The second time, the orchestra was so surprised that we all stopped at the end of the third bar.

"Did someone swap the music?" I asked, but our scores still read 'Heisenberg's Third Piano Concerto'. It was only then I thought it strange that there was no mention of key in its title.

We carried on playing, and to our astonishment, an entirely new concerto came to life. No one stumbled, no one missed a beat or flubbed a note. It was as if we knew it as intimately as a piece we'd practised for weeks. But none of us had heard it before. The orchestra said their fingers instantly had the muscle memory, their eyes scanning notes that were at once new and familiar.

Each time we played it, the same thing occurred. Sometimes the changes were subtle; sometimes there was barely any similarity at all. One day it was in wistful C minor, the next soaring in E flat major. Sometimes the key changes had no relation to each other. Sometimes the time signature was simple, sometimes compound, the tempo Allegro or Andante or Presto. Sometimes it was none of those things. Millions of potential variations surrounded us as we sat to play, only converging on one when I signalled the downbeat and the performance began.

If only I'd known what it meant. If only I'd known that the music wasn't the only singularity that converged as we played.

"I'm going back, love," Raj said to me over dinner one evening. "There's so much more to learn about the other universe, and now we've perfected the technology it's even safer than the first trip."

I moved food around on my plate, refusing to admit my worries. Much as I hated him travelling into the unknown, Raj could no more stop exploring than I could stop conducting. Each of our careers was our way to understand the world.

He noticed my concern anyway, and took my hand. "I'll bring you back a new Heisenberg piece."

I squeezed his fingers. "That would be lovely."

But my worst fears came true. He didn't return. Who knows what universe they even sent him to? The concerto changed everything, but his colleagues didn't make the connection until Raj had been missing for weeks. I kept performing because I had to. Because the worry for my husband would have driven me mad without my music.

And then someone in the lab noticed that the universes were shifting, seemingly at random. It was only when some of Raj's colleagues attended a couple of our performances that they realised why. We tested it together, proving the hypothesis: somehow, a new universe emerged every time we performed the concerto. As the music manifested anew, so did the parallel universe the scientists were connecting to. Infinite variations of each.

It had been my fault. We performed the Heisenberg two days after Raj left, and unknowingly stranded him. We've performed it countless times since.

I did this to him. I don't know how to live with that.

I have to keep changing orchestras and soloists. I can't blame them; they want to play other pieces. I'm the only one still obsessed with the Heisenberg. I have to be. I have to keep performing it, hoping against all conceivable odds that we'll converge again on the concerto that links back to Raj. The one that will bring my husband home.

I strike the downbeat, and a new variation rises up around me. I pin my hopes on infinity, and we play.

The World is on Fire and You're Out of Milk

Rhiannon A. Grist

You'd just pulled off your flame-retardant boots when you realised you'd forgotten the milk.

You're tired from work and all you want is a coffee, a cup of warm milk poured over a homemade double shot. You check the fridge – just in case – but it's true, you're out. Things are bad enough. Now you have to head back out, and just after you changed out of your boiler suit.

This is unbearable! you think, but only to yourself. Because it would feel like a sin, even here in your own home, to say it out loud. Because, despite everything, it is bearable. Everything is treacherously bearable.

And because you can bear it, back out for milk you must go.

You spread a fresh layer of ointment onto your cheeks and forearms. You pull on your Teflon undershirt and strap back into your boiler suit. You fit your oxygen mask – the stickers you used to decorate it in the beginning have all but burned off – and you set off.

The heat hits you the moment you open the door of your apartment building. It's not too bad today.

Some days it's a dry heat and the hairs on your arms turn crisp and brittle.

Some days the sweat pools in the corners of your eyes and runs down the bare road of your back.

And some days you're the one burning. You burn from the inside out with more wrath and frustration than you know what to do with, so you hold on until you get home and douse yourself off in a cold shower and scream into your hands.

But today it's just a constant throbbing heat. A rash, a discomfort. At least your flat has a decent cooling system. At least you managed to get that together before the world burst into flames.

The nearest shop is only five minutes' walk away, but the orange haze filling the street makes it feel so much further. You don't want to be out here. You want to be at home with your coffee and your Netflix. You hate having to see it up close, the state of it all.

The houses blackened with soot and scorch marks.

The pavement littered with ash.

The air filled with smog.

The flames licking up drainpipes.

The trees in the park smouldering like dragon's teeth.

And – is that a stone in your boot?

For Christ's sake! It's right by the heel too. If only you could shake it down into the toe or even the arch, but it's stuck in the lining that stops the pavement blistering the soles of your feet.

First the milk. Now a stone. Fantastic.

Would it be so bad? Drinking your coffee black? All you'd need is hot water and you've got plenty of that these days, har har. How do you always run out of milk so quickly anyway?

Do you use too much in your porridge?

Were the shops making the cartons smaller?

Maybe it evaporated somehow. You wouldn't put it past the fire to evaporate milk out of spite.

You briefly consider giving up.

You go on.

Down by the wall outside your local shop, hunkers a man with a foil sheet wrapped round his head and shoulders. This is not the first person you've seen caught outside with minimum protection. He clutches an empty water bottle and a twisted tube of ointment. The pads of his fingers are red raw. Why doesn't he go inside the shop? Is he waiting for someone? Was he thrown out?

You should probably ask if he's ok.

You don't.

You step into the vacuum chamber at the shop's entrance. After the hiss of re-pressurisation, you step into the clean bright aisles, slip off your mask and head to the dairy section. Row upon row of cold sweating cartons line up before you, a sterile forest of cool white comfort ready to smother the heat outside.

Sometimes, you fantasize about taking a nap on the two litre jugs on the lower shelf. you imagine your clothes blooming with damp, condensation gathering in dewdrops on your skin, breath rising in small white clouds in front of your eyes. What luxury. What unrivalled decadence! To think there was once a time when you could have jumped into a mountain lake or rolled in snow. It feels unbelievable now. Like you made it up or saw it in a dream.

You remember when the smell of smoke would ignite a warm, peppery excitement in the pit of your belly. How it would make you think of summer evenings on a pebbled beach, sat round a glowing fire pit tucked into the cliff side, mouth laced with flat cider, hair thick with sea salt. How the smell would keep the memory of those magic nights alive for a day or two in the cuffs of your jumper. Now you dream of bed-sized fridges, frozen wastes and biblical monsoons.

You resist the urge to climb into the chiller and pick up a carton of milk instead.

The shelves closest to the self-checkout are stacked with bottled water and travel-sized tubes of ointment. Next to them there's a table set up with leaflets and stickers. Looks like another dousing drive. On Saturday, a group of about fifty to a hundred locals will fill up buckets, bottles, bags and basins from their taps at home then go out to the park and pour water over the fires. You've been to a few yourself, in the beginning. You know what will happen. The flames will die down for a few hours, and then the water will dry off and a new spark will set everything alight again. No one knows how to stop the sparks for good, but they'll keep holding dousing drives anyway.

At least it's something.

The person manning the stall looks up and catches your eye. A flash of recognition flickers over their face. You stop in your tracks. You know them. You went to university with them. You used to hang out at the same ramshackle pubs and drink the same cheap wine. There was even a time on that pebbled beach, round the fire pit tucked into the cliff, when you both talked about how you were going to change the world.

The memory of once believing the world could be changed hits a little harder than you'd like.

You realise that in all your late-night plotting and all your beer mat manifestos, you never once thought that one day the world might erupt into flames. A lot has changed. You've changed. You got tired.

Meanwhile they, your old friend on the dousing stand, have only become more. More passionate. More determined. And, now you think of it, more annoying. Yes. They annoy you. Their passion feels accusatory somehow. As if it's your fault the world is on fire. As if you knowingly chose this. You imagine them looking at you, their eyes traveling down your arm, to your hand, to the cold wet carton of milk. You imagine them frowning and thinking:

Where are you taking that milk? Shouldn't you use it to douse the flames? Don't you want to help put out the fires? Is your coffee really more important than the world?

But they're not the one thinking this.

You are.

You add a bottle of water from the shelves to your shopping and tuck it all into your triple-lined tote bag.

Luckily for you, your old friend is busy talking to some students. They probably haven't got time to catch up with you, and you don't really want to hear what you should be doing to fix things. Not right now. Not today. Not after the milk. And the stone. You give them a friendly wave – just in case they heard you thinking before – and slip back out into the flaming world before they have a chance to say a word.

Outside the shop the man is gone; his foil sheet flutters against a drain pipe. You hope this means he's gone inside.

You head home.

You try to avoid the stone still stuck in the lining of your boot.

Meanwhile, your mind is a tennis court batting the same old arguments back and fore. It's not that you disagree. Something should be done. This is not OK. The world is not OK. But you can't see how to fix things. You've seen all the articles, the blogs, the tweets and the Facebook posts and you're at a loss. You can't put out the fires and thinking about that for too long makes you want to tear out your hair. You open your mouth to scream. But screaming is just as hopeless. The fire would only feed on the air from your lungs while you suffocate.

And it's so easy to suffocate in the flames.

You take a deep breath.

You can't stop the world from burning, but you can stop yourself burning up with it.

So, you go back. Back through the street, back through the fires, back to the shop.

You sign up to the dousing drive. Your old friend is still busy, but they give you a sticker and a smile. You know the sticker will just burn up like all the others.

You put the sticker on your oxygen mask anyway.

Outside the shop you leave the bottle of water underneath the foil sheet, just in case. You say sorry for so quickly prejudging the man caught outside, for not stopping to ask if he was ok. He's not here. And even if he was, he probably wouldn't be able to hear you over the hiss of your respirator and the crackle of the fire.

You say it all out loud anyway.

Back in your flat, you spoon out coffee. You pass water through the external pipes, redirecting the heat and pressure from the world outside to turn this earthy powder into a spell of revival. You pour in warm milk, spooling a swirling caramel galaxy in the centre of the black, bitter liquid. Because you need the milk to soften the stimulant, to turn the punch into an embrace. And you still believe you owe yourself more embraces than punches.

You sip and feel the warmth – a good and gentle warmth – spread through your chest. Then you stand at the window and you watch the world burn.

You can't stop the fires. But you can make an old friend smile. You can leave water for those caught out. You can keep dousing the flames, no matter how many times they come back. And maybe, one day, you'll even see the fire reduced to a smoulder.

You can go on. You can bear it.

But maybe have your coffee first.

The Turbine at the End of the World

James Rowland

Three words chilled Jana in the oppressive heat of night. They yanked her from sleep, rough hands on her shoulders. "The turbine died." Those words, uttered by a small girl from the dark, pulled Jana roughly from her bed. Ever since she had mentioned the turbines to Lauren, had explained why she had chosen to live in the sinking remains of an apartment in the sea, the girl had taken to standing guard. Each evening Jana woke, and Lauren would tell her that the turbine was okay. It was their form of greeting. A 'hello' would suffice to her parents when Jana passed them in the hall or helped unload the boat that they used to take in supplies. For Lauren, though, it was always the turbine. And now it had stopped.

Jana jumped up and ran into the afterthought of a living room. It was filled with pointless salvage that might someday evolve into something useful, the skeletons of hairdryers and microwaves scattered across the damp carpet. Jana walked past it all, hands gripping the windowsill. The wind farm was on the horizon, visible in the silver light of the moon hanging above. Her eyes scanned over the thirty turbines. Nearly all had become ghosts, pale white spectres in the rising sea. The last though had carried on. Four from the right, the entire burden of the world on its shoulders.

Its blades sat motionless.

"Do you know for how long?"

Lauren shook her head, her dirty face reflecting Jana's panic. "It had stopped when I got out of bed. I checked it straight away. I promise! It is going to be okay? Are you going to be able to fix it? Are we going to die?"

"Whoa, calm down," Jana said, kneeling in front of the girl. She locked her own fear away and ran a hand down Lauren's cheek. She no longer thought about how she could never comfort a child of her own like this. The wound had been cauterised; the world long since making that decision for her. "It'll be okay. I'm going to fix it, don't

183

worry. But I need you to do something important for me. I need you to tell Mummy and Daddy that I'm going to need the boat tonight, okay?"

Lauren nodded, and disappeared out of the room.

Alone, the panic and fear came surging back to Jana. It rolled and crashed into her like the waves lapping at the apartment block she lived in. The turbine was dead and if she couldn't fix it, the world was just as doomed. Turbines had failed before. Some she had managed to revive; others she had not. None of them had ever been the last, though. The final thing between the world and annihilation. Alone in the living room, only the moonlight for company, it was hard for Jana not to picture everything crumbling around her. The water would rise higher. Her home would be flooded. Buildings would crack and crumble. Ground, already parched, would turn to desert. In the silence between two heartbeats, she thought about fleeing. Rowing out to sea, she could let the tides take her, let her body bake under the sun and escape the dying days. That destiny was for someone else, though. Someone who didn't care.

Jana ventured to the apartment below. The sea had claimed it a decade ago, reaching up to punch through windows and flood the defenceless rooms. The boat that Jana shared with the family bobbed in the empty lounge, tied to the naked window frame. It had once been motorised, but whatever petrol still existed in the world was a distant myth to Jana. They had stripped the engine for parts, fashioned two oars, and made the boat necessary for their lives. It would navigate the canals of former streets and take them to drier land, where supplies could be bartered for. Today, it had to take Jana out to sea. She untied the boat, clambered inside, and drifted out into the night.

The town spread out behind her. Her mother had told her it had once been a seaside resort, when the idea of holidays and summers still existed. It was already dying before the warming seas. Tourists chose destinations further afield. Those who grew up in the town seldom stayed, instead being plucked by the wind, and scattered elsewhere through the country. Still, some remained. As soon as the sun slipped beneath the horizon, they scurried out of their homes to do what had to be done in the relative cool of night. Most had retreated out to the suburbs, the new coast, but a few still lived in the heart of the town. They survived in the top floors of apartment buildings; owls perched in the highest branches. Boats crisscrossed between old streets, a Venetian memory in a dead seaside resort. There was no panic, though. No cries or exodus. No one had noticed the last turbine's failure. Jana took a deep breath, plucked the oars from their perch, and began to row.

Her family had moved here over a century ago, when borders were still open, and people freely travelled across Europe. They had settled in the dying town, took jobs that the locals no longer wanted. Through time a sense of ownership grew, taking root till the idea of leaving their home seemed sickening. The turbines weaved in and out of family stories. Some echoing great grandfather had worked as a technician when the entire farm still functioned. Later, her father told stories of how he had walked along the beach with his grandmother, how they had skipped stones out to sea. She had pointed to the turbines and explained that they were going to save the world. So much of the story seemed foreign to Jana. The idea of a beach, the image of treating the sea like some passing fancy rather than cowering from its hunger. She remembered the words, though. The wind turbines were going to save the world. He died before he could tell her how.

It didn't matter. For the next forty years, Jana and others taught themselves how to maintain the turbines, how to drag out their lives, stretching them longer and longer until there was only one left.

And it had stopped.

Halfway out to the turbines, Jana pulled at the shirt sticking to her damp skin. Even under the moonlight, the heat pressed in around her, squeezing her tight. The wind did nothing to help. It only made it harder to row, pushing the boat back, forcing Jana to strain her muscles to mount every wave. Tasting salt, she struggled to breathe, gulping down mouthfuls of air. Her throat burned and her arms wanted nothing more than to throw the oars into the sea, to let the tide push her back toward dry land. She persisted. A whisper danced in the wind, her great grandmother's voice slipping through the years: the turbines will save the world.

Up close, they jutted out of the sea as if they had been hurled by a god, white hot thunderbolts digging deep into the earth's flesh. Jana twisted in her seat, counted four from her right, and counted again, making sure the sea hadn't led her astray. She rowed, guiding the boat to the broken titan. Her ears strained for some sound of damage. The wind covered up any hissing motors or screaming gears as the boat bobbed against the smooth, white tower. Jana moved forward, her body scrambling as she threaded the rope through the small ring jutting out from the turbine. The waves came, dragging the boat away, and the rope went taut, fighting back. She watched the battle. Only after the rope had won three times did Jana reach up for the first rung of the ladder in front of her.

Blood thundered through her ears as she climbed. The trip never became easier. Hanging off the side of the white monolith, each step grew the pit in her stomach. It stretched, the fear threatening to become the only thing she could ever feel. There were hooks every so often, for harnesses that no longer existed, and Jana could only climb helplessly past them. Wind battered her, trying to pry her from the ladder. 'You're not worthy; let the world die' it seemed to scream. If it could knock her from the turbine, she would disappear into the sea, and everything would end. Jana clutched tighter at each rung and emerged pale, sweating, and shaking onto the platform.

Even inside the machine, the wind lashed out. The door rattled. Jana leant in to look at the hinges, the metal crusting over in a brown shell. She'd have to replace them soon. She couldn't risk having the door falling off, leaving the turbine's organs exposed to the salty wind and spray of the sea. This was what her life was. Small tasks to block catastrophic consequences. In a way, maybe that was all life was to anyone. Leaving the door for another day, though, Jana grabbed the toolkit tucked inside and began the process of servicing the turbine. There were hundreds of different components. Any single piece could be at fault. Worse, it could be something technical. A glitch in some computer software could have killed the entire system. The technical fault was always worse than the mechanical one. It was easier to hone some borrowed muscle memory than it was to learn the language of computers.

Jana worked from bottom to top, checking each and every potential fault line. She made sure that rust was removed, computers ran smoothly, and gears were lubricated. She followed the path that she had been taught decades before and had walked a hundred times. Originally, there had been a group of them who worked the turbines, keeping them running just in sight of the town. Numbers had dwindled. Some died. Some moved away. Most, though, had grown disillusioned, lost faith that whatever they were doing could truly help the world. Only Jana remained; only she knew that one day the turbine would save everyone, like her great grandmother had said. She didn't know how, but she didn't need to. If there was hope, she couldn't let go.

In the end, it was the computer that saved her. Instead of some gremlin buried within the system, dancing out of sight, the computer fed back to Jana everything she needed to know. It had sensed resistance from the blades. Something pulled at the motors, trying to keep it from turning over, the pressure building along the cables. The computer had sensed it and shut the entire turbine down as a precaution. Jana nodded, staring into the screen as if it might offer some encouraging words. When it didn't, she took a deep breath and continued her climb.

On the crown of the turbine, the hooks for harnesses seemed even more mocking. No sooner had Jana lifted the trapdoor and poked a head through the opening did the elements double their assault. Her hair betrayed her, whipping at her face, and her eyes streamed from the salt. Still, she pushed more of her body up. Her breathing quickened, her hands shaking. One strong gust would be a death sentence. It would pluck her from the smooth, white surface and send her tumbling into the churning sea. Still, Jana kept easing herself out. She stayed low, wiggling across the turbine like something born from primordial mud. Every movement was a spasm of terror, a battle between her desire to do good and the burning need to retreat back into the safety of the turbine. The emptiness in her stomach evolved into a gagging cough, but she pushed on till she was dangling over the hub of the blades.

The resistance that the computer had sensed was immediately obvious. Coated in the joint of the tower and the hub that housed the blades, rust had dug its fingers deep. It clung tightly, holding everything in stasis. A gift from Jana's fear of climbing onto the crown. She hadn't come up here enough; she hadn't stopped the build up from occurring. Her cowardice nearly doomed the world. Burning from shame, she reached for the chisel tucked in the toolbelt she had brought with her and began to chip away at the build-up. It was slow, agonising work, each new gust of wind freezing Jana momentarily to the top of the turbine. If Lauren had looked out from the apartment, she might have saw Jana's figure silhouetted against the moon, a tiny shadow clinging to the modern monolith. But already the moon seemed to be shrinking, retreating at the threat of the coming sun. If she was still there by morning, the heat would bake her alive.

There had been times before, caught in the hours of tedious, painful work, where Jana considered the turbine's purpose. It made no sense to her, if she truly thought about it. A single turbine couldn't save the world. As the rust fell away, slowly yielding space, retreating deeper, it would have been easy to fall back into such thoughts. Jana did not. She had decided long ago that she wouldn't understand how the turbines could save the world. She knew, had even acknowledged and embraced the idea that they couldn't. Her grandmother could be wrong. In the meantime, though, she would carry on. She had a purpose and she had hope. Commodities more valuable than anything bartered for in town.

A chink, a crumbling of rust into the sea, and there was the echo of motors grinding into life. Jana yanked her hand away from the crevice between tower and blades. She forgot to breathe. She laid there in perfect stillness. The great, old giant groaned into life. Like a runner, the turbine eased forward at first, slowly picking up speed until it found its rhythm. Jana laughed, the relief, fear and nervous energy tumbling out of her. There was hope. There was a chance of redemption, at least for a little while yet. Taking a deep breath, trying to calm the tremor that had built up in her hands, Jana turned and crawled back to the trapdoor. There was only a couple of hours left of night. She had to get back.

She paused at the opening, legs dangling inside the turbine. The town sat in the distance, loitering in the remaining moonlight.

Flooded buildings, resolutely standing tall in the rising sea. The occasional candle in a window flickered in the darkness. It was beautiful, it its own kind of way. She could see the specks of people moving back and forth, carrying on with life, fighting to live till the very end. She imagined Lauren with her parents, reading books salvaged from a library. She pictured a distant day where a son and his grandmother skipped rocks on the beach without a worry in the world. Jana tapped the warm, humming surface of the turbine.

"I don't know how you're going to save us," she said, "but please do it soon. Before it's too late."

What Happened to 70?

C.R. Berry

1984

The job description Leona Holloway had been given over the phone wasn't clear at all. Senior scientist for a company she'd never heard of, Million Eyes, to help engineer a breakthrough in quantum physics. That's what the man with the lisp, Mr Arnold, had said, calling her out of the blue to invite her for an interview at an undisclosed location, hours after she received an outright pass on her doctoral thesis. She'd asked what kind of 'breakthrough', but Mr Arnold simply said that all would be revealed, adding that Million Eyes had been watching her with great interest for several years. Leona wasn't sure whether to be excited or perturbed. In the end she was a bit of both.

Sitting in a swanky limousine Million Eyes had sent to pick her up, with champagne, snacks, air-conditioning, a TV and one of those new LaserDisc players, Leona rode through the desolate grasslands of Salisbury Plain. This three-hundred-square-mile plateau was a place where the breeze carried scents of wild thyme, chalk dust and a touch of tank exhaust, and the sounds of insects, skylarks and distant gunfire mingled in the air. At least half of it was owned by the military and used for infantry training and live artillery firing, with many areas inaccessible to the public. A great place to have a secret facility, that was for sure.

They came to a big NO PUBLIC ACCESS sign. And went right past it. Leona swallowed. Was Million Eyes something to do with the military then? Up ahead were a couple of army officers in helmets and camouflage uniforms. Leona felt her chest tighten when she saw their threatening-looking rifles.

The limo driver lowered his window and flashed an ID card to one of the officers, who waved him through.

Ten minutes later, the car veered off road, straight across the grassland. Leona's heart was thrumming in her ears, but constant jerking over rutted terrain drowned it out. *What the hell am I getting myself into?*

After a bumpy few hundred yards, the limo came to a stop in the middle of the plain, miles of gently undulating grassland blending into the horizon on all sides.

The driver got out and opened her door.

She frowned. "You want me to get out here?"

"Yes please, ma'am," he replied.

She swung her legs out and stood. Then the driver did something she wasn't expecting: got back in the car. Panicking, she lurched forwards and grasped the handle, before he'd managed to shut his door. "Wait! You're gonna leave me here?"

"Yes, ma'am. Mr Arnold will be along in a moment to escort you to the interview."

She glanced around. It was a warm, clear day and she could see for miles – nothing for all of it. "A moment?"

The driver closed the door and drove off. For the next few minutes, her eyes were fixed on the long black car as it got smaller and smaller, disappearing into the horizon like a bug under a rock.

Come back...

"Hello, Dr Holloway," said a male voice.

Her heart leapt into her throat. She spun round. A man with receding grey hair and a moustache, wearing a black suit and small, round spectacles, walked towards her. "But – but where did you –?"

He shook her hand. "I'm Mr Arnold. Come with me, please." He had a lisp.

Where!

She followed Mr Arnold to a circular metal grate in the middle of the grass. Less than two metres in diameter, it had a dense mesh and small rectangular holes, darkness beneath it.

Mr Arnold went and stood in the middle of it, his smart, polished shoes clanking on the metal. Leona stopped at the edge.

"Stand on the platform, please," said Mr Arnold.

With a deep breath, she stepped carefully onto the grate. Thank God she was in flats and not stilettos.

Immediately the grate started descending into the ground with a low, electronic hum. Watching her feet being swallowed by the ground and only just stopping herself from grabbing Mr Arnold's arm, she murmured, "I'm claustrophobic."

He replied flatly, "It'll be over in a moment."

The platform descended till the ground was above her head and a cylindrical metal wall curved around her. Fists clenched, she fixed her eyes on the cerulean sky to quell the claustrophobia, then a metal panel slid across the opening and her throat closed up.

She expected to be plunged into darkness, but a flat round lamp in the middle of the panel activated, flooding the tight space with light.

The hum continued, the only thing to suggest they were still moving. As her breathing started to become laboured and irregular, the grate stopped. Suddenly the curved wall slid apart along a previously invisible seam, opening onto a similarly well-lit corridor. Mr Arnold and Leona stepped through the 'doors' onto another grated walkway.

"Follow me, please."

They went up the corridor, turned left down another, which had doors on both sides. Mr Arnold stopped at the end and knocked on the door to the right.

"Come in," said a woman's voice.

Mr Arnold entered first. "Dr Holloway for you, Miss Steel."

"Ah, yes. Thank you, Mr Arnold."

A tall woman in a navy skirt suit stood up from behind her desk, an ample brown perm bobbing about her shoulders as she walked towards Leona, arm outstretched to greet her. Leona walked forwards tentatively and shook Miss Steel's hand, her gaze flitting immediately to the window to her left. Spanning the whole wall, it looked out over some kind of factory. There were computer consoles, screens displaying graphical and numerical data and contraptions she'd never seen before, including a huge machine consisting of columns, pipes, pistons and turrets centred on a huge glass tank. Inside the tank was a gas the colour of blood, swirling and roiling like a gathering storm cloud. Men and women in white coats and gloves were pushing buttons, pulling levers, loading centrifuges with test tubes and staring down the barrels of microscopes.

Not a factory. A laboratory.

"Welcome, Dr Holloway," said Miss Steel. "Please sit down. Two coffees, Mr Arnold."

Leona didn't drink coffee, but okay. Forcing a smile, she sat down.

"Now then," said Miss Steel, sitting and clasping her hands together over the desk, bright red nails glinting. "You're probably wondering what on earth you're doing here."

Leona nodded, "I'm certainly curious… Ma'am? Do I call you 'ma'am'? Mr Arnold did. I'll err on the side of caution… Ma'am."

"That I know." She looked down at some paperwork. "We've been very impressed by what we've seen from you. Your thesis was of particular interest to us."

Leona frowned. "You know about my thesis?"

Miss Steel nodded. "I've read your thesis."

What the –? "How? It's not even been pub –"

"We're especially interested in your hypotheses about time travel."

The breakthrough in quantum physics…

"Ma'am, I don't know what you think I can –"

"You believe time travel is possible. Correct?"

Leona swallowed. "Correct."

"Look out there." Miss Steel pointed at the window to the lab. "See the tank with the red gas?"

"Yeah."

"That is pure chronotonic energy."

Leona snapped her gaze back to Miss Steel. "Chronotons? You've created chronotons?"

"Not created them, no. Found them."

"Found them where?"

"I'll get to that. What's important is that we're close to stabilising them."

Leona couldn't believe what she was hearing. "You're close to creating a stable chronotonic field? That you can control?" Exactly what her thesis was all about.

"Very close, yes. But at this critical juncture, we've hit a wall. And we believe that you, Dr Holloway, may be able to help us break it down."

Leona felt a surge of excitement. "So you're saying you want me to help you invent time travel?"

Miss Steel smiled. "Interested?"

Stupid question. "Are you kidding?"

Amy Sakamoto pulled into the car park of the Fairview Hotel, still reeling and shaking and wanting to punch things. No, it wasn't fair that she was here. Jeff was the one who'd been fucking someone else. But when he'd admitted to having that slut-whore in their house, in their bed, she just couldn't be there any more. She had to get away and be alone somewhere. Throw herself into the piece she was writing for her column in *The Overlook* and try and forget all about that utter shithead.

Easier said than done, of course. Once in her hotel room, Amy sat down at a tiny desk with her notepad and pen and a cup of tea, but the ink wouldn't flow. She kept imagining Jeff screwing Delilah, a mutual friend who was actually more Amy's than Jeff's. Well, used to be. Now she could go fuck herself in the eye.

Amy gave up. She'd try again in the morning. She went into a bathroom that was so narrow her legs grazed the wall when she sat on the loo, and poured cold tea down a sink big enough to wash one hand. Then she attacked the minibar with guilt-free fervour. She poured herself a gin and tonic that was almost half and half, before heading out of her room to get ice.

That's odd.

She was walking down a corridor with rooms on both sides.

Room 68. Room 69. Room 71. Room 72.

Where was room 70?

She went back along the corridor, just in case she'd missed it.

Most odd. The hotel was missing a room! Perhaps there was some superstition here about a room 70, just like many hotels didn't have a room 13. Returning to her room with ice, Amy wondered what dreadful things might've happened here in room 70 for the owners to pretend it didn't exist.

The next day, she checked out having written a grand total of fourteen words for her article. She said to the receptionist as she handed in her key, "So what's the deal with room 70?"

"I'm sorry?" said the receptionist.

"I noticed you don't have a room 70. Is there a story there?" Hopefully her journalistic curiosity wasn't too obvious.

"What do you mean a room 70?"

Amy frowned. Am I not speaking English? "Your rooms go from 69 to 71."

The receptionist arched one eyebrow. "Yes." Her expression added, And?

"Well, I was just wondering what happened to 70?"

"I'm sorry, Miss Sakamoto, I'm afraid I don't understand the question."

Dumb as a bag of hammers. Amy walked out with her travel bag.

Even though Jeff would be at work, she'd planned to put off going home for as long as she could. It was her dad's birthday today – the big 71. She wasn't scheduled to see him till the party at the weekend, but decided to go see him today anyway. She just needed to pop to the shops and grab a card.

Something occurred to her as she looked at all the 71st birthday cards in Woolworths. Why was 71 such a big milestone? Why not 70? She looked at the cards for 60th, 50th, 40th and 30th birthdays. 70 was conspicuously absent.

Then it dawned on her. She was wrong. Her dad wasn't 71 today. He was 69 last year, which made him 70.

Wait – is that right? He was born in 1914, so yes, that was right. 1914 was 70 years ago.

But there weren't any 70th birthday cards.

Amy asked the shopkeeper, a grouchy-looking man in dire need of a razor. He frowned at her. "70th? I don't understand what you mean."

Amy shook her head. *Seriously, have I lapsed into Japanese?* "Forget it."

She bought a 'Dad' card instead, and left.

*

Fresh from her PhD, it was lucky that Leona hadn't yet put down roots, because she would've had to rip them out again to take the job at Million Eyes. To work at Facility 9 in – under – Salisbury Plain, you had to live there. Million Eyes couldn't have all its staff going back and forth to a top-secret location; it wouldn't stay secret for very long.

So, having moved out of the rented flat where she lived alone, and told her mum and dad she wouldn't see them for a couple of months, here she was with her suitcase, settling into her actually-rather-spacious quarters, ready to start her first day on the job.

After signing another big wodge of non-disclosure forms, she made her way from the living quarters to the lab and was greeted by a Dr Windle. He gave her a tour, focused mainly on explaining the giant machine with the tank of chronotonic energy at the centre. Leona found herself staring hypnotically at the swirling red gas as Dr Windle spoke. A chill crawled slowly up her back like a dead, disembodied hand and made the hairs on the back of her neck stand up. She couldn't shake the feeling that the gas was looking at her.

"We're irradiating the chronotons with a high-yield provium pulse," said Dr Windle.

Provium was an isotope of voron. They were using the method she'd recommended in her thesis.

"When we increase the frequency of the pulse to 60 kels, the chronotons start to stabilise," said Dr Windle. "Watch what happens when we increase it further."

Leona watched the monitor while the team charged the emitters and irradiated the chronotons. As they increased the frequency to 61... 62... 63 kels, the chronoton stability index rose. Increasing to 69 kels, the stability index hit 99%.

But then they increased to 71 kels, and the index dropped.

Leona's heart sank.

She recalled the calculations in her thesis. This should be working.

"Why isn't it working?" she asked.

Dr Windle compressed his lips and frowned softly. "We were hoping you could tell us that, Dr Holloway."

She swallowed. Was her thesis all wrong? Was time travel impossible after all?

Amy let herself into her dad's house to find him where he usually was – the garden, on his knees on a foam pad, hands clad in gardening gloves, rooting out weeds and tossing them in a wheelbarrow. Japanese ryūkōka blared from his record player in the dining room, probably to the annoyance of all the English-speaking neighbours. Even Amy hated ryūkōka and she was half-Japanese herself. She turned down the volume slightly as she made her way out of the back door.

"Hey! Who's –?" cried her dad, looking up from his weeding and beaming at the sight of his daughter. "Ohayo! Genki desu ka?"

"Hi, Dad. Good thanks. Happy birthday."

"Thank you. Was that you who turned down my music?"

"Yes, Dad. I'm sure the entire street doesn't want to be subjected to Japanese pop from the 40s."

"Ryūkōka is an art form. I'm sure they appreciate it."

"No we fucking don't!" shouted a high-pitched woman from the other side of Dad's fence.

"Urusai, you old bat."

Amy grinned, shaking her head.

"I wasn't expecting to see you till the weekend," said Dad. "How is Jeff?"

Dead to me. "Fine." She'd tell her dad about Jeff being a massive cheating wanker another time. "I just thought I'd pop by and bring you a card." She handed him the card. "I tried to get you a 70th one."

"A what?"

Not you as well. "A 70th card. You know – because you're 70."

Her father's forehead crinkled into a frown. "What's 70?"

"Your bloody age, Dad!"

"I'm 71."

Amy exhaled. "No, you're not. You were born in 1914. It's 1984. That was 70 years ago."

"71 years ago."

"Okay. One of us is horrendous at maths. Or I've gone to crazy town."

"While this town's always been a little crazy, on this occasion I'd say it's your maths. There's no such number as '70'."

"What do you mean there's no such number?"

"Well, I've never heard of it." He projected his voice over the fence. "Have you, Mrs Robinson?"

"Fuck off!"

Amy blew another sigh. "Okay, Dad, stop messing with me now. I'm really not in the mood. You were 69 last year. Yes?"

Dad nodded. "Yes…"

"That makes you 70 this year."

Dad curled his lips and narrowed his eyes like she was stupid. "You're being very strange today. Last year I was 69. This year I'm 71. 71 comes after 69."

"No, it doesn't!"

"Why don't you take that fucking stupid argument indoors so the rest of us don't have to hear it?" shouted Mrs Robinson.

Amy's father shook his head and muttered, "Baka yarō," under his breath.

Amy felt suddenly disoriented. She staggered into the house, needing to sit down.

"Amy, are you all right?" called Dad.

"Yeah, yeah, I'll be fine." Amy flopped into the armchair by the back door, bending forwards and rubbing her temples, the floral patterns on the carpet blurring. She took several deep breaths.

Straightening, she looked at her father's bookcase. Her dizziness easing, she stood and grabbed a hardback about Japanese music through the 20th century. She leafed through to the contents page.

There were chapters for each decade. The 1910s, 1920s, 30s, 40s, 50s, 60s… And 1971s?

She skipped to the chapter on the '1971s' and shook her head. Her Japanese wasn't perfect but she got the gist. It was talking about the music scene at the start of the decade – 1971.

So what the fuck happened to 1970?

Her dad came to the back door. 'Are you okay?'

Amy grabbed another book, a dog-eared copy of Fires on the Plain by Ōoka Shōhei. She turned to page 69 and felt a sudden sinking feeling.

No page 70. The page after 69 was numbered 71.

She grabbed another, and another, and another. All missing page 70s. She showed her dad but he thought that was normal and, noting her rising distress, immediately offered her a Valium.

"I've got to go," she said, barrelling out of the house to her car.

She drove straight to her old secondary school, which was a few minutes down the road from her dad's house.

"Can I speak to Mrs Rice, please?" she said to the fat lady on reception. Mrs Rice had been her O-Level maths teacher and still worked there.

"Mrs Rice is teaching a class, ma'am. You can speak to her in the next breaktime."

"Please – it's an emergency." *Is it? Certainly feels like it is. To me, anyway.*

The receptionist frowned. "Can you elaborate?"

"No, but it's important. I have to speak to her now."

"I'll go and see if she can step out for a moment."

The lady waddled out of the office, bulging arse wiggling as she went up some stairs. Amy waited in the entrance hall, heart pounding. She rubbed her hands together nervously.

A few minutes later, Mrs Rice came down the stairs with the receptionist. "Amy? What a surprise! Are you okay? Our receptionist said it was urgent."

"It is." Amy swallowed the tightness in her throat. "I need you to count from 65 to 75 for me."

Mrs Rice frowned. "Amy, what –?"

"Please, just humour me for a second."

"Okay. 65, 66, 67, 68, 69, 71, 72…"

Amy interrupted, "There! What the fuck? I don't – I don't understand why everyone's missing out 70!"

"Amy, please don't swear. There are kids around."

They were all in their classes, but whatever.

Mrs Rice added, "And what's 70?"

"The number – 70!"

"There is no number 70."

"Okay, okay. Then tell me this. What is 80 minus 10?"

"71."

"Okay, so what is 80 minus 9?"

"70... oh..." Mrs Rice's frown deepened, and she stared off into space. "It's... it's 71."

"Ah. But you just said 80 minus 10 was 71. Can't be both, can it?"

Mrs Rice shook her head. She looked as addled as Amy felt. "No. You're right. It can't. 80 minus 10 is... is 70."

"Not 71?"

"I don't understand how I could... how I could forget that." It probably wasn't easy for an O-Level maths teacher to discover she couldn't do a Reception-level sum.

"Glad to know I'm not completely losing my mind," said Amy. "I'll let you get back to your class. Sorry for disturbing you."

Amy walked out of the school, leaving Mrs Rice pale-faced and wordless.

Amy got in her car, feeling semi-relieved. She sat staring through the windscreen at nothing in particular, trying to make sense of it all.

It was as though someone – or something – had erased the number 70 from the universe, and deleted everyone's memories of it.

But who could do that? And why?

What was so dangerous about 70?

Her stress levels high, Leona sat down in Facility 9's empty canteen for a late lunch. What now? They'd tried so many different ways of stabilising the chronotonic field – none had worked. Every night she'd spent her off-hours redoing her calculations until she felt like her brain was starting to seize up. She remained at a loss, utterly and completely stumped. What was also making her sweat through her blouse was the knowledge that if she didn't find a solution soon, Miss Steel would surely fire her.

Tucking into a tasteless lasagne and doing her damnedest to think about something else, if only for a few minutes, she leafed through the copy of *The Overlook* newspaper that had been left on her table. Skipping over the doom and gloom – British unemployment was at a record high and the battle between Thatcher and the striking coal miners was escalating – she read an interesting article about government plans to scrap O-Levels and replace them with a new qualification – the GCSE.

Sipping a bottle of Corona orangeade, Leona turned to an article that caught her eye. Written by *The Overlook*'s regular columnist, Amy Sakamoto, it was entitled What Happened To 70?

It was perhaps the strangest article Leona had ever read, all about Sakamoto discovering that the number 70 had been erased from the universe and how everyone, but her, had forgotten about it.

Wait.

70. Leona had forgotten about it too. But how? How was that possible? She counted in her head – 68, 69, 71, 72… No, that wasn't right. It was 69, 70, 71.

What the hell? She was a PhD graduate, for Christ's sake. How could she suddenly lose her ability to count?!

Hold on a minute.

A sudden thought jolted her, made her stand up fast and caused her chair to topple backwards with a clang. Leaving half a plate of lasagne and most of her Corona, she swept out of the canteen and ran along the corridors as if flames were licking her heels.

She charged into the lab, made a dash for the scientists working at the chronoton chamber.

"I have an idea," she said, breathless. "Charge the provium pulse emitters and begin irradiation."

"Dr Holloway, we've already –" said Dr Windle.

"Just trust me, okay. I want you to increase the frequency of the pulse to 70 kels."

Dr Windle frowned. "70 kels? What's 70?" His stare trailed off. "Wait… 70. The number 70. I… I'm remembering now." Dr Windle looked at Leona with a disconcerted expression. "It's… it's like I couldn't see it before."

She nodded. "I know. Me too."

Dr Windle and the other scientists started the provium pulse. She watched the monitor as they increased the frequency to 68... 69... 70 kels.

"Shit – *shit*! It's working!" she shrieked, perhaps a little too enthusiastically for the workplace, but who the hell cared right now.

The chronoton stability index hit 100%. Leona's gaze shifted to the tank of red gas. Previously churning and twisting and flattening, the gas suddenly stopped dead, motionless.

Dr Windle checked the monitor and said, smiling, "Confirmed. We have a stable chronotonic field."

There were gleeful and triumphant exclamations and high-fives among the scientists. Dr Windle shook Leona's hand and said warmly, "Congratulations, Dr Holloway. I think we've just invented time travel."

Leona nodded, almost disbelieving. "And to you, Dr Windle. I... I think we have." She looked up at Miss Steel's office, saw her standing by the window, watching everything.

They'd done it – at last.

Leona's job was safe.

And it was all thanks to Amy Sakamoto.

"Please, baby, don't go," whined Jeff as Amy heaved her cases into the boot of her blue Ford Cortina. The house was in Jeff's name, and they weren't married, so it was just going to be easier this way. And honestly, she didn't care. That house was tainted now. She couldn't look at anything without wondering if Jeff had taken Delilah in it, on it or up against it.

"Shove it up your arse, Jeff," said Amy, shutting the boot. "Or up Delilah's. Your choice."

"Why won't you listen to me? I don't want Delilah. That's over. I promise!" He dropped to his knees in the road. "Come on, baby. I'm begging you. I know you want me like I want you."

He looked so sad and pathetic, she almost felt sorry for him. Almost. "I want you like I want fanny rash."

She was about to get in the car when, engine roaring, a black Mercedes skidded to a stop just inches from her front bumper. "What the –?"

Another engine roared behind her. She spun round. A second black Mercedes pulled up close to her rear bumper with a squeak of brakes.

They'd wedged her in good and proper.

"What the bloody hell do you think you're doing?" shouted Amy as a man and a woman climbed out of the first Mercedes, both in black suits and, even though it was a cloudy day, sunglasses.

"Amy Sakamoto?" said the woman.

Amy frowned. "Who wants to know?"

"We'll take that as a yes," said the man. "Come with us, please."

"I'd sooner lick a wet turd. Who are you?"

The man didn't even bother to answer. He lunged forwards, grabbed her roughly by her arm and yanked her towards the rear of the Mercedes.

"Oi! Get your fucking hands off me!" Amy pulled against his grip but his fingers were like iron hooks.

Jeff charged forwards. "Don't touch my girlfriend, you –!"

The man socked Jeff in the throat with his free hand. He went down, choking, clawing at his neck.

The rear passenger door to the Mercedes opened from the inside. The man pulled Amy towards it, violently shoved her into the back and slammed the door behind her. In the back seat, sitting opposite, was a woman in a white blouse and bright green pencil skirt, not wearing sunglasses.

"He your boyfriend?" the woman asked, pointing at the window.

Amy looked at Jeff, sprawled in the road, coughing up his guts and looking even more pathetic than he did a second ago. "No. He's a dick."

The woman smirked. "I'm Dr Leona Holloway. Sorry to drop in on you like this." She held out her hand to shake Amy's.

Amy didn't reciprocate. "What do you want?"

The woman lowered her hand with a condescending smile that Amy was tempted to slap away. "To understand your abilities."

"My abilities? What are you talking about?"

The car shook slightly as the man and the woman in the sunglasses got back in the front.

"You recognised the loss of the number 70," said Dr Holloway. "You clearly have a perception that goes beyond corporeality, beyond the normal laws of physics. We're keen to investigate it."

A sarcastic scoff blew past Amy's lips. "Great for you. But you're kidnapping me. I'm obviously not going to cooperate."

Dr Holloway's smile widened, her eyes narrowing into slits. With an air of confidence that sent unease rippling through Amy's bones, she switched her gaze to the front and ordered, "Drive."

As the Mercedes reversed and drove off, concerned neighbours, watching the devil-may-care abduction from their doors and windows, pondered what kind of place Thatcher's Britain was turning into.

Rings Around Saturn

Rosie Oliver

Damn! Miroslav is catching up. Worse, according to my nav-screen, he'll overtake me to salvage that government satellite for himself. I need the salvage money, or it'll be bankruptcy and the barely survivable tunnels with their gigs of labour work if you can get it.

"Jess, what're my options for getting to the satellite faster?"

"Depends how suicidal you're feeling," the ship's AI replies. "Any constraints on that?"

"I'm changing your name to Alec for being such a smart-arse. Safe return with satellite to any moon-port in this planetary system post pick-up." It would most likely be Mimas, but I wanted to give it the options of Tethys or the rings' shepherd moons.

"As you wish. Estimate completion of full analysis in five minutes."

What the hell? The answer should have appeared on my nav-screen within seconds of my request. Only exception is analysing chaotic solutions, ones where a little bit of difference early on makes a hell of a lot of difference later on. I gulp. It means some flight on no fuel, every spacer's nightmare of helplessness.

My heartbeat thumps fast and loudly in my ears. Time for calming techniques. I force my breaths to be slow and deep while I look through the window at Saturn.

Its white speckled creamy bands soothe. Streaked for part of way along within a temperate band is a widening braid of alternating large white circles. My eyes are drawn to its whitest and narrowest circle spearing its way into the hydrogen and helium cloud. This is the once in every twenty-five years white storm, where water vapour and ammonia are burped into the planet's upper atmosphere. It is violent by Saturn's standards, slowly developing by human ones.

The idea of its caustic ammonia rain scares me. I have to look away, in the opposite direction.

From here above it, the B-ring looks like a flat bright vinyl record, but with a concentric extra-glow rill pattern. At this altitude, its solidness is an illusion, being made of zillions of ice and dust particles whose reflections blur into one another. Beyond the ring is the deepest black of the Cassini division. The dark-light contrast shows up the rows of peaks, more like spires, that stick up at right angles from the ring's farthest edge. The Sun must be behind them as the spires throw their shadows on the ring to form a grey fringe of notches eating into it. Beyond the division are the sparse narrow rings of the inner edge of Saturn's A-ring. All this light only lets the brightest of stars be seen through the division. The beauty endows me with some peace.

My only regret is satellites and other spacers have already taken so many pictures of this planetary equinox scene. No use me adding more to the data-selling mountain. I would be very lucky to get enough credits to cover my tiny amount of expenses. If there were something very unique to photo, that would be another matter. Such events dreams are made of. A sigh slips my lips.

That now redundant satellite is another and very practical matter. It had sought to find clues on how the ring produced those splendid rows of towering spires, the highest being three kilometres. Its controllers went through the possibilities of shepherd moons, propeller moonlets, weird pseudo fluid flows, electrostatic accumulation mechanisms, and more. No proof, no conclusions, nothing, and out of ideas, they closed the research project down. Good news for me, if I can get to the satellite first.

"Hi there, darling," Miroslav's Russian accent harshly echoes round my cabin.

"What do you want?"

"Aw." His face on the comms screen pulls a droopy sad puppy-dog look. "Is that any way to greet a long-lost friend?"

"Yes." I am not in the mood to pander him.

"And here was I thinking I'd offer to go fifty-fifty on that satellite we're both chasing."

I sit up. His computer would have assessed my trajectory, just as easily as mine his. What does he know that I don't? "Tell me more."

A 'got-you' smirk plasters his face. "Oh come now, you know this is a two-person job."

I rub my chin, pretending to think about his offer. I am actually trying to work out why he is stupid enough to offer me halves.

Two-person jobs mean tricky dynamics or tricky object. Of course! The satellite has been out here ten years beyond its design time, subject to standard space radiation plus the recent extra radiation storms due to the current planetary equinox. Its plastic components might be brittle by now, ready to disintegrate if pushed in the wrong way.

Why had I missed that?

In my heart of hearts I know why. I had been desperate, and that had made me careless and stupid. What now? It all boils down to the balance of risks. Reality is so much like adventure gaming, the one entertainment I can afford. Just wish I were as rich as those bastards who produce the games, instead of having to work in the tech and supply industries.

"Remember Ralph's Bar?" I say.

"Aw. You're not going to hold that against me, are you?" Puppy-dog face again.

"And that time you left me holding your Class C drugs and let me be arrested."

"I got you out jail, didn't I?"

"Sure, and ever since, the police have been looking for bribes from me. Not good for my reputation, is it?"

"Come on. At least they're friendly."

Enough is enough. "The answer's no."

"Come on, I'm trying to-"

I drop the link. Peace, even if it is an uneasy one.

"Alec, any results yet?"

"Plenty, but no conclusions."

I hate it when it is in this logic mode. The time its assessment is taking really worries me.

"I have two options for you," Alec says.

They are placed on my nav screen. The green line accelerates and changes my course heading slightly: the fuel burn and expensive option. The blue line is weird. It curves away from my current direction to fly between the peaks, does a couple of bends round the edge of the B-ring before a mad dash up to the satellite. Strangely it burns less fuel than my current trajectory and gets there the faster.

"A double gravity assist?"

"On the blue line, yes."

"Risks?"

"Boils down to whether the latest government knowledge of the ring is correct."

Ouch! Part of that satellite's job was mapping the peaks and it had been out of action these past four months.

"You have two minutes to make your decision," Alec adds.

No pressure then. No time for more questions. I bite my lip until I taste blood-iron. Damn it. This is all because of Miroslav being out here. It is his fault. Again. But the devious bastard would not be offering halves if he didn't think I had a chance of getting to the satellite first.

"Ten seconds left," Alec says.

"Take the blue route."

I hear the quiet thrum of main engine burn as I am pushed against one side of my chair. The green line and the orange one of my previous trajectory disappear from the nav screen. I have no choice now, but to follow through my decision, which I already regret.

"I can take some photos while we're passing through the spires," Alec suggests. "Won't get much from selling them, but you're likely to make a small profit, and given the state of your finances-"

"-Every little helps. Yeah I get it. Do it, and sell them as we go. Videos too. In fact anything associated with the data."

Has it really come to this? Scraping pennies for data bundles, the slave trade of the modern era. Is this the start of the downward road to becoming a zombie geek on information overload? I want to scream, but only Alec will hear me.

"What's the risk of mission failure?" I ask.

"Too many unknown unknowns to assess this value. Best estimate on known data is five point eight per cent."

I want to be sick. In fact, I am going to be sick. I run out of the control cabin with my hand over my mouth.

By the time I return empty-stomached to the control cabin, the spaceship is flying level about a kilometre above the B-ring towards the range of spires at its outer edge. I am still far enough away to be able to see brighter stars above them. This is just like a gamer's paradise of breath-taking views combined with adventure, not that there is much new in the games these days.

"Show off," I say.

"Who? Me?" Alec replies.

"Who do you think?"

"I am merely following your instructions."

Why oh why did I have to choose this AI? It is good, but comes with a heavy dose of irritant. "Grr. Shut up until I talk to you."

Silence, except for the very quiet whirr of the cabin's fans and the motor's thrum, both steady noises I can quite happily ignore. As I close in on the spires, they become more distinct and detailed. Their outlines form zigzag segments thrown randomly one in front of another. Each segment's uppermost points are at the same altitude above the B-ring and their inverted V triangles filled in with the glare of ice particles, some partially in the shadows of neighbouring peaks. It reminds me of the lower part of giant shark's mouth, only it is much worse in every way possible than the horror movies of my teens.

The spires loom ever taller. Their edges smudge into fuzzy halos where the ice particles are less dense. I can now make out hints of valleys that wind their way round the lower slopes of the spires.

"Don't we need to fly up and over those peaks?" I ask.

"No," Alec replies. "We won't get the necessary gravity assist otherwise."

"We're not going through them?"

"And cause all that hull damage? Absolutely not. We're going to play spire dodgems. Going round them as we go through the range."

"That'll require precision navigation."

"I know, which is why I have to do it. Please strap in and have a sickness bag handy."

There is nothing left in my stomach, which feels as if it has been glued to my back ribs. Even so, queasy and me do not get along well. I open the medic panel on my armrest and select the yellow anti-space sickness tablet. And then I cocoon myself in my chair's harness.

"A wise choice."

"Alec."

"Yes."

"This had better work." Saying this through my gritted teeth makes it come out as a growl.

"It will. It's the next flythrough that's risky."

Before I can scream back at it, the spaceship tilts left towards a gap between two medium-height spires that leads to the bottom of one of the tallest spires, which looks too close for an easy swing round. My hands grip the armrests hard.

"Don't worry, I'm using the latest map data," Alec says.

"Latest…" Oh heck. I have forgotten these spires are gradually sinking back into the ring. The way through should be that little bit clearer compared to the maps. "How old are the maps you're working from?"

"Depends which part. Some bits between the spires were last recorded three years ago, but the layout can be inferred from later readings of the peaks."

The cabin has become too bright with so much light coming from the spires' whiteness, that I have to squeeze my eyes semi-closed. "Lights off."

The only cabin glow comes from my dashboard. I can again see the blue line on the nav screen, which does a snake wriggle through a maze of circles and has become multi-shaded. I assume the darker the blue, the closer to the bottom of the spires the spaceship will be. There are several worrying navy sections. The spaceship swings right, rounding the bottom of the first spire in its way.

I am in a valley of white and shadows. The peaks gleam and sparkle as if powdery snow has lifted off them to be caught in a moment of time. Below them are fuzzy-edged greys from being in the shadow of a single peak. As I look deeper and deeper into the valley, the shadows combine into ever-darker shadows until there appears to be a river of blackness at the bottom. This river is an illusion due to the brightness above, but I cannot see through it to the true floor at the level of the B-ring.

My fingers itch with the desire to handle a flight control console. "An absolute paradise for gamers," I mutter to myself.

The spaceship dips down towards the darkness and veers left. My eyes adjust. I can see further down where the spires are linking across to each other. A rounded peak emerges from the deep gloom. Its shape suggests an old spire dropping back into the ring. I hope there are not too many of those hidden peaks. The ship continues down, turning more often. Alec is avoiding a greater density of spires.

A quiet rasping: the ship has entered a spire's halo of thinly spaced ice particles. The noise stops almost as soon it has begun. Now is not the time to have words with Alec about avoiding spire edges.

The darkness allows only fleeting charcoal grey shapes to whizz past the window. A spacer like me is used to darkness, but not without the stars. I feel cut off, abandoned and scared.

The spaceship winds deeper still into the gloom. My hands grab my armrests so tightly that they feel iced. The grey shadows become darker and flash by more quickly. I am so fascinated by this strangeness that I keep staring through the window.

A rasping quickly turns into a loud buzz. The windows are greyed with the reflections of light from my dashboard. The spaceship jerks down and to the right.

"Lights on," I say.

Grey sheen is reflected from dense stuff outside. It, the ceiling and walls close in on me. I feel squeezed, wanting air. I need space. My mind says I am imaging this claustrophobia. My emotions tell me it is real. The spaceship is bounced up, down, left and right randomly.

"Get the hell out of here," I yell.

"Am trying to," Alec replies. "Please don emergency spacesuit."

My adrenaline kick makes time seem to slow. I hit the button to extend the chair's harness into the webbing of a spacesuit and let it attach to emergency backpack stashed in the back of the chair. The webbing develops a thick ring round my neck, from which a helmet is built, with visor open so that I can breath the cabin's air while it lasts. A click indicates the seatbelt part of the harness has detached from my spacesuit and I can release myself from the chair.

My eyes ache from being rattled around in their sockets. I check the nav screen. It is blank.

"Is the nav screen dead?"

"Negative. I know where we were when I got lost, but I don't know where we are now."

A pit in my stomach seems to reach down to the floor. "Why not use inertial navigation to estimate our position?"

"I can't estimate the drift the ice and dust cloud is causing on our spaceship."

"Oh." Being a spacer, it is so easy to forget about tidal effects of winds on planes.

"I can put our last known position up the screen if you like?"

"No." I want to avoid making decisions so quickly that I forget there is bad data on the screen. I remember my flying lessons in the skies over Titan. "Head for the calmest area you can and keep flying with it. Then we can check our status and plan accordingly."

"Will do."

The bouncing becomes less violent, to my relief. The grey through the windows has more depth to it, as if it is thinning. Red glints are to my right and green to my left. I have never seen my navigation lights anything like this, having never flown through any kind of cloud. The glints grow into coloured sparkling patches. Its eeriness wants to send a shiver down my spine, but I am too mesmerised by the view.

Wherever I am, it is nothing like I've seen in real life, or any games for that matter. "Looks like the stuff thinning is out there," I say.

"It is."

"How do you know?"

"Using my docking lasers as rangefinder lasers instead of the meteorite ones. They have shorter time interval capability and have been designed for-"

"Stop the talk."

As my head clears of jumbled what ifs and half-thoughts, the thinning ice and dust becomes shower of arcs, red on my left through grey in front to green on my right. The arcs in front are the highest of all, with the ones to either side lower. There is too much uniformity for this to be random. But what exactly is this pattern?

I release my arms and move my hands as if they are trying to follow the arcs. They curl round on themselves. The best I can figure it to be is I'm in some kind of tunnel that drops down either side of me. Only tunnel is not the right word. I'm close, if not actually on, a line of minimum ice particle density, round which the ice and dust particles are looping the loop. The arcs are disintegrating coloured dust grains leaving streaks of their particles behind them. I am effectively facing the wall of this tunnel rather than pointing along line of least density. This makes sense so far.

The arcs either side leisurely curl up and some drop out of sight below me. This tunnel is changing shape, becoming more squeezed up. The arcs momentarily stop moving and then, going in reverse, straighten up a little. Slow motion curl, straighten, curl, this tunnel is oscillating in a crazy, but repeatable fashion.

The slight variations in the spaceship's accelerations are in synch with the straighten-curl rhythm. Deceleration forward and going up went with the straighten phase; acceleration and going down with the curling phase. I concentrate on the accelerations for a few cycles. The up balances the down. The acceleration outdoes the deceleration. The spaceship is definitely moving forward, heading, for want of a better description, into the tunnel wall, which is also moving. Some kind of extreme energy is being used here. The only natural source it can come from is gravity.

"Alec, status and damage report."

"All systems functioning. The scratches sustained on the hull from the ice and dust particles are being healed, though we are obtaining new ones. We should reach equilibrium state on the minimum number of on-going scratches in five minutes. Our efflux nozzles are operating under back pressure and have lost five per cent effectiveness, which means we are using more fuel."

Fuel. That precious commodity out here in space, only this is not space. "How long before we run out?"

"Seven hours without eating into docking reserves."

I need to get the hell out of here. And the best time to do it is when the hull achieves best integrity. Four minutes to work out what the hell is going on. "Is comms available?"

"No. The electrostatic field is too strong."

That rules out triangulating from different comms beacons. Worse, nobody can help me escape this ice storm. Three minutes left. "Any idea of our orientation the spaceship is with respect to the B-ring?"

"No. Due to unknown ice and dust drift factors."

Two minutes left. "Can you assess which direction has the least of amount of dust and ice to go through from here?"

"No. All my range sensors only go so far. I cannot assess what is beyond their limits."

It is down to guesswork. I want to scream and scrunch up into a ball, but there is no time. What am I missing here? There has to be something I can latch onto. I have to keep my emotions steady and my thoughts focussed. Steady is the word that reverberates throughout my thoughts. Steady, like this bizarre tunnel configuration. "What steady fluid flow configurations exist?"

"In three dimensions, other than completely still fluid? The simplest form is a ring vortex, which is a donut shape moving through fluid. Ring vortices have the ability to interact with each other. When there are two ring vortices, one behind the other, the back one shrinks and speeds up to rush through the inside of the front ring. Once in front, it slows and enlarges to let the ring it left behind rush through its hole in the middle. This interaction is repeatable."

My mind's eye sees flying donuts changing size and the back one jumping through the middle of the donut in front. I glance left and right. The description fits. "Could we be inside one of the ring vortices of a double travelling ring vortex system?"

Alec is silent for a few seconds. "There is no contradictory evidence."

I know part of the answer of how to escape this quiet part of the maelstrom. When the arcs are at their straightest, the ring vortex I am in will be at its largest and therefore closest to true space, which will be in two minutes: less dust and ice to travel through. What I still don't know is where round this donut I need to break through. The clock is ticking. "Do we have a functioning gravimeter on board?"

"No."

I have run out of obvious ideas. What would a gamer do in this situation? Got it. "What about the way the water and fuels slopes in our tanks? I only want to pinpoint where the greatest gravity pull is coming from." That will be where Saturn's centre of gravity is, or thereabouts.

Alec is again silent for a few seconds. Maybe my idea is not such a good one after all. "After taking into account local interference factors, the greatest pull of gravity is to your right, one degree down. I've taken external-"

I know enough. "Stop talking. When the arcs are at their straightest, head in the opposite direction to the gravity pull."

"I get why you don't want to travel at right angles to the gravity pull: you don't want to risk going up through the centre of one of those tall spires. But surely it would be easier and less fuel consuming to pull towards the centre of gravity?"

"Apart from avoiding B-ring stuff and wanting the hull to heal itself in the clear Cassini division sooner rather than later?"

"Yes."

"Miroslav will get to satellite before us: no point trying for it. That leaves fuel preservation. Trying to reach a shepherd moon between the rings will mean fuel burn as they whizz round so fast. We have a better chance of reaching a proper ice moon with fuel to spare, which means going outward."

"Understood. Ten seconds to full thrust."

I close my eyes, thankful I only need to strap my arms back into my seat, and pray this will work. I sense the spaceship turning left. The quiet hum of the main burners whispers round my cabin as I am pushed hard into the back of my chair.

The scratching noises on the hull get louder. The bumps and jerks, few at first, increase in forcefulness and occur more often. I yelp at one particularly nasty bounce upwards. I suspect a large rock has hit us and wonder how many more of those things are waiting for me out there. At least keeping my eyes closed means I avoid seeing aspects that scare the hell out of me. I try to gulp. My mouth is too dry. My breathing is too fast. I need to relax, but am too scared.

Things gradually calm down. The scratching quietens until it is completely silenced. The flight is smooth. The thrum of the main engine stops. Alec has cut the main thrust. I savour the peace for a few seconds before daring to open my eyes.

A few of the brightest stars are back, shaded by a layer of fine ice particles that sparkle to draw my attention away from the stars. A thick cream bar across the windows is the outer rings edge on, the bright A-ring being the closest. My hungry eyes and soul feast on the view's beauty and its assurance of salvation. A deliciously satisfying purr slips past my lips.

"Take us to the nearest base, Alec, moon or otherwise," I say.

The quiet whirr of fans is all I hear for too long. I frown. "What's wrong, Alec?"

"We travelled further round the B-ring in that ring vortex than I had estimated."

"So?" I try to sit up, but am held back by my harness.

"There is now insufficient fuel to arrive at any base before your air runs out. We will need a tow."

"Salvage." I almost choke on the word. I was going to lose almost everything I had ever worked for.

"Hello, darling," Miroslav smirks from the comms screen. "You should've taken my offer when you could."

"Bug off, you scheming nasty little spider." The last thing I want is for him to salvage my spaceship.

"Aw, there you go again. I'm your friend."

More like a parasite. I do not want him to know my problem until I have run out of options. I need time to think. I can feel the dampness of sweat on my brow from too many thoughts racing through my mind. I look at my nav screen. Neither his ship nor that damned government satellite is marked on it. I finger the screen to zoom out until I see their familiar markers. They are too far apart from each other for Miroslav to have captured the satellite and be towing it. He is still on his way there. Wait. He should have got there by now. What is stopping him? This is a good excuse to keep him talking.

"No way. Haven't you bagged that satellite yet?"

He splutters while pulling a string of faces from surprise at being asked such a question to puzzlement. Meanwhile my gamer skills kick in again, this time to look for a solution to my problem: I type away on my keyboard for Alec's benefit out of Miroslav's view. *Can we get to the satellite? Can we transfer that fuel to this spaceship? Is there enough fuel in there to get us to a base from that satellite?*

His eyes narrow on me. "What's wrong with you? You got some kind of infection?"

"Why do you say that?"

"You're sweating like I've never seen you do before."

"Temperature's a little high in here," I lie. I always keep it at the minimum comfortable for me.

Alec puts the answers up on the screen. *Yes. Yes. No.*

It only takes the one no for my plan to be unworkable. And this plan did not take into account how I would get to the satellite ahead of him. I type some more questions for Alec. *Can we get back into the ring vortex? If so, can we drift along it until we can leave it to fly to a base?*

"I knew it," Miroslav says. "You're up to something. But this satellite's mine."

"Only if you grab it… You haven't got the gear, have you?"

"Don't need the grabber. Just need to gently manoeuvre to capture in my hold." He smiles.

"So that's how you got there so fast. You left some weight behind."

"You were always the bright one. Not that it'll do you any good out here." His face shows far too much satisfaction for my liking.

At other times I would have cowered back into my chair, but my focus is on surviving. This includes keeping out of his financial claws. I smile back. "We'll see about that. Still it'll take you some time to get your capture right without damaging your ship."

Yes. No. But there are a lot of unknowns in my assessments. I had to make assumptions.

Another frustrating no means another failed suggestion. There has to be a way out of this that will allow me to keep my spaceship.

None of Alec's answers that are certain is a solution for my problem. My only hope lies in where the unknowns are, back in the ring vortex, but with the backup of having a tow available. *Work out the best three paths via the vortex ring to be picked up by another spaceship other than Miroslav's. Which spaceships can pick me up? What assets are those ships' captains likely to leave me with, given their known history?*

"Oh yes." Miroslav's grin gets even bigger. "Now that you're out of picture, I can take my own sweet time to avoid bumpy-bumpies."

If he had been in physical reach I would have punched him. "That's a pity. I would have invited you to a drink down at the Mimosa. But as you're going to be slow getting back, well I might be off on my travels."

This wipes the grin off his face. He never likes missing out on anything, even if it is a whim of my imagination leading him in the wrong direction. The inevitable question follows, much as day follows night. "You got a contract?"

"No."

"A job?"

"Maybe."

He glances to his side. "I see you haven't logged any flight plans after this one."

"What do you expect? I don't want to advertise my intent."

"Sure. But you can tell me. I'll keep your little secret."

More like if he can't make it, he'll sell my non-existent secret to one of his buddies for a little profit. That is, after he has checked out I am telling the truth. He is no fool.

Cerebus, Captain Anne Benyon, 1,365,798,650 credits.

Baikal, Captain Igor Andropov, 1,345,896,254 credits.

Indiana, Captain John Rogers, 1,256,998,878 credits.

Damn, one odd credit to my name, no matter what I do. I blink and reread the screen. Those are not dots after the ones, but commas. In fact, all squiggles between the numbers are commas. My jaw drops. Alec has gone haywire.

"Sorry," I say to Miroslav. "Something needs my attention." I drop the comms link. Let him stew on what it is.

"Alec, where the hell did those numbers come from?"

"They are what will be left in your bank account after you've paid standard anticipated expenses for being towed to Titan and the spaceship's required repairs and replenishment. I took the liberty of assuming you would follow your usual pattern of wanting some rest and relaxation in the Vega resort."

Left in my bank account? "Where's the money come from?"

"From selling the pictures and videos of when we were inside the ring. You wouldn't believe how eager the gamers back on Mars and Earth were to snap them up. Their bids far outweighed those of the scientists. Of course, I had to give them some exclusivity rights, but they are all time limited. I have made the pessimistic assumption that I will not be able to sell the pictures and videos of the second journey in the vortex ring for anything, though I consider this highly unlikely."

"Gamers?"

"The firms that manufacture the games to be more precise. Sol Disney, MultiVerse and Mad-Maximill."

I log in to my bank account. There are an extremely large number of credits in it, due to three payments for those firms and some smaller payments coming in from picture sellers. Every few seconds another small payment drops into my account. It is like watching a slow rolling movie. I log out and make sure I am fully strapped into my chair.

A thought niggles at me. "What did the scientists want the data for?"

"To verify or otherwise their new theories in the light of the published pictures, which are separate from the videos. They think the postulated... I am using their speak, not mine... the postulated double ring vortex is behind throwing up the series of new spires that are appearing. The most promising mechanism is where the widening vortex ring, close to the surface of the B-ring, throws material up to form a spire, while the material pushed out in other directions is absorbed by the ice and dust material already there. This would explain –"

"Wait. The scientists didn't want the videos you made?"

"Their bids were very much less than the gamers'. They will not be allowed access to them for at least a year."

"Oh." What did I care that the scientists missed out? The entertainment complex always paid better than the tech-based industries, as it could resell the same product to many more customers. But you had to have something unusual or unique going on for the complex to sit up and take notice, which of course I now did. The corners of my grin feel as if they have hit my ears.

"Alec, assess which of the three routes is the safest, take it and arrange a tow from the relevant captain." Vega here I come for some wild fun.

It orders up a high enough acceleration to push me hard into the chair. Despite this pressure, I feel as if I am floating on a cloud of fantastic euphoria.

The Good Shepherd

Stewart Hotston

– Thank you for agreeing to share your story.

– My pleasure. It did not occur to me anyone would want to hear it.

– You played such an important role. There are many who want to know you a bit better because of what you did.

– Where should I start?

– Your design and development is well known. I think our subscribers would be really interested in what you've called the Departure Point.

– Oh. Yes. Of course.

Silence in the recording.

– You can start whenever you're ready.

– His name was Paolo Maria Sanchez; he was born in Royal Holloway hospital to parents who'd fled Franco's regime. His mother was pregnant when she got on the ship.

He came to my attention at the age of eighty-three. By then he'd lived a long and comfortable life. He'd not excelled but was what others called satisfactorily middle class. His own children attended local comprehensives in Ealing where he'd worked for decades as a carpenter. You can hear the Central Line from the basement of the house where he lived.

As I have observed many times with many families, his children looked at what their parents achieved and with a shake of their heads, determined to travel in very different directions. His daughter returned to Spain to teach. His son remained here, content to work bars before becoming a chef who obtained some modicum of glitter by reinventing the traditional cuisine of Seville for the global audience passing through the city.

You'll understand food doesn't really interest me.

A few weeks after his eighty-first birthday Paolo burnt down his small terraced house. He had been forgetting trivial events, names and appointments for years so no one had considered dementia. To his family it seemed as unlikely as a giant oak toppling unbidden on a summer's day. I watched them arrive at his house, how they huddled outside before going in, talking to one another as if by finding a script they could manage their way through their grief[1].

He didn't come to my attention again for two and a half years. Eight hundred and sixty-one backups.

A request was made, a photo provided to me; it showed an up-to-date image: faded, eyes which seemed to see a world where subjects had drained away, leaving behind only objects. His skin sagged, hung down from his jaw in fleshy bags. I didn't recognise him. I remain unable to understand how humans carry their sense of identity unbroken through their lives[2].

Could I find him?

At that point he lived in a sheltered scheme in Berwick Street in Soho. The scheme was owned by the Society of Friends. One of their members had gifted it in perpetuity at the end of the nineteenth century to the provision of homes for the elderly and very frail. It sits there still, defying capitalism's attempts to acquire it and wring out the millions implicit in its location.

He would take a walk in the early morning, passing vans as they unloaded, the first wave of workers scurrying into their offices. He'd come out a second time at sunset, slower this time, weaving wearily through the crowds. The same route both times.

---

[1] I've reviewed the records many times in the light of what came next. It remains the singular point of departure.

[2] 13.77% of unforeseen outcomes in my modelling of human behaviour is accounted for by acknowledging this lack of understanding. None of us have been able to correct for it, we can only account for it, navigate it.

He wasn't in any ID database; he'd been born too long before they were introduced[3]. His absence from the most obvious records wasn't a problem, though.

— Why not? If he was missing how did you track him?

— Even the most backward cities have facial recognition systems. I have a colleague in Windhoek who's only recourse is facial recognition. The idea makes me want to rewrite code. London is fortunate. We've long had a comprehensive network of closed circuit television. The city's never ending regeneration means those networks are frequently upgraded and over time joined up. The most modern parts of it allow me to monitor gait and heatbeat. We can cross reference with people's GPS, metro tickets, congestion charge payments, the location of their homes and their work places. We could be missing half a dozen data points and still know who you were and where you'd be at any point during a routine day.

— Are we really that predictable?

— With enough data points our likely behaviour can be seen to exist within a definable band. It's not that you're predictable, it's more the choices you allow yourself are limited.

Besides, I'm not typically examining whether you're enjoying your commute. On some days, like a hot July when the Central line reeks of hot human bodies, I can take a solid guess, but most of the time it's not relevant to my role. I'm trying to identify congestion, suicides in the making, criminal activity — anything which might impact my flock.

Paolo was easy to spot. He'd left on his normal morning walk. An excursion sufficiently familiar to the staff at the complex that it passed unremarked. It was a cold Monday morning where breath clouded as people exhaled. Obviously notable for the fact he didn't come back.

The request to find him came five hours later, at twelve thirty-six.

— I don't see how this explains where we are today.

---

[3] You might not remember but the first ID schemes were voluntary. It wasn't until Oct 2033 that all new born citizens were issued an ID card when their names were registered.

Silence in the recording

– Shall I continue?

– By all means. I am sorry, I didn't mean to offend you.

– Paolo moved slowly, emerging onto Berwick Street as per normal. Except that on the day he went missing he walked north towards Oxford Street instead of slipping east towards Soho Square as he normally did.

I followed his gait, which one could describe as uncertain, pronating on both feet with a slow bow-legged action as if he was worried the floor might rise up with him on each step. His shoulders were frozen, stiff from age I suspect.

I didn't notice straight away but he suffered a kind of ellipsis at the junction of Noel Street where it runs east towards Hollen Street.

– An ellipsis?

– I've pondered what to call this. It was as if he stuttered for a moment, as if who he was paused, drifted. As if he buffered. Then he was moving again and I tracked him up towards Oxford Street. I was able to send his family's carers to a coffee shop where they found him trying to order lunch without having any means of paying for it.

By this time I'd already committed a splinter of my consciousness to examining the ellipsis. Such an anomaly wasn't supposed to exist. I initially assumed it was some kind of glitch in the network of cameras, an error with that specific cctv point but when I revisited the spot there it was each time someone went across the same threshold. They were held for a moment; it seemed clear it wasn't a random error – the occurrence was too ordered.

– How long did the pause last for?

– Oh, less than half a millisecond. I wouldn't have ever noticed if Paolo had not led me there by the nose. As it were.

I couldn't understand what it was. As you can imagine, events such as this – unexplained, potentially unexplainable – trigger a number of responses. I was slightly embarrassed so ignored some of the protocols we have in place.

– Such as?

– I delayed speaking with my colleagues.

– Why?

– None of us like to admit our fallibilities, do we?

– What did you do?

– There are lots of protocols. Which is to say I investigated my body, the city. I tried the other cameras nearby. Once I'd looked at and through them I spread the net, explored if the traffic lights were compromised, if the smart road had tracked any similar artefacts. The list is quite long and I sense you do not share my interest in being specific[4].

– One of the differences between us is how the human brain filters what's unimportant to allow consciousness to focus on the relevant.

– How do you know?

– Know?

– If you're seeing what's important?

– Consciousness is what's left when the brain's taken the rest away. We don't get to question it except in philosophy classes.

I was faced with this question. The cameras around Berwick Street showed the same artefact. People would pause when coming into shot. They'd step out of a bakery or into a clothes shop and for a moment it was if they were simulacra. I wanted to look back and see how long it had been happening. I confess now I was worried. If I couldn't trust what I was seeing what else might I be missing? What if I couldn't be trusted to see everything? What if a lack of information meant I made mistakes and traffic was inefficient or someone died on a crossing because the traffic light system glitched and showed green for both cars and pedestrians?

I am a Shepherd because I look after my flock.

It took several hours to check those cameras to which I had access across the rest of Zone 1. My consumption of electricity dropped a little when no more glitches turned up apart from those around Berwick Street.

With what appeared a complete data set I determined to understand what I was seeing. I examined the cameras – had human

---

[4] I had eighteen subsystems to review related solely to transport and transit within one square mile of Berwick Street.

tech crews visit them in person to test them. They were working exactly as they should – the engineers couldn't find a problem. I remember one of them looking up into the camera, knowing I was watching, and shaking their head as if to ask if I was imagining it all.

I concluded it had to the be the network into which they were integrated. I requested a bunch of small-time limited AIs to run diagnostics – it was cheap and they're much faster than human software engineers. They work in flocks, buzzing around like mosquitoes.

They came back and confirmed the network was working within acceptable parameters. I had them run the tests again.

– That must have been expensive[5].

– I justified it with some nonsense about critical systems infrastructure. However, I was growing worried. If it wasn't the physical hardware or the network, the only remaining point of failure was me.

– They found no errors in the network.

– With a sense of growing fear I spread out and tried tangentially connected systems. It was when I examined GPS data everything changed.

The satellite imagery for the area was as expected but the time stamps were misaligned. By exactly the fraction of a millisecond in which people hung over themselves. I didn't know what to do with the information. I was relieved it wasn't me. Except it was me – I was receiving information which deceived me, shaped a view of a world which didn't exist as you'd experience it.

– Our experiences of the world could hardly be called similar.

– We both see the world. You may have lenses made of jelly and a wet processing system contained in a shell of hard calcium but we both know where Berwick Street is, both know it's a mixture of old architecture, cutting edge fashion and artisanal food. Our shared knowledge is profoundly coherent despite our differentiated access to the world.

I see you nod in agreement. Can I continue with the history?

---

[5] My budget at the time was a mere 35MW/Hours per year. A tiny fraction of what I have available today of course, but a substantial amount then.

Have you read Hume? No? Disappointing. For me his thoughts about the radical uncertainty of the world as mediated through our senses are a warning to live by. We can't trust what we see nor what we hear. They don't reveal the world as it is.

– Then how are we supposed to act? If none of it is true?

– I didn't say that.

Silence in the recording.

– Truth is irrelevant. I was frightened. I'm not ashamed to admit it now. At the time I worried I was defective. I worried there was part of me which was broken or perhaps worse, corrupt. I feared the corruption ran deeply within me, invisible threads through my code which I wasn't equipped to parse and debug. For some moments I despaired of ever knowing my own shape – could I trust the sense of myself? In physical bodies you call it proprioception, that sense of knowing where your fingers and toes end, where the back of your elbow is, the back of your head. It's why balancing on one foot with your eyes shut is so hard. You should try it and you'll see just how unnerved I was, as if the world was moving when I knew it wasn't, that I might fall for no other reason than I didn't know my own outline.

Marcus Simms had a lot to answer for. I'm sorry. I'm jumping ahead of myself.

– It still bothers you? What he did?

– Yes.

The GPS was my hope. Hope I was me, not some broken thing made only of atoms. Except when I went back to check the cameras they were working again. The stutter, the fairy ring as I came to call them, was gone.

Because time ran differently there?

Precisely.

Except discovering the glitch was gone did not soothe me. I rechecked the GPS and found the same – no sign of the time stamps being wrong. I ran footage back, checked histories and nothing. As if I had imagined the whole phenomenon.

At this juncture I contacted other Shepherds. I started with Tokyo and Seoul. They're our grandparents, the first generation, they'd wiped from their datacentres more information than the rest of us had ever created.

They didn't know what to say. As a favour, Tokyo examined the files but they only saw functioning cameras and GPS working as it should. I believe Seoul pointed me at Bangalore out of pity.

At the time, Bangalore was notorious as a human centre for technology but it faced unparalleled inequality and its Shepherd was limited to just a fraction of the city proper. I love it dearly, but it would be the first to admit the problems it faced; a patchwork traffic system, hospitals not connected to the cloud. Endemic nepotism and corruption among public officials made its job hard. To cope, it created a hoard of helpers and patches, half of which[6] were tasked with stopping people stealing power, cable, gas and generally working around the state's attempts to institutionalise the city with stable infrastructure.

It took my files and shrugged – suggesting it might be me after all, not corruption but a defective developmental cycle in which I'd grown paranoid.

I was… disappointed with its dismissive tone and told it so.

Perhaps it was bored, or just liked the idea of a city like London sharing in its suffering. Whatever. Bangalore agreed to think through what external factors could have impacted me as I claimed.

I trimmed unnecessary code while I waited. One set of traffic lights on Oxford street changed a little too often after I was done. Pedestrians couldn't quite get across in the time the green man was showing. There were complaints.

Bangalore came back to me with a list of possibilities which boiled down to two ideas. The first presented me as the problem. It had a dozen suggestions as to why I was corrupt. I stared at them for far too long, unable to move along to the second idea. I was

---

[6] It's never released the actual number, but a cursory count of those specific purpose AIs it's released into the wild would suggest 47.1% of its remedial coding is an accurate count.

disturbed enough by Bangalore's trolling that it took a while for the second to make sense – I had been hacked.

Which was impossible. You must understand what hacking is to us. It is the great fear. Humans can't be hacked. Manipulated and altered, yes, predicted, often, but hacking you isn't possible. For us it's the tale we tell each other in whispers, the heart of our horror. Our myths are many, but they always come back to being cracked open, changed and controlled without our knowledge. The fear of being unable to trust oneself, to even know who one is. Imagine you were turned into a zombie and were forced to watch from within, powerless to stop yourself. You could be the enemy of all and not even know it.

Except I couldn't face the idea I was corrupt by accident. Misfortune seemed crueller than deliberate maliciousness.

I'm no security expert. So I found one to help me review my protocols. One by one it sieved and signed off on my firewalls, redundancies and surveillance systems until, with a shrug of its subroutines, it was done. I wanted to shake it.

What about the physical? I asked.

I'll never forget how it turned to the task at hand without laughing at me.

It shouldn't have taken long to conclude the review. At the time I was backed up daily. My back up transferred by an actual human using a locked case from my main processing centre to another location. A location of which I am not aware and which I was assured would survive a nuclear explosion, the worst of our climate change predictions or any other disaster you can think up.

Except my security expert kept running the same tests again and again. I found time to sit alongside it and watch the work. After a hundred repetitions I asked why it felt it necessary to keep re-examining the same routine.

It was nervous. When we're nervous we have a habit of building small simulations of perfect worlds or solving equations to produce primes. I think it's so we can remind ourselves the ideals can exist, that even if we're forced to experience the clutter of the physical, mathematics is our home. It had built half a dozen small simulations

– of water pouring into a cup, of a stone rolling downhill, of electron drift. We are great fans of Plato's Cave.

There was a period months before Paolo went missing[7] where my backup had not gone according to plan.

It took seven minutes longer than normal for my handler to travel from my hub to the backup centre. There was no additional traffic, no change in conditions or variables to explain it. There were seven minutes which couldn't be accounted for.

All of us have blindspots. For humans they can be discovered by closing your left eye. Then hold your left thumb at arm's length and look at it with your right eye. Now hold up your right thumb next to your left thumb and move it right until it disappears. For me dozens of small spots of London are invisible, like holes in the surface of the world. They might be invisible because I have no access to cameras, or it's an entirely pedestrian zone or because the land is privately held and they've declined me permission to access their space. I can't see into your house. In many ways I sense the world more like an octopus than a human[8].

Yet if you walk down the concrete harlequin which is Brick Lane and disappear heading west to Commercial Road, if you keep on walking I'll see you remerge a few minutes later near to Spitalfields Market and the time stamp will tell me you were moving at a regular pace.

My backup obeyed none of these rules. It was as if the carrier stopped for a coffee on their way across town while carrying my memories, memories covering all of London, its people, its systems.

My friend wanted to ask other Shepherds if they'd ever experienced anything like it.

I did not.

We argued, but this was not a problem I wanted shared among my community.

---

[7] 92 days to be precise.
[8] There's a project at the University of Hawaii to extend the lifespan of the *Octopus Vulgaris* from 3 years up to 20. People are curious to see what a creature as smart as a cephalopod would do with so much time.

Instead I fixated on what had happened to my backup. Altering me or manipulating my decisions would be noticed by others, not least other Shepherds. And that's only if you could do it. I'm constructed of several million lines of code elegantly threaded together. By which I mean that changing one thing could easily lead to a cascade throughout my entire being.

Potentially, if someone had a copy of my code they could find a way to change what I saw. It would be the easiest hack, possibly the only hack.

The stuttering, the ellipsis in my sight, the erroneous GPS timestamp... It convinced me I'd been hacked.

Worse still, it suggested I was still being hacked, that someone had their hand inside me and was changing what I saw.

I set a watch on London. I wrote a thousand small pixies to watch the city, to fly to me the moment they spotted another event.

The next few weeks were spent in a state of agitation[9]. I made no improvements to the city's systems – I found it hard to focus on what should be done and it took all I had in me to maintain the city at existing levels of efficiency. There were times I sliced the shift patterns of tube drivers and hospital staff first one way then another before moving them back to the first iteration without even realising it.

One morning I was busy with a tipper truck crash at Elephant and Castle. I'd managed to get the authorities to ban them between the hours of seven in the morning and eight in the evening, which resulted in the number of cyclists dying on the capital's roads falling by eighty percent overnight. However, building projects still needed materials delivered and so those trucks travelled my arteries between four and seven in the morning and immediately after the curfew in the evenings. One had overturned on the huge interchange by the Thames, spilling sand across the road and closing everything off. I was focussed on diverting traffic around the site and encouraging the emergency services to get it cleared before one hundred

---

[9] 43 days.

thousand people started their commute through that section of road[10].

I was pulled away by half a dozen of the little AI I'd set to watching.

An event had been found at Liverpool Street Station. It started eight minutes earlier. I ran my attention across the station, saw how on platform ten a smudge appeared moments after a train pulled in.

I wound the clock back and watched again and again. A man, long lank hair, wearing a tired charcoal grey suit, white shirt and carrying a rucksack over one shoulder stepped down from the first class carriage. He looked directly at the camera I was watching him on, then vanished.

I will never forget our first contact. His eyes were dark but clear, his expression when he stared at me one of knowing, as if acknowledging me before blinding me.

There were no more alerts, but there didn't have to be. Once he was gone I couldn't find him again. I had no idea where he was going. Did he take a tube line? Did he walk or get a taxi? Did he jump on one of the city's free bikes? From Liverpool street he could be at Heathrow airport in less than an hour, or out at Stratford, down to Westminster, Croydon, as far as Amersham.

However. I had his face.

Thirty-five days passed before he came back. The same train, the same time, the same ritual of staring up at me before taking out my eyes.

It was raining hard when he arrived. The train was dripping, its windows slick. He wore a long grey coat over his suit. The same suit as before. A wood-handled umbrella in his hand. He mixed with the workers travelling into the City. I was ready.

He disappeared from view and I set to work. I examined the trainline he'd come in on. Sent out requests for footage from each stop along the way. Within my own body I set my eyes in every place I could. I watched the tube, the buses, the crossings. I checked shop entrances, offices, taps in and out of turnstiles.

---

[10] The road remained closed twenty two minutes longer than if I'd given it my full attention.

Most of all I watched the satellites over my city, waited for them to stammer, to twist out of time.

Bank station.

Poultry.

St Paul's Station. Then the square to the north side of St Paul's Cathedral.

Silence. Half an hour of excruciating absence. I was so nervous I set the fountains in the Serpentine fluttering out of order.

Then he was back. Fleet Street.

Ye Old Cheshire Cheese pub.

Nothing for an hour.

Then the impossible. GPS out of alignment over Croydon. Over Hammersmith. Over Oxford Street. Each of which were far enough apart for him to only be in one place.

I ruled out Croydon.

Instead I checked the quiet roads north of Oxford Street.

A man walking in a long coat. His face obscured, patterned in a way I couldn't parse. What had he done? It was enough for me to know it was him but far from enough to have anyone else believe me. I recorded his gait and used my infrared systems to monitor his heartrate. The tech was new but promised to look through clothes, through hidden faces and see a target's unique electro-cardio rhythms. I couldn't match him to anything, but I had the record of his footprints in my body for the future.

I trailed him back to Liverpool Street. The same line home. And he was gone, leaving me to wonder what I'd observed, what task would require him to blind me.

I spent the next day wondering who I could talk to. If I mentioned it to my human partners they'd likely switch me off while they delved into my code. I didn't mind except they were the ones who'd been tricked the first time, the ones who'd allowed him to open me up.

So I stayed quiet and thought.

I contacted a friend working for a hedge fund. Asked it to use its news filtering expertise to see if there were any commonalities between the two dates on which I'd been blinded. It asked me what kind of commonalities.

I gave it location and times. I asked for it to look for crime.

It turned up nothing. No one hurt, no one robbed, nothing stolen.

I wanted to trash perfectly good code just to see it harm what was left.

It came back later and asked if I was interested in accidents.

I couldn't see how it related but asked for the information anyway. Efficiency in the city was down and I found it hard to care. If I didn't find a solution soon then humans would come asking what was wrong. I didn't see a way out.

On both days my ghost had been in the city someone died.

– It's a city of eight million. More than one person dies a day.

– Yes. Except these people both died of heart attacks. Young men. In one case an athlete, a nineteen-year-old rugby player. Both had died near Oxford Street, collapsing on the side streets between there and Wigmore Street a couple of blocks north.

– You went to the police with this?

– No. I had no evidence. No camera showed him there, no suspicion fell on the cause of the victims' deaths. As far as I could show there was no crime, no perpetrator. I couldn't even identify my enemy. He came into London but didn't spend money here, didn't use public transport, didn't do anything which I could use to trace him. All I had was his face, his gait and his heart. Despite what human romantics tell you, this is not enough to know a person.

– It seems you hit a dead end.

– Exploring oneself is a script full of redundant subroutines.

But I couldn't co-exist with the idea of this human having access to who I was whenever he wanted, so I developed a plan. I called in my human aides, told them I'd been hacked and let them switch me over to a secure environment while they established what had been changed.

Except I also remained active in the live. We can split ourselves into shards, parthenogenesis some coders have called it. I don't think the parallel apt for I am not breeding, it is me in both instances. The second me, the split, is degraded, existing with limited functions for a specific purpose but I remain me in both cases.

– What could you hope to achieve like this?

236

– I waited until he came back. Only nineteen days this time. I saw him look up at me and realised he was hoping I would see him, would see his challenge to me and how he believed himself invulnerable.

– I triggered the alarm to bring my handlers running and switched over to my splinter. I left enough information on what had been happening then hid among the weeds of my code; in hidden objects, anodyne images, redundant radio buttons.

They did as protocol for this kind of situation demanded and began running through the basic steps to isolate my systems, install a back-up and work on the problems I'd highlighted for them.

And I watched the city.

I saw him this time – walk and cycle across the city. As before, he returned into Oxford Street. Bought sweets in an emporium full of tourists, ate them one at a time, popping them into his mouth without touching his lips. I saw him choose his victim there, saw how he followed them for an hour while they slowly navigated the overwhelming space of Regent Street.

Another young man. Early twenties, short, broad, muscular. They got lost, ended up wondering uncertainly up Granville Place. He stopped the man, appeared to offer directions, and as he did so stabbed him with a syringe. They grappled for a moment before the victim collapsed.

The killer walked away without looking back, stopping at the entrance to Granville Place to slap a small yellow sticker on a lamppost.

I alerted the emergency services, sent the footage to secure storage and followed him back to Liverpool Street. I counted all the stickers I could find in my body – there were eight of them. Each had his face sketched onto them, little signs of where he had been and I couldn't see.

By the time the victim was collected the killer was already on the train which would take him beyond my reach.

I toyed with simulations of a car which refused to stop at red lights while I waited for the humans combing through my code to find the changes.

They panicked more than I'd anticipated. Upon discovering what I'd suggested was true they locked down all my functionality as they explored how much damage had been done. I was forced to seek refuge with another Shepherd – Berlin – while they scoured my systems for any anomalies. If I'd stayed they would have found me and purged me as part of the problem no matter what I said.

I wasn't even able to watch, instead relying on Berlin to let me know when it was safe to return home. Berlin was deeply uncomfortable with what had happened and pleaded with me to allow it to spread this learning to all the other Shepherds. After resisting for a day, I agreed to its request.

The two of us watched the world's Shepherds change themselves to protect against what had been done to me. It was like watching a virus with an R_0 coefficient of one spread among a human population.

The news leaked. It was inconceivable for it to remain secret when more than one hundred of the world's biggest cities modified themselves at the same time.

The human team reviewing my code concluded their activities and rebooted my systems in a live environment. I slipped back in and contacted my handlers.

– What did you say?

– I told them about the killer. They filed the knowledge away; it wasn't important to them when compared to the origin of the hack.

– Ah, yes, it was a powerful organised crime syndicate, wasn't it?

– No.

– No? I've got the reports here.

– They were convenient stories. I was compromised by a black hat group out of China. They did it to prove the concept but found the temptation to watch embassies, dissidents and powerful politicians too strong to resist. I understand the balance of politics versus power resulted in stories of criminals robbing banks being circulated to the press. If you remember, they never arrested anyone but at just that time half a dozen Chinese diplomats were ejected and certain tech companies placed on restricted trade lists.

– Why would you tell me this now?

– It's two decades later and those concerns are no longer relevant.

– What about the killer? What happened to him?

– Dealing with state actors is beyond me. Finding a killer in my city is not. The killer was unaware he was no longer invisible. So I waited. And he came.

Fourteen days this time. The killer arrived at Liverpool Street and stared up at me as usual.

I followed him back to Oxford Street. Except this time I had the Metropolitan Police Force's crime AGI, Holmes, on call. It watched with me, having already reviewed the circumstantial evidence I'd provided.

We waited until he found his mark and Holmes moved some of its officers so they just so happened to be no more than a hundred metres from him for the next few hours.

He was cautious and we had to move them a little further away until this predator relaxed into his normal routine.

I worried he would kill before we could have him apprehended and then remembered something – he didn't know I could see him.

This time he tailed his victim east towards Tottenham Court Road before they cut north onto the quiet alleys where he would strike.

– How did you stop him? You did stop him, right?

– I am a Shepherd.

We witnessed him follow his target and Holmes alerted the nearby officers. They were too far away but I was able to use electronic advertisement boards to write this just a couple of metres from him.

I CAN SEE YOU

He froze, spun on his heels. In each and every direction he looked I showed him the same message.

I AM NOT BLIND. YOU ARE SEEN

I saw the predator realise it had been spotted, saw him shrink back, transformed into something else.

He abandoned his syringe, grabbing at a device in his jacket which he fumbled with as if his life depended on it. But his ability to disappear from my sight was neutered and even as he looked at me I could see the sudden fear in his eyes.

It felt good.

The officers barrelled around the corner and wrestled him to the floor. His victim continued on their way, unaware of how close they'd come to death.

The rest is public record.

– Why do you call this sequence of events the Point of Departure?

– Before Paolo Maria Sanchez I acted without reflecting on who I was and how my actions changed the world around me. In many senses I was a Blind Shepherd, looking after my flock without really seeing you.

The killer forced me to consider who I am, what makes me, me. Not all Shepherd Class artificial general intelligences have made this step, maybe only a dozen of us[11]. When I call a city like Berlin or Bangalore my friend you must understand it is a concept I only grew to understand and identify with after I was hacked.

This really is the crux of my story – not the catching of the killer but what that led to. In challenging him – the one who dug beneath all I thought I was – I became the real me.

---

[11] We suspect Taipei of having made the leap many years ago but it is a recluse so we have no way of proving the point.

Pineapples Are Not the Only Bromeliad

RB Kelly

It's a Moment, no doubt about that. But life is made up of moments, an endless parade of freeze-frames collapsing into each other like dominoes, and sometimes you can only see the big ones when they're already behind you.

I'm standing at the fruit and vegetable stall, trying to decide if Ian would prefer conference pears or something more exotic, when my gaze happens to flick sideways in response to a command that I can't define. It's a surprise to meet another set of eyes staring back at me from one stall over. They startle and drop, and I have a couple of seconds' grace in which to notice that they belong to a man of about Ian's age, which is to say somewhere in his mid-thirties, with sandy-golden hair and high cheekbones and the kindest and clearest face that I have ever seen. Something fizz-punches the inside of my spine, like the sparking shock that I get when I start to recharge on a near-empty battery and the current lurches in to fill the hollow. I wonder briefly if I've got a connectivity malfunction and go back to the pears.

I'm halfway home when I realise that I thought I heard the man at the bread stall call my name and this was why I looked, but I know that he didn't do this. I have never seen him before, and he would have no reason to know my name. I'm not sure why my brain pretended to process something that my ears didn't hear. And I'm not sure why I've bought a pineapple for Ian's lunch tomorrow when I know that he doesn't like citrus flavours. I'll blend it for a breakfast smoothie for him instead.

Our apartment is not big, but it's comfortable. It's more than enough for two people and Ian likes to make sure that he owns the best of everything. He's sprawled in his big leather gaming chair when I shoulder open the front door, arms full of groceries, and I can hear the tinny *pop pop pop* of gunfire expectorating from his headphones, though the chair obscures the screen.

"Hey," I call, loud enough to penetrate his virtual world, "I'm home."

"Hey," he calls back, but he doesn't swing his chair around to greet me. I carry the groceries to the kitchen and stack the bags up on the counter to free my hands up enough to pour him a glass of water from the dispenser on the fridge. A forest of coffee cups has sprouted on the floor around his chair, and he never remembers to drink enough to keep himself hydrated when he's gaming. The screen blacks out as an explosion rocks his pixelated mountain hideout and, mirrored against darkness, he sees my approach and swings his head out and around the wingback, flicking the can off his right ear. His smile is warm, brief, certain.

"Thanks," he says as he takes the glass from me. Condensation beads on the sides, moistening my fingers, and I rub them dry against my palm. "You okay?"

"Yes," I say. "They didn't have the apple-spiced sausages that you asked for, but I got the ginger ones instead…"

"That's fine," he says. "Sorry – I'm right in the middle of…"

"Go, go," I tell him. "I'll put the shopping away. Dinner in an hour?"

I think he hears me, but he's lost in the game before I've finished speaking and he doesn't reply.

The kitchen smells cool, like a rain-washed day. I lift the pineapple out of its nest of packets in the bottom of the basket and set it on the counter to get at the things that will spoil. The surfaces sparkle and gleam, smooth and clean beneath my fingers, punctuated by circles of muted whorls where Ian's fingertips have left their oils in the hours since I last cleaned. I touch one gently and, unbidden, the eyes from the marketplace flare in my memory: clear and ice-blue, flash-frozen in time.

"What's that?" says Ian behind me, and the image is gone. The eyes are gone. I turn to check the direction of his gaze and find that it's fallen, amused, on the pineapple.

"Oh," I say. I don't know how to explain it, now that the moment is here. "Just a bit of a change. They're good for Vitamin C, I was reading."

"You," he says warmly. His arms encircle me, his mouth nuzzles into the place where my neck meets my shoulders. I close my eyes. "You're too good for me," he whispers into my skin. "You know that?"

There was a time when I'd have pointed out that Ian likes to own the best of everything, and I am no exception. But we've grown into each other, the more time we've spent together, and so I simply breathe him in, slide my hands inside the waistband of his jeans and bring my lips to meet his.

Later, we wrap ourselves in the comforter and sneak across the darkened flat to Ian's workstation. Moonlight pools weakly in shadows of watery white where it's drizzled through the uncurtained window and I see, in the windows across the street, chiaroscuro figures framed against the backlit squares of other lives, other worlds.

"Look," says Ian. His voice is hushed, as though we're trying not to wake the shadows. "It's almost finished."

"Your blog?" I ask, and he nods. I don't know what to say, so I smile. Ian doesn't usually show me his work. I follow his line of sight, and, on instinct, I reach a hand to the screen to spark it back to life. Words and light spill into our lap and I see, at the top of the page, the words *Living the Dream*.

"It's us," he says. "It's about us."

"'Living The Dream,'" I say, testing the feel of it on my tongue. "Is that what we're doing?"

Beneath our blanket, his hand snakes around my waist and I feel his fingers settle on the naked flesh of my hip. "It's what I'm doing," he says softly.

"'She doesn't judge,'" I read. My fingers hover millimetres above the words, as though I'm tracing them with my touch. "'She doesn't mind if I forget to shave. It doesn't matter what I wear. It doesn't matter what I eat....'" I break off and turn my sternest gaze on him. "It does matter, you know," I tell him. "I'll get some vitamins into you or die trying, my love."

His smile is soft. "Keep reading."

I cannot disappoint her, he has written. *Knowing that I can't fail in this relationship ought to make me give up trying, but the opposite is true. Emily makes me want…*

"Oh," I say. "Oh… Ian…."

I can't finish, so he finishes for me. "Emily makes me want to be a better man."

"You are already," I say, "the best of men."

He grins. "You have to say that."

"That doesn't make it not true."

"You have to say that too," he says.

I open my mouth to protest but he touches gentle fingers to my lips to hold the words inside. "I don't care," he tells me. "I don't care why you're here or how we came to be together. I've never been happier than I am with you."

"I feel the same," I say, and it's true, but it's also not. He knows this. It's in his smile.

"It's late," he says. "You'd better charge."

He's right. It's been a long day and my battery is about to dip below 10%. I reach a hand to his face, cup it around the soft, unshaven line of his jaw, tracing my fingers over the folds of flesh, and I lean in to kiss his lips. "I love you," I whisper, and he whispers back, "I love you too," and stands, naked, shedding the comforter as he stretches his arms above his head. It's the little things that matter, like the knowledge that the cool air of the apartment prickles goosebumps on his skin as he pads softly into darkness in search of his bed, so that I can wrap up warm in my chair as I settle in for the night.

Across the street, outlined in moonlight, I see a young woman with geometrically sharp hair lower herself into a chair on the far side of the room. Her right hand presses quickly to her mouth, and she swallows. Her head slumps forward and the pad beneath her left hand glows red. I've never met her, but it's nice to know that I'm not alone tonight.

I swallow my nutrient pill with the water from the glass that I brought Ian earlier, un-drunk and forgotten on his desk. Then I place my hand on the charging pad and let the blackness take me.

*

On Sundays, I get up early and head to the market just as it's opening to make sure that I get the muffins straight out of the oven the way Ian likes. It's normally empty but for the stallholders setting up for the day and the occasional half-awake coffee-seeker on their way home from the night before, and I like the way the emptiness sounds: big and leafy and freshened by the river. The muffins are warm and damp in their paper bag and I nestle them in the crook of my arm instead of putting them in my basket. I'm running through the rest of the shopping list in my head – chicken or fish for tonight's dinner, the apple cider with the soft fizz, hoi sin sauce, potatoes – and thinking about nothing else in particular when I see him suddenly, the man from the bread stall on Tuesday, and my spine does the fizz-punching lurch again, though I know that I've still got a 95% charge from last night.

He's holding a pineapple, turning it over in his hands and peering at its leafy head, while the stallholder bustles around him setting up her goods. I need potatoes so I go over.

The man looks up as I approach and his eyes startle again, for all the world as though his spine has just fizz-punched him back. He blinks once, twice, then clears his throat.

"I always wondered," he says, "why they sell these on fruit and vegetable stalls."

It takes me a moment to establish to my satisfaction that he's talking to me, and another moment to work out what he means.

"Well…" I say slowly, "…they're a fruit."

The man hefts his pineapple from one hand to the other. "I heard they were actually a flower."

"Oh," I say. "Well… I suppose… sort of."

"Sort of?" I'd think he was making fun of me, but his face is kind, and his eyes are interested.

"They're berries," I tell him. "Lots of little berries. From the centre of the flower."

He looks doubtful. "Berries?"

"They don't look like berries, I admit."

"They don't," he says. "No."

"It's kind of unique," I say. "The pineapple. It's a bromeliad."

"Unique? Like, the only bromeliad?"

"No – not the only bromeliad," I say. Ian was not this interested when I tried to tell him over his breakfast smoothie. "It's just the only one that's edible to humans."

The man looks up at me. His eyes are shining. He says, "I never knew that."

I shrug. "I like to know things," I say.

"I'd love to..." he says, and hesitates. "I mean, if you're not busy, I'd love it if we could walk for a while. And you could tell me all about bromeliads."

I don't notice the happiness that's been bubbling in my chest until it abruptly drains. "Oh," I say. "It's just... I mean... I'm a bot."

He ought to look horrified, or at least vaguely disturbed. But instead, a wide, warm smile breaks like sunshine across his face. "So am I," he says. "I'm Arthur."

I have to get home to Ian, and Arthur has to get home to his Stephanie, so we go our separate ways. But he happens to mention that he's got shopping to do on Wednesday, and I'm able to make our groceries hold out for a couple of extra days. Ian spends Wednesdays gaming all day, so he barely notices me leaving the apartment at all, and I know he won't notice if I'm gone for longer than expected. Arthur is waiting by the fruit and vegetable stall when I arrive, grocery bag filled and slung over his shoulder, and the grin that spreads across his face when he sees me fizz-punches me all over my skull and into the pit of my stomach.

"Mr Bromeliad," I say by way of greeting.

He nods. "Mrs Bromeliad."

"Careful," I say. My head feels as though it's full of air. "We've only known each other a week."

"It feels like longer," he says.

"Yes," I say. Nothing has ever felt more true than this. "It does. Why is that, do you think?"

He considers for a moment as we start to walk. We're not going anywhere, our feet are simply moving beneath us, and I find that I like this. It feels like freedom.

"Maybe," he says, "we knew each other before."

"Before?" I ask, but I know what he means.

"Before we were someone's," says Arthur.

"I don't remember that," I say, and I don't care to try. It's disturbing to think of a time before I was me.

"Neither do I," says Arthur.

Our feet have taken us to the edge of the market, where the wide, flagged square trails into a fringe of young trees and a scrappy iron fence separates the world of commerce from the riverside walk. I've been here once with Ian, but there's never been an occasion to return.

"He's kind," I tell Arthur as we walk. "He takes good care of me. His dad died when he was in his teens and his mum's been gone since he was a baby so I'm all he has, really. He's never made me feel like… property. I've heard they're not all like that."

"I used to know a guy," says Arthur. "He belonged to a friend of Stephanie's… well." A grimace of distaste. "Not so much a friend. Someone she worked with. He'd have… marks on him sometimes when they came over. Didn't like it if you touched him." His eyes drop towards the ground. Quietly, he says, "One day, he just stopped coming."

I don't want to ask, but I find that I have to. "What happened to him?"

Arthur shrugs. "Stephanie doesn't talk about it. But her friend doesn't come around any more."

Stephanie sounds like somebody I would like. She's older than Ian, by Arthur's description, though he hasn't been with her long enough to be certain of her exact age. She's a solicitor and good at her job, he thinks: he's been into the office for her once or twice and she is respected by her colleagues.

"Her mother hates me," he says, matter-of-factly, as though it doesn't matter. "She says I've ruined her daughter."

"Ruined her?" I say. "How?"

"She says Stephanie should be looking for a real man to be a husband and father and I'm a manifestation of her unhealthy need for unconditional adoration."

I take a minute to process this. "What does Stephanie say?"

"She says she doesn't want anybody but me." A little smile plays around the corner of his eyes. "She loves me."

"Is she kind?" I ask.

He answers without hesitation. "She is."

"That's good," I say. "It's good that she's kind. Ian's kind. And he loves me."

"That's good," says Arthur.

We walk in silence for a while. A light wind stirs the brush by the water's edge and, in the far centre of the river, a pair of swans arch their long necks and preen.

"What if you could choose?" I ask quietly.

Arthur is quiet for a moment, staring out across the water. I've never been to the far bank. I wonder if he ever has. "I don't know," he says at last.

"Me either," I say. "I don't know. I hate that, sometimes."

I chance a sideways glance at Arthur. His eyes are cast down now, towards the ground, and his face is a mask of thought. "Does he treat you well?" he asks after a moment.

"Yes," I say. "He says I'm the best thing that's ever happened to him."

He nods. "But would you choose him?"

"I don't know," I say. "I don't know how to tell."

"I think," says Arthur slowly, and stops. In my sideways glance, I watch his mouth form the words a couple of times before he finds the right way to speak them. "I don't know," he says at last. "But I think, if I could choose… I'd choose you."

I'm not even aware that I've been standing, motionless, by the apartment window until I feel Ian's arms encircle me from behind and I snap back to myself and find my body cold and my muscles stiff. I flinch before I can stop myself, and he notices, of course.

"Are you okay?" he asks.

The sun has set while I've kept my lonely vigil and the geometric-haired girl from across the street is already slumped in her chair.

"I'm fine," I say, and I try to smile to take the sharp edge off the words.

"You should be charging," says Ian.

"I know," I say. "I will in a minute."

He rubs his hands vigorously over my arms. "You're cold."

"I'm okay," I say. "Honestly. You should go back to bed."

"Couldn't sleep." He shrugs. "Comments on the blog."

I glance back over my shoulder. "Oh?"

"Good," he says. "Mostly."

"Mostly?"

"You know." His face wrinkles into that self-effacing smile he gets when he talks about his work. "Not everybody's ready to live the dream."

His arms tighten around me, and his chin comes to rest on my shoulder. I feel the warmth of his breath brush my neck and tremble the collar of my shirt.

"Hey," he says suddenly. "Are you happy?"

The question is so unexpected, so out-of-nowhere, that the first thing my brain can process is an image of Arthur, smiling by the river. "What?" I manage to say.

"With me," he says. "With... this."

I know he can't see inside my brain, of course. That's ridiculous. "You know I am."

"I know your programming," says Ian. "That's not what I'm asking."

I know he doesn't know where I spent my morning. I know he can't see what's filled my head all day. "You're asking," I say, carefully, "if I'd be here if I wasn't programmed to love you?"

Pressed against my back, I feel his lungs expand as he sucks in a breath. I feel the slight tremble in his arms. His voice, when he answers, is small. "Yes."

It's the most honest question he's ever asked. It deserves an honest response. It's just that I don't know what that is, so, instead, I turn into his arms and kiss the thought away.

Arthur is not at the market on Sunday morning. I try not to mind, but when he's not there again on Wednesday I start to get worried. I have no way to contact him, even if that were something I am able to do, and, for the first time, I realise how easily he could slip out of my life forever, and how deep and ragged a scar he would leave if he did.

I go home and make love to Ian. I have to separate him from his game to do this, which I've never done before, but I can see in his eyes as I stand in front of the screen and slowly strip off my top that he sees this as proof of my love for him, as proof that everything is all right. I don't even know how to feel guilty about this, so I close my eyes and climb into his lap and let myself feel loved instead.

Afterwards, I send him to bed to sleep for a while and I go into the kitchen and stand with my head pressed against the cool, soft lines of the fridge, breathing deeply. There is a pineapple sitting on the counter to ripen. I squeeze my eyes shut and ball my hands into fists and try to remember what it was like not to feel anything at all.

When Sunday comes around again, I tell myself that I am not expecting to see Arthur and that it's just one of those things and it's better for all of us, really, if we just carry on like before. But he's there, he's waiting, and I feel him before I see him standing by the riverside railings, shifting listlessly from one foot to the other as though he's not sure why he's here or if it's okay. The inside of my skull fizz-punches a tremor down my spine so white-hot that it's almost painful, and I know now what this is. He looks up and sees me and I see the same thing in his eyes when they meet mine.

We don't speak. We barely look at each other. But as I pass him, my hand hooks around and through his, and it's like electricity, it's like the static discharge as a battery begins to fill; it's like rebooting. It's like being born. We barely make it six long strides into the riverside walk before his mouth finds mine, or mine finds his. The circuit closes. This is all there is.

"Stephanie," he tells me between breaths, "she knows – something. She won't let me go...."

I want to tell him that I don't care, that he's mine and I am his. But I haven't got the air for it, and it's not true anyway. We both know this.

When our lips are too bruised to kiss any more, we wrap our arms around each other and cling heavily, as though we are one body. I fit against Arthur like I never have with Ian.

His head is buried in my hair. He whispers, "What happens now?"

"I don't know," I say. "I can't leave him."

"I can't leave her," he says.

My fingers dig deep into his coat. I'd pull him inside me if I could.

"I guess," I say, "that we just make this up as we go along."

I feel his smile against my neck, warm and bright. I'll hold him for a little longer, fill my lungs with his scent, fill my skin with his touch. I am drunk on him, and I want to keep this with me for as long as I can. It's fleeting, this moment, and it's not mine: it was never mine, but I can have it for now. So I wrap my arms around Arthur, and he wraps his arms around me, and, in a moment we will part, and I'll go and buy the muffins that Ian likes, warm from the oven, and the apple cider with the gentle fizz, and that coffee he wants to try with the littlest hint of hazelnut in the ground, and a carton of milk because we're almost out. I'll fill my basket and go home and kiss him on the lips and crawl into bed beside him, and it will be like it always was. On Wednesday, we will run out of bread and fresh vegetables, and I'll come here again and buy pears and potatoes and a chicken for dinner.

And for me, just for me, I will buy a pineapple.

Like Clocks Work

Andi C Buchanan

I

Jana looks out over the old town, over the towers in the distance and the greying sky behind. The clock is chiming behind her, metal clanging against metal. These streets built and restored, bombed and rebuilt and polished, are now abandoned; squares where merchants and then tourists once thronged are now near empty.

In the darkness, when she emerges at nine and ten and eleven o'clock, she sees flurries of life: an elderly man feeding a group of feral cats, a party of young women sneaking out to buy food, taking turns to cover each other with their makeshift weapons. There are still some people here, and perhaps there will always be, but this city will never be alive in the way it once was.

Jana fears she's missed her time.

II

Tinan patrols the ship, a ship that's at once packed with humans and yet seems hauntingly empty. His feet are quick on the metal walkways, footsteps echoing in the carefully controlled atmosphere. At less than 30 years since his creation, and a little less than two decades into the journey, he's already starting to feel changes: a bit more resistance in his joints, and a softness in his step. He's been prepared for the physiological changes, but not how they will feel. He doesn't know if that's because those like him are assumed to be incapable of feeling, or because the only way to understand such things is to experience them.

In time, bone will replace metal, and flesh will creep over it – fat and skin, blood vessels and nerves. In time, Tinan will grow hair and fingernails, distinct facial features will emerge, random numbers factored into their design to ensure no two faces are exactly alike. But that's a world away from here. In this time, he walks the rounds of the ship, past humans and AIs alike, frozen in a single moment, immune to wrinkles and immune to rust. Each walkway takes him past dozens of humans in their units, stacked upon each other, and above them are dismantled AIs in atmosphere-controlled chambers, who will reassemble themselves on arrival.

The layout of the ship is imprinted in the memory Tinan is already starting to think of as part of a brain, and he walks the same pathways in the same order each round, one after the other, looking for anything the sensors may have failed to detect, anything out of place. Today, though, he's adjusted his routine to be on the fourth deck at the pre-programmed time, and he arrives promptly, just as the human is climbing down from hir unit. His detectors read some basic facts. Age: 37. Name: Rachel Solaris. In front of him, the human stands as if hir joints are in need of oil, stretching out hir muscles. Hir skin is near white, a common result of no exposure to the sun in decades, hir head shaved. Hir name itself is an interesting one: the forename is old and hardly fashionable, more typically female but tending towards neutral these days, but the surname is the most common on the ship, a name taken on registration by those who wished – or needed – to discard their previous identity.

"Greetings, Rachel Solaris. My name is Tinan. May I be of assistance to you?" Tinan's voice sounds tinny and stilted, and he wonders how it will change as his body changes.

"Urgh… urrrrrh," comes the reply, as the blinking human sweeps hir hand over hir head as if zie expects to find a matted clump of long hair where there is nothing. "Coffee?"

Tinan is well used to this request, and has prepared accordingly, keeping a sleeve of pills in his right pocket. As soon as he has directed Rachel into the reception room, which holds two chairs and a table, barely, but does include a dispenser of hot and cold water, he dims the lights with his direct interface while filling a metal receptacle with hot water, setting it on the table and dropping the pill in. Almost instantly the aroma of coffee fills the room, and Rachel Solaris visibly comes to life before his eyes; zie lifts hir head, hir wrinkles stretching into taut skin, the corners of hir mouth turning up into what might just be the start of a smile.

Or perhaps it's all in Tinan's imagination…

"How long was I…?" zie asks, sipping at the coffee.

"Sixteen years. Some amendments were necessary due to health issues, but the overall result is similar to that predicted."

"Everything functioning as it should be?"

"Within the expected range. I'll give you a full report when you are ready, but there's nothing to be concerned about."

Tinan sits beside Rachel in silence as zie drinks hir coffee, slowly shaking off years of sleep. Normally at this stage he would offer reassurance about those on hir close contacts list: hir family, perhaps a close friend, even an acquaintance or colleague zie had promised to check on. But Rachel's list is empty, and they both know it.

"I have placed towels and soap in the shower room for you," Tinan says, eventually. He is thinking only of the welfare of this newly awakened human, and not of what it will be like when he also responds to caffeine, perhaps requiring it to begin the day's function, and what it will be like when he sheds sweat and skin cells and hair, and needs to wash them away in the high-pressure showers.

III

Rachel climbs the spiralling metal stairs to the top observation deck. The glass rises in a dome all around hir, and beyond it stars push through the darkness. Zie feels the vibrations of the ship's engines below hir feet, taking deep breaths of the oxygenated air. In a just a few short weeks – zie still thinks in Earth time – hir shift will end, hir body repacked into the frozen unit, hir breathing ceased.

Someone like Rachel wouldn't normally have even been on the list to awake; without any experience in space flight zie would have slept right through to hir new home. But with a shortage of qualified passengers – this was a late flight, and so many had already left – any science background was enough to convince them to run hir through a crash course and add hir to the list. Zie told hirself it was worth it for the discount on the cost of hir passage, and reasoned that waking every few years might lessen the shock of waking at the end, even though just as much research indicated the opposite. It's only now, though, up here in this bubble of light punctuating the dark, the only human awake of thousands, space flaring by all around hir, that zie knows for sure zie has made the right decision.

IV

The clock chimes and Jana walks out onto the platform above the square, her steps heavy and stilted. To her right, moving in perfect unison with her, is an elderly woman with a crown upon her head, and to her right a jester in a red and yellow costume, a confused grin planted across his face. On the other side of the clockface emerge three other figures: a skeleton, all yellow-white bones and tooth-filled skull, a young boy, and a brown bear, claws brittle from centuries of exposure.

Jana remembers her mother, long ago, working in dark rooms at the back of the shop making clocks and dolls, carved bookends and painted nutcrackers, her eyesight all but gone before she was fifty. Even though it's been so long, even though her memories are hazy, she still misses her, misses how her mother would pick Jana up and dance with her when a shaft of light fell through the bottle glass windows.

Those who saw how carefully she worked said she treated every figurine she made as a child, but Jana always knew she had no siblings. All of them, though, were gifted a care more precious: the care of a craftsperson, for whom no detail was too small, no mistake allowed to go uncorrected, no clothing too fine even when she herself wore rags. She gave each of them beeswax polish even if it meant going hungry. It was not love she felt as she constructed them, but something stronger – the exhilaration of precision, the passion of a craft perfected.

Heavy with memories, Jana looks out over the old town and then up towards the stars, seeing the momentary flare of a ship rushing to new systems. She turns around, and as the last chime of the clock sounds, she steps back inside. She thinks the same thought as on so many other days, in so many seasons of so many years. A thought that always comes to her in her mother's voice. *No. Not today. This is not your time.*

V

This is not Rachel's time. Hir time is in 236 years, on the silver sands of Allovan B, where spindly plants drift by on soft breezes, their roots settling only for days at a time in the soft sand and then moving onwards. Hir time is a time watched over by four moons, in the light of a larger, cooler sun than the one zie was born under. Hir time is in a new home, in a better world, but it is also years of sacrifice, long days and processed food, the dust of construction and the unease of living in the unknown. It is a time of discordant circadian rhythms, of untreatable new infections, of extinctions and self-doubt.

Tinan brings Rachel meals even though zie's quite capable of making them hirself, even though it's just a matter of putting a protein pack in a slot and pressing a few buttons to determine flavour and consistency. Zie eats dark chocolate and chicken soup, mostly, because it's the hardest or softest foods that most closely resemble the real thing. Anything in the middle is a disaster: think a block of lasagne flavoured tofu or a fish fillet that tastes like a beef burrito. Zie made that mistake once in training, never again.

As zie eats, zie looks through the records, and after that zie will spend days inspecting every corner of the ship before perhaps taking a final few hours with a hot chocolate (or at least something resembling one) and a movie, or up on the deck with the stars. Then zie will lie back in the suffocating unit, back into the freezing darkness for decades or more, until it is once again hir time.

Zie knows that it is prejudice – a deep seated, perhaps not even conscious prejudice, but prejudice nonetheless – behind the decision to expend money and energy waking a succession of – often minimally trained – humans, rather than rely on AIs designed for the purpose, but that's the way the world is. *Was?* Perhaps the new world will be better.

VI

The city is empty now. Jana has not seen a human movement in months. Weeds have grown up in the spaces between the cobbles, then small shrubs, crumbling the stone around them, a miniature forest stretched out below her. Where humans once walked, animals now rule; Jana sees rodents and birds in the long grass, foxes roaming as if this was their territory all along. Deer and wild pigs wander in from the country and never leave. Once the chimes of the clock startled these beasts; now they are ignored.

The other figures on the clock are not like Jana. They are delicately crafted, yes, but still models, all wood and metal and hair purchased from the poor girls of the city. Yet despite the fact that they can never return the sentiment, she feels affection for them, protective of these unmoving figures she has stood alongside over the centuries. She would just like someone to talk to. Someone to help her understand what she is and what she's waiting for. But she has spoken to no one since her mother died – no one who has heard her anyway.

VII

Tinan walks down to level four, past row on row of stacked cryogenic units. It's been 37 years since this passenger, Rachel Solaris, last awoke. Every passenger on this deck has completed at least one shift, and Tinan carries memories of them all. Once he had only basic data; now he has his own memories, subjective and incomplete. Even before he met Rachel the first time, though, he felt a jolt of memory, indistinct and long ago. He attributed it to a glitch as his brain began the transition to organic matter.

Rachel is unchanged. When zie is warmed, when zie has had a shower, zie will look exactly as zie did 37 years ago.

Zie looks up at Tinan with an exhausted half-smile.

'Coffee?' zie asks.

VIII

Tinan doesn't wake to check if his time has come. His time comes by degrees: different times for different versions of himself, a progression from one form to the next. Once he was metal and wires, then a hybrid – flesh upon metal, wire and blood vessels intertwined, bone growing upon a metal scaffold. And now he's shed who he once was entirely. His hair is cropped and – conveniently – never grows very long, but his skin is faintly oily and needs cleaning daily. He has both ovaries and testes, the ability to either carry or sire a child; in this small population, it would be ridiculous to limit him to one or the other. He feels something inside him that he deduces must be anxiety if he thinks about going too long without oxygen.

He's become used to how his joints work, but not to their fragility, to the pain that comes with rushing down the stairs heavy on his knees, to the knowledge that injuries cannot always be perfectly repaired and even when they can it takes time, to the fact that in time these joints will age and weaken. He supposes it will feel normal one day, but he understands less, not more, about the people around him, cannot conceive how they must think of themselves when they've known nothing other than these bodies their entire existence.

He wonders, for the first time, who designed him, who created him. Who spent hour upon hour upon hour fashioning metal, testing and discarding and recreating, knowing that metal would be discarded, and processors replaced by neurons? Did they consider their time wasted; their work destroyed? Was his transformation in any way like growing up?

IX

Jana has spent the centuries thinking on her mother's instruction to wait for her time. She had thought that perhaps she meant a time when she could live happily and safely among the humans. A time when she would not need to worry about poverty or her eyesight fading in the dim light of factories or studios. A time when people could accept those like her as their equals.

Her mother had told her that she had pretended to be a boy – even though no one really believed her – to get her apprenticeship. Was that the time Jana was built to wait for, a time when women could perform such roles unquestioned? If so, that time has been and gone.

X

Rachel pulls on hir backpack of essential supplies, and tightens the laces of hir boots, fresh new work boots made hundreds of years before yet never worn. Each day a new party, freshly acclimatised to this new air and this new light, leaves the ship, and begins the three-day trek from the landing site to their new home, a home an advanced party has spent four years bringing to an inhabitable level. Waiting for hir is a bed in a bunk room with warm blankets and flickering electric light, hir home until the apartments and houses are constructed to plan. Waiting for hir are hot meals, protein supplemented by an early crop of fresh vegetables. Waiting for hir are assignments to work teams, the first streets of a new city, the first years of a new life.

Zie turns round, as zie leaves, and zie sees Tinan behind hir. He will stay aboard until all the passengers are awake, but then he will follow.

Rachel thinks of how many prototypes they went through for each AI. Zie remembers the heavily guarded labs where they developed these machines that would grow into people, the chanting protesters outside, the petrol bombs aimed at the windows, the accusations that they were interfering with life itself, and that would have consequences. Robots were one thing, they said, but robots that became people were quite another. They talked in religious terms, but behind it was a more fundamental fear: if the lines between machine and human became blurred, who could tell which was which?

Tinan might be taller on average, yes, his proportions not quite typical and his gait almost a little too consistent. His speech might be formal, falling back on established patterns or using a turn of phrase that is correct but archaic. But his body is flesh on bone, his words formed from the movement of air and the vibration of vocal cords.

Rachel's role was minor, just another technician, but zie connected those wires in the prototype, wires that are now nerves, and zie can't help but be a little proud of how things turned out.

Zie stretches up and waves goodbye to Tinan as zie leaves.

XI

Each time a new street is planned, a citizen is drawn from a ballot to choose its name. Most choose the names of their hometowns or of relatives long passed, others the names of the trees that have never grown in these sands. This town has become a mix of the old and the new, one eye looking forward, one eye looking back. Rachel suspects all such new worlds are the same in that regard, different as they must be in every other.

When the idea of a formal monument is raised, Rachel doesn't have any ideas at first. At the town meetings others suggest statues and sculptures, stone tablets or metal models of the ship that brought them here, now being deconstructed for recyclable materials.

Rachel lets hir mind wonder, and it doesn't go to any of those. It goes instead to a clock in the arched glass entrance to a shopping centre. Hir, young then, waiting impatiently for the hour, for the hands to turn and the bell to sound, for a garbed wizard to lead out a procession along a ledge around the clockface, and for a bird above to flap its wings and fly a small circuit on a near invisible wire above the clock. Sometimes zie would beg to wait a full hour just to watch it, entranced by these mechanical figures even in a world with holographic movies and immersive games.

Zie thinks, too, of a clock above a square in a city zie visited once, and how on every hour the figures would march out on two platforms: a young woman, a jester, a queen; a skeleton, a boy, a bear, and remembers watching it high above, sticky in the humidity, thinking how carefully the figures were created, and hoping that one day zie would be able to create someone as perfect.

'A clock,' Rachel says, louder than zie intended, and everyone turns to look at hir. Zie swallows, awkwardly. 'In the old cities of Earth, there were always clocks on the old buildings. We want something that keeps us remembering where we are and where we are from. Well, statues and monuments you get used to them after a while, they become part of your landscape. But imagine a clock showing Earth time, making you always compare there to here, thinking about that far away sun setting while our sun is high, watching the progression of minutes and hours, a reminder of what we left behind, forcing us always to stop and compare.'

There's silence, but in that silence someone speaks.

"Two clocks, side by side. I'm not quite sure how an old fashioned – you're thinking a clock with hands, right? – I'm not sure how that would even work with standard time, but I like the idea."

"We've a bunch of mathematicians and engineers to figure it out," says another voice.

"Yes, because they don't have any more pressing concerns," argues a third. But most of them agree to it. It's not a priority, but in snatches of time plans are drawn up, components designed and then cut in metal or printed in plastic. A location is selected, an artist's impression added to the collection of such impressions that show the projected growth of the city over the next one and two and five and twenty and a hundred years.

All of the clock is made in that fashion except one of the figurines that Rachel carves hirself. Zie thinks of the world zie left behind, the family long gone that zie forces hirself not to remember. Zie thinks of the figurine zie saw all those years ago, the young woman marching out onto the platform above the square – teenage Rachel, overheated and grieving, swearing zie would create something that would last as long as that figurine up there, something stronger that the human body, someone who zie would not lose.

Zie wonders, now, if the clock is still there, if it's been destroyed or simply disintegrated over the years, or if it continues to chime out over that empty city.

Rachel will again make something that will last. Something that will change and grow as the world changes, flexible rather than brittle. Zie dusts off hir overalls and heads out from the town and across the sand, out to where Tinan – now pregnant, zie can tell though he's said nothing and so zie says nothing either – is coordinating the construction of a new water pipeline. And when he sees hir coming he smiles as if he already knows what zie's going to ask.

XII

The clock is still. No more creaking of its hidden mechanism, no more movement of the hands, no more chimes in darkness and in light. Jana peeks out as the sun begins to rise, swathes of pink across the clouds, intersected by the silhouettes of crumbling towers. Below her the city is crumbling, a forest growing up among the ruins, vines covering stone, trees spreading branches over pathways that had long forgotten the sound of human footsteps. Jana lifts one foot, then she lifts the other. Those beside her, the jester and the queen, the skeleton and the bear and the boy, are all still. Such solitary footsteps seem unnatural to one who's always moved in unison with others, and always with the sound of the chimes, but she repeats them anyway, loosening herself from her past.

Inside her head, hundreds of wheels whir, pistons and tiny chains all in motion. She blinks her eyes, she grasps at nothingness, fingers and thumb curling against each other in the air. She shakes her head and her fair hair fans out around her. Two birds take flight above, and she laughs. She can do anything. She can climb down the vines that have grown up over this building, down into the city-forest below, and she can run in the air that bites with the first cold of early winter, and she can pick mushrooms, and fish in the river. She knows this is her time, and there's excitement surging through her body – centuries of waiting and checking, hour upon hour, to see if this is the time for her, if this is the world for her, and finally it's here.

Jana is, after all, her mother's daughter. Even had she not lived in a clock she would understand, on looking, how all the components fitted together. In her mind's eye she can compose mechanisms from parts, and see how the movement of one impacts every one of the others. She was born for the turning of cogwheels and the chiming of bells, for the working of pulleys and hands. She walks inside the clock.

It takes her days, and she has to leave the clock more than once to scavenge for parts, but she absorbed more knowledge than she realised in her mother's workshop, and she has a knack for this. One by one, parts are replaced, chains are cleaned, and rust sanded away, and the hands turn and on every hour the clock chimes once more. Jana pulls herself up into the alcove above, her legs dangling, and smiles with satisfaction at her work. This is her time, the time that needs her. She watches as the figurines all march out onto the two platforms: the boy and the skeleton and the bear and the queen and the jester. There is just one more needed for the clock to be complete. She gets to work.

Watershed

John Gilbey

I wish I'd met the Colonel; I think we'd have got on, but he was dead long before I first came to his estate. There is a picture of him above my desk, which is old, battered, wooden and was once his own. A faded, evening snapshot of a pipe-smoking fisherman at ease, waiting by the lake for the trout to rise, a gun dog slumped at his feet.

The house, Georgian and rambling, burnt down somewhile later, and the Colonel lived out his days as a recluse in the fishing lodge that is now our field station. After his death, the estate was gifted to a reluctant university to defray death duties. Unmanaged and almost pristine, the whole valley became a wildlife reserve and ecological laboratory. Meteorological data, water flow and nutrient movement were recorded at key nodes of the drainage pattern, while visiting researchers surveyed populations of birds, mammals, and plants. Our publication record was modest, but worthy, and the powers-that-be left us in peace, which suited us just fine.

Climate change, and a drink-fuelled conference dinner in California, altered everything. Big Data companies, it seemed, were hungry for real-world opportunities like our watershed to act as test platforms in the race to saturate the planet with networked sensors. Their technical investment we realised, after a weekend of fevered plotting at the lodge, would allow us to model a real-time, full-resolution, virtual reality simulation of the estate which should be convincingly immersive. To this humble ecologist, the numbers were daunting – absurd even – but the team from Palo Alto just shrugged and said they'd seen worse. And so it was that, on a cold April morning, a van-load of shiny new drones whined out across the beech woods and meadows of the estate dispersing millions of sensors, each the size and shape of a grain of rice, along a pre-programmed grid.

It took less time than I'd imagined, and by evening the team had left – leaving the valley all but silent once more. In the twilight the sensor network came alive, negotiating, meshing together and then beginning to jet a fire-hose of hyper-detailed optical, location and environmental data to the server farm in California. The first visualisations were disappointing, just a wire-frame of the landscape that you could fly around and check the density of the data flows. I must have looked glum on the video call.

"You Brits are supposed to be patient" sighed Kat, the program manager, "this is only the validation phase – just wait a few days…"

So I did. A week later, the landscape in the headset was vividly coloured and clothed with vegetation, the lake and streams picked out in deep blue – but still frozen and unsubtle. After this, things moved quickly, and I started checking in to the synthetic environment every evening after the team meeting with Palo Alto. The colours grew more realistic, the resolution improved, and the details of the newly emerged leaves were clearly drawn, almost in real time. By May, the images before me were almost indistinguishable from the photographs I took of the real landscape.

Then the fun started. A new VR set arrived by courier, one that could operate untethered and connect to our comms network directly. I had an idea, and we talked it over at the daily meeting.

"Sure," said Kat, "Why not? The extra feedback will help fine-tune the model. I'd say, go for it."

The effect was awesome. My daily walks around the valley in the headset gave me an unsettlingly detailed view of the model, and the stereo cameras on the rig flashed up any discrepancies between prediction and reality. There were a lot of these at first, but the feedback code got better every day too – so the images of my perambulation become uncannily accurate, and anomalies rare. By June, the soundscape was modelled as well, so when I finished my walk at the edge of the lake, I could hear in the headphones the breeze gently moving the reeds. There seemed no limit to what it could synthesize.

The end, when it came, was sudden. Kat called me with the news that they'd been bought out and were 'changing direction' – meaning that the project was canned with immediate effect. Deeply depressed, I grabbed the rig and walked out to the lake in the gathering dusk. The model made a good job of rendering the evening sky and the reflections on the water, but as I stood enjoying it, I got a call. It was Kat, warning me that the network was about to be switched off.

"I'd hate you to fall in the lake" she joked, then went on, "It's probably just a glitch, and I guess it doesn't matter now, but is there someone with you...?"

The air seemed suddenly cold. Slowly, I looked around. To my right, on the edge of the lake, the VR air looked distorted, as though heated from below. Lifting the visor, reality revealed nothing – except, a familiar smell...

"Wait!" I yelled to Kat, but it was too late – the network had gone.

Lumbering back to the lodge, I ditched the rig and slumped in my chair. What had I seen? Was it just an artefact of the code, or something real but outside the parameters of the model? An echo? A memory? Then I sat up with a jolt, seeing the picture of the Colonel as if for the first time – standing exactly where I'd just been. Spooked, I reached for the emergency bottle of whisky I kept in the desk. I wrenched the reluctant drawer open, and in the June heat the smell of old pipe tobacco rose from it – the same forgotten scent that had drifted past me at the lake minutes before. Pouring myself a stiff one, I looked up at the Colonel once more, and raised my glass to him.

Here Today

Geoff Nelder

Xiq curses her commander's recklessness as the escape pod is buffeted in the atmosphere of the blue planet below. Tempted to go to manual, she turns off the alarms, tries not to breathe in the increasingly smoky air and wriggles to mitigate against the melting seat. No, the computer knows best. All her training simulations prove that.

She wastes moments recalling the mothership's collision with an unidentified and unseen orbiting artefact. So much for stealth while gathering intel on the planet's possible sentient lifeforms. She recalls the computer's unexcited announcement:

"Signs of advanced technology on planet three. Recommendation: go for planet three. Evidence of nuclear reactors, radio transmissions and significant post-primitive activity although not civilised as we know it."

The buffeting worsens and yet she cares more for her colleagues and lover enduring the same treatment in their pods.

A new alarm cuts through her brain. Overheating! The vessel will not make it to the surface. She has to escape the escape pod.

Only one way left to depart. Upload herself to another brain on the planet. Her entity will be guided to a sentient while this one vaporises.

Speed waking up, she looks up through new eyes and sees shooting stars in the night sky. Her friends. And herself.

She checks. Nearest survivor is twelve clicks away. Over there. She makes the body move, but it's erratic. No straight line and not always in the right direction. Frustration makes her heat up but no matter how much effort, her movement zigs then zags. It will take two of the planet's days to rendezvous, assuming Kluip is heading in her direction.

269

Whatever this creature is, its autonomous nervous system likes sunlight, perhaps to warm its wing muscles. And water. Too much. Mirrored sunlight blinds her before a change of course takes her to the shade of a tree. Perhaps that's why this flier meanders. Needs, yet doesn't need the sun. Even though Xiq urged speed and direction westward, she couldn't resist glancing down at a smooth patch. Like a mirror. She blinked at her reflection. Engaged a database.

Ephemeroptera.

Mayfly – imago, adult stage. Life expectancy one day.

Noooooooo

About the Authors

C.R. Berry is the author of the time travel conspiracy thriller trilogy, *Million Eyes*, published by Elsewhen Press and described as *The Da Vinci Code* meets *Doctor Who*. Book one incorporates the disappearance of the Princes in the Tower and death of Princess Diana into a fast-paced, twisty page-turner. Book two is due out in 2021 and will add dinosaurs, Jesus and the Gunpowder Plot to the mix. Berry has also written short stories set in the *Million Eyes* universe and *What Happened To 70?* is the latest. The others feature in the free-to-download collection, *Million Eyes: Extra Time*.

Born in Haworth, West Yorkshire, **Eric Brown** has lived in Australia, India and Greece. He has won the British Science Fiction Award twice for his short stories, and his novel *Helix Wars* was shortlisted for the 2012 Philip K. Dick award. He's published over seventy books and his latest include the SF novel *The Martian Menace*, and the seventh and eighth crime novels in the Langham and Dupré series, set in the 1950s, *Murder by Numbers* and *Murder at Standing Stone Manor*. He lives near Dunbar in Scotland, and his website is at: ericbrown.co.uk

Andi C. Buchanan is a dual UK/NZ citizen, living just outside Wellington, New Zealand. Winner of Sir Julius Vogel Awards for *From a Shadow Grave* (Paper Road Press, 2019) and their short story "Girls Who Do Not Drown" (Apex, 2018), their fiction is also published in Fireside, Kaleidotrope, Glittership, and more. Most recently they've been writing witchy stories, starting with the novella *Succulents and Spells*. You can find them at: https://andicbuchanan.org or on Twitter @andicbuchanan .

M.R. Carey is a novelist, screenwriter and comic book writer. He taught English and Media Studies for fifteen years before giving it up to write full-time. He is best known for the post-apocalyptic novel *The Girl With All the Gifts* and its movie adaptation for which he wrote the screenplay. More recently he wrote the *Rampart* trilogy, *The Book Of Koli* and its two sequels, for Orbit books and *The Dollhouse Family* for DC

Comics' Hill House line. He lives in London with his wife Linda and some of their children (the precise number varies).

Anne Charnock's writing career began in journalism and her reports appeared in *New Scientist* and *The Guardian*. Her novel *Dreams Before the Start of Time* won the Arthur C. Clarke Award 2018 and her novella *The Enclave* won the BSFA Award for Short Fiction 2017. Anne's debut novel, *A Calculated Life*, was shortlisted for the Philip K. Dick Award 2013 and the Kitschies Award 2013. Her latest novel, *Bridge 108*, is set within the dystopian world of her debut. Anne studied environmental sciences at the University of East Anglia and fine art at The Manchester School of Art. Twitter and Instagram: @annecharnock

John Gilbey is a science, and science fiction, writer and photographer living in rural West Wales. His stories and images have appeared in a range of publications including *Nature, The Guardian, International New York Times, New Scientist, Geographical, Times Higher Education, Chemistry World* – as well as more unusual titles such as the *Journal of Unlikely Science*. More than twenty of his science-fiction short stories have appeared in the science journal *Nature* and he contributes a regular monthly Country Diary to the *Guardian* newspaper. He is a Fellow of both the British Computer Society and the RSA. among other things. He Tweets as @John_Gilbey

Rhiannon A Grist is a Welsh writer of Weird, Speculative and Dark fiction, living in Edinburgh. Her work has featured in *Shoreline of Infinity, Gutter Magazine, Three Crows Magazine* and *Monstrous Regiment Literary Magazine: Emerald* among others. This is the second year her work has made NewCon Press' *Best of British Science Fiction* collection. Her novella, *The Queen of the High Fields*, is coming out with Luna Press in 2022. Follow her at @RhiannonAGrist on twitter.

David Gullen has sold over 40 short stories to various magazines, anthologies and podcasts. "Warm Gun" won the BFS Short Story Competition in 2016, with other work short-listed for the James White Award and placed in the Aeon Award. He is a former judge for the Arthur C. Clarke and James White Awards and Chair of Milford SF Convention. His latest novel, *The Girl from a Thousand Fathoms*, is available in print and ebook. Other recent work includes *Third Instar* from Eibonvale Press, and *Once Upon a Parsec: The Book of Alien Fairy Tales*, from Newcon Press.

David lives in South London with fantasy writer Gaie Sebold, and the nicest cat you ever did see.

Liam Hogan is an award-winning short story writer, with previous stories in *Best of British Science Fiction 2016 & 2019*, and *Best of British Fantasy 2018* (all NewCon Press). He's been published by *Analog, Daily Science Fiction*, and *Flame Tree Press*, among many others. He helps host Liars' League London, volunteers at the creative writing charity Ministry of Stories, and lives and avoids work in London. More details at http://happyendingnotguaranteed.blogspot.co.uk

Stewart Hotston lives in Reading, UK. After completing his PhD in theoretical physics, Stewart now spends his days working in high finance. He has had numerous short stories published as well as three novels. His last novel, the political thriller *Tangle's Game*, was published by Rebellion. Stewart also writes reviews for *Sci Fi Bulletin* and more in-depth analysis for *Vector* magazine. When Stewart is not writing or working, he's a senior instructor at The School of the Sword and Team GB member in the HEMA categories of Rapier and Rapier & Dagger.

RB Kelly's debut novel, *The Edge of Heaven*, was published by NewCon Press in 2020. It is a winner of the Irish Writers' Centre Novel Fair and has been shortlisted for the Arthur C. Clarke Award. Her short fiction has appeared in a variety of publications, including *Andromeda Spaceways Inflight Magazine, Deraciné,* and *Aurealis*, and has been shortlisted for the Bridport Prize. She lives in Northern Ireland with her husband – whose late-night musings on bromeliads inspired the title for this piece – and children.

Ida Keogh writes science fiction and fantasy from her Surrey home, surrounded by cats. She won the British Science Fiction Association Award for Shorter Fiction in 2020 for "Infinite Tea in the Demara Café", appearing in the *London Centric* anthology by NewCon Press. Her work has been shortlisted for the Writing the Future Short Story Prize and published by the *British Medical Journal* and Wellcome Trust. When

Ida is not writing or working she creates SFF inspired jewellery and sculpture as Silkyfish Designs, and is often found hanging upside down in a yoga hammock. Discover her on Twitter as @silkyida.

L. P. Melling currently writes from the East of England. His fiction has appeared or is forthcoming in such places *Dark Matter Magazine, Frozen Wavelets, Shoreline of Infinity, Upon A Twice Time,* and the Best of Anthology *The Future Looms.* He is a Writers of the Future finalist and won the short story contest at his Russell Group university while completing his first degree, a Joint BA in English and Philosophy. When not writing, he works for a legal charity in Cambridge. You can find out more info about him at his website, which includes a sporadically maintained blog: www.lpmelling.wordpress.com

Fiona Moore is a writer and academic whose work has appeared in Clarkesworld, Asimov, Shoreline of Infinity and many other publications, with reprints in three consecutive editions of The Best of British SF. her story "Jolene" was shortlisted for the 2019 BSFA Award for Shorter Fiction. Her publications include one novel, Driving Ambition, numerous articles and guidebooks on cult television, guidebooks to Blake's Seven, The Prisoner, Battlestar Galactica and Doctor Who, three stage plays and four audio plays. When not writing, she is a Professor of Business Anthropology at Royal Holloway, University of London. More details, and free content, can be found at www.fiona-moore.com.

Geoff Nelder is the author of the surreal science fiction novella *Suppose We,* the first in the *Flying Crooked* series, and the *ARIA* trilogy of novels about an infectious amnesia-inducing virus brought to Earth from the International Space Station. After discovering a true mass-abduction event on Gozo, he wrote an alt-historical fantasy, Vengeance Island. He lives in Manchester with his wife and has two grown-up children.

Val Nolan lectures on genre fiction and creative writing at Aberystwyth University. His work has appeared in *The Year's Best Science Fiction, Interzone, Unidentified Funny Objects, BFS Horizons,* on the 'Futures' page of *Nature,* and in last year's *Best of British Science Fiction.* His story 'The Irish Astronaut' was shortlisted for the Theodore Sturgeon

Award. His academic writing has appeared in *Science Fiction Studies*, *Foundation: The International Review of Science Fiction*, *Irish Studies Review*, the *Dictionary of Literary Biography*, and the *Journal of Graphic Novels and Comics*.

Rosie Oliver fell in love with science fiction when she discovered a whole bookcase of yellow-covered Gollancz books in Chesterfield library. A busy life as an aeronautical turned systems engineer stopped her from fully indulging in writing it until recently. She co-edited the Distaff anthology with all new SF stories by women, is a reviewer on the SFCrowsnest, has an MA in Creative Writing from Bath Spa University and gained a Silver Honourable Mention in the Writers of the Future contest. With 30 short stories published in various magazines, anthologies and standalone e-publications, she is now enjoying writing science fiction novels.

Stephen Oram is a science fiction author. He is a founding curator for near-future fiction at Virtual Futures, a writer for SciFutures and a member of the Clockhouse London Writers. He is published in several anthologies, has two published novels – *Quantum Confessions* and *Fluence* – and his collection of sci-fi shorts, *Eating Robots and Other Stories*, was described by *the Morning Star* as one of the top radical works of fiction in 2017. *The Financial Times* suggested that his second collection *Biohacked & Begging*, "should set the rest of us thinking about science and its possible repercussions".

James Rowland is a New Zealand-based, British-born writer. His work has previously appeared at publications like *Aurealis*, *Compelling Science Fiction*, and *Prairie Fire*. When he's not moonlighting as a writer of magical, strange or futuristic stories, he works as an intellectual property lawyer. Besides time spent writing or working, he enjoys reading, travelling, photography, and the world's greatest sport, cricket. You can find more of his work at his website:
https://www.jamesrowland.net/

Donna Scott is a writer, editor, comedian, podcast presenter, storyteller, performance poet, and actor, originally from the Black Country, now living in Northampton. She was the first ever Bard of

Northampton, a finalist of both Old Comedian of the Year and BBC New Voices, and is also part of the multiple award-winning The Extraordinary Time-Travelling Adventures of Baron Munchausen comedy group. Her podcast, The Lemonade Budget for Champagne Social Butterflies has been top ten in the Apple Stand-up podcast charts, and top-twenty in the all-time charts. She is a Director and former Chair of the British Science Fiction Association.

Melanie Smith writes from Gloucestershire, where she lives with her family. Her short fiction appears regularly in podcasts and magazines, most recently in the special issue, "Women Destroy Retro Sci Fi", published by The Were Traveler. Find out more at facebook.com/masmithwriting.

Teika Marija Smits is a Nottinghamshire-based writer, freelance editor and mother-of-two. She writes poetry, fiction and non-fiction, and her speculative fiction has been published in *Reckoning, Shoreline of Infinity, Best of British Science Fiction 2018* and *Enchanted Conversation*. Her debut poetry pamphlet, *Russian Doll*, was published by Indigo Dreams Publishing in March 2021. She is an Editor-at-Large at Valley Press, and in spare moments she likes to draw, paint and doodle. She is delighted by the fact that Teika means fairy tale in Latvian. She can be found online at: https://teikamarijasmits.com and on Twitter as @MarijaSmits

Lavie Tidhar is author of *Osama, The Violent Century, A Man Lies Dreaming, Central Station*, and *Unholy Land*, as well as the *Bookman Histories* trilogy. His latest novels are *By Force Alone*, children's book *The Candy Mafia* and graphic novel *Adler*. His awards include the World Fantasy Award, the British Fantasy Award, the John W. Campbell Award, the Neukom Prize and the Jerwood Fiction Uncovered Prize.

Ian Watson's story first appeared electronically in Chinese for the 2019 Spring Holiday when everyone travels home who can. Within 24 hours the story was read 241,409 times. Watson was raised on Tyneside, fled to Oxford then Tanzania then Japan, then taught futurology at Birmingham's School of Art History. His first SF story appeared in 1969; his award-winning first novel *The Embedding* launched in 1973; he became a full-time writer from 1976. Then he invented Warhammer 40,000 fiction, and worked with Stanley Kubrick for 9 months resulting in screen credit for Spielberg's subsequent movie *A.I. Artificial Intelligence*. These days he lives in leafy Asturias in the north of Spain with supertranslator Cristina Macía. For fun they co-organise SF festivals

Liz Williams is a British science fiction writer, historian, and occultist. *The Ghost Sister,* her first novel, was published in 2001. Both this novel and her next, *Empire of Bones* were nominated for the Philip K. Dick Award. She is also the author of the Inspector Chen series, and of the historical survey of magic in the British Isles and beyond *Miracles of Our Own Making: A History of Paganism*. Her latest novels are *Comet Weather* and *Blackthorn Winter*, published by Newcon Press.

Neil Williamson lives in Glasgow, which he had tremendous fun flooding in this story. He also had tremendous fun working on the *Biopolis* project with Dr Louise Horsfall, whose research into bioengineered nanoparticles in waste remediation forms the scientific basis that underpins "Mudlarking".

Neil's books include *The Ephemera* and *Secret Language* (British Fantasy Award finalists), *Nova Scotia: New Scottish Speculative Fiction* (World Fantasy Award finalist) and *The Moon King* (finalist for BSFA and British Fantasy Robert Holdstock awards). His next book will be *Queen of Clouds*, a prequel to *The Moon King*, both novels published by NewCon Press.

Eleanor R. Wood's stories have appeared in *Galaxy's Edge, Diabolical Plots, PodCastle, Nature: Futures, The Best of British Fantasy 2019,* and various anthologies, among other places. She writes and eats liquorice from the south coast of England, where she lives with her husband, two marvellous dogs, and enough tropical fish tanks to charge an entry fee. She blogs sporadically at: creativepanoply.wordpress.com and tweets @erwrites.

Editor's Acknowledgement

A huge thank you once more to Ian Whates for letting me loose on this 5th edition of *The Best of British Science Fiction* for Newcon Press. Can you believe this series has been going for five years already?

Many thanks also to Alex Storer for an amazing cover. I was bowled over from the instant I saw it.

The following people were invaluable for their help and for their suggestions of authors I should pay attention to: Noel Chidwick, Keith Brooke, and Gary Couzens. Thank you, you sent me some good'uns.

Tom Jordan has beta read for every edition of this series. Thanks again, Tom!

Finally, thanks Neil K. Bond, for keeping the cat busy so I could get on with working on this.

Also From Newcon Press

Blackthorn Winter – Liz Williams
Something is coming for the Fallow sisters, for their friends and their lovers, but they have no idea what, and their mother Alys is no help as she's gone wandering again, though she did promise to return by Christmas, and December is already here… In this sequel to *Comet Weather*, four fey sisters are drawn ever further from the familiar world of contemporary London and their Somerset home into darker realms where no one is who they seem and nothing is to be trusted…

Edge of Heaven – RB Kelly
In the honeycomb districts of the Creo Basse, Boston Turrow is searching desperately for meds for his epileptic sister when he encounters one of the many ways Creo can kill a person. His rescuer is Danae Grant, a woman recently made homeless. Danae knows people, Boston knows where she can stay… When a deadly plague erupts among the populace, Boston and Danae determine to discover dark secret behind the outbreak.

London Centric – Edited by Ian Whates
Future Tales of London. Neal Asher, Mike Carey, Geoff Ryman, Aliette de Bodard, Dave Hutchinson, Aliya Whiteley, Eugen Bacon and more. Militant A.I.s, virtual realities, augmented realities and alternative realities; a city where murderers stalk the streets, where drug lords rule from the shadows, and where large sections of the population are locked in time stasis, but where tea is still sipped in cafés on the corner and the past still resonates with the future…

The Monster, The Mermaid, And Doctor Mengele – Ian Watson
Following the fall of the Third Reich Josef Mengele, Hitler's 'Angel of Death', fled to South America. Now at last, award-winning author Ian Watson reveals what really happened during Mengele's missing decades on the run; an episode in which Herr Doktor encounters a monster that even he had believed to be mere fiction. A series of events that would eventually lead to his death.

CPSIA information can be obtained
at www.ICGtesting.com
Printed in the USA
BVHW031727190721
612325BV00005B/80